The Shattered Curling Stone

Stone
A Novel
David S. Florig

David S. Florig

Book cover design by David S. Florig.

Ocean Park, Maine.

Cover picture "Eglinton Ladies 1859" copyright © The Scottish Curling Trust. Used with the kind permission of the Scottish Curling Trust.

Library of Congress Control Number: 2024913599

ISBN: 979-89885545-1-6 (Hardback)

ISBN: 979-89885545-2-3 (Paperback)

ISBN: 979-89885545-3-0 (eBook)

1. Fiction – historical – general   2. Sports & recreation – winter sports – curling

BISAC: FIC014000 Fiction/Historical/General   FIC121010 Fiction/Scotland/19th Century   FIC038000 Fiction/Sports

Printed in the United States of America

10 9 8 7 6 5 4 3 2 1

www.davidflorig.com

To my wife, Nancy, who not only had to endure the writing of *The Stones of Ailsa Craig*, but now this, as well.

Foreword

The Shattered Curling Stone is not just a tale of a young girl carving her place on the ice in 1880s Scotland; it is a celebration of the rich history and resilient spirit of women in curling. As we journey through the fictional, yet deeply rooted story of this young Scottish girl, we are reminded of the profound impact of sport on personal and societal levels. This book brings to life the often-overlooked history of women's curling, illuminating the courage and determination of those early pioneers, such as Ailsa Maclaren, who paved the way for future generations.

Growing up, I was one of the fortunate girls who did not succumb to the statistic that sees 70% of girls drop out of sport by the time they are 17. I had the unwavering support of my parents and friends, who pushed me to continue playing, shaping me into who I am today. This support was instrumental in my journey, from competing at two Olympics to winning a silver medal for Canada at the 2010 Vancouver Games.

Sport has taught me invaluable life lessons: resilience, determination, and the courage to pursue my dreams. These lessons have transcended the rink, enabling me to serve as a board member on numerous organizations, as the current CEO of Canada's Sports Hall of Fame, and as the Honorary Coach for the 2025 Special Olympic World Games. These opportunities were not only a result of my sporting career, but also the confidence and fortitude I gained through sport. In sport, you learn to fail, pick yourself up, and try again. You never truly lose; you either win or you learn.

My advocacy for girls staying in sport extends beyond winning championships and medals. It is about the character that sports build, the opportunities sport creates, and the values learned. Through my 45+ years in curling, I have witnessed firsthand the obstacles and struggles women have faced to gain full acceptance and equal participation in the game and the broader sports world. While I encountered some of these challenges, I am heartened by the progress we have made. Today, we see the culmination of the efforts of countless women who fought for gender equity, equal access, and recognition in curling and all women's sports, including hockey, soccer, and basketball.

We stand on the shoulders of those who came before us, championing each other and leaving the sport better than we found it. The future of curling excites me immensely. *The Shattered Curling Stone* is a tribute to the legacy of women in curling and a beacon of hope for the generations to come.

As you turn the pages of this book, I hope you are inspired by the tenacity and spirit of the characters, much like I have been by the real-life heroines of this sport. May their stories encourage you to push forward, embrace the challenges, and celebrate the triumphs, knowing that through sport, we build not just champions on the ice but champions in life.

Enjoy the journey.

Cheryl Bernard is a two-time Olympian, 2010 Olympic silver medalist and business leader. At just 23, she founded an insurance brokerage and, within eleven years, transformed it into a multi-million-dollar enterprise. By 43, she had led Team Canada to a silver medal in curling at the 2010 Vancouver Olympics.

"Follow your dreams, they know the way. Let your own story come out. Dare to be your best. Reach beyond your grasp, and surround yourself with people who believe you can, and know that you hold the pen when it comes to writing your own life story."

Today, Cheryl is the President and CEO of Canada's Sports Hall of Fame. A firm believer in leveraging her athletic achievements for greater good, Cheryl has been a dedicated curling broadcaster with TSN from 2014 to 2023. She continues to serve her community through board memberships with Tourism Calgary and Special Olympics Canada and was also named Honorary Coach of Team Canada for the Special Olympic World Games in Italy, March 2025.

Cheryl is deeply committed to inspiring others to pursue their goals and realize that life is shaped by the choices we make.

Preface

The Shattered Curling Stone is my follow-up novel to *The Stones of Ailsa Craig*. Like the latter, it centers around the 500-year-old Scottish sport of curling. Also like *The Stones of Ailsa Craig*, it is set largely in 1880s Scotland, toward the end of the Victorian Era. *The Shattered Curling Stone* is not a sequel, per se, and does not rely on the reader having read *The Stones of Ailsa Craig*, although a few characters appear in both works.

Curling is certainly a niche sport, known primarily from being featured on television every four years during the Winter Olympics. Most people are wholly unfamiliar with it, or know it only as a curiosity. For those people, I suggest reading the Appendix first, which provides a primer on the game's long history, how it is played, the equipment that it is played with, and the surface that it is played on, which, you may be surprised to learn, is not at all like hockey or skating ice. A little understanding of the game and its history dating back more than five centuries to the lochs, rivers, and ponds of Scotland will help provide context to the story. There is also a Glossary of some Scottish and curling terms which can be consulted, if necessary. If you don't know what "cauld" means ("cold") or what "sooping" means ("sweeping"), you can look it up.

The Shattered Curling Stone is a work of historical fiction, which can be a tricky genre to both write and read. As with most historical fiction, some of the persons, places, and events are, or were, real. In this particular case, Her Majesty Queen Victoria, the Reverend John Kerr, Henrietta and John Gilmour, and Mrs. Maxwell Durham were all real people. The rest of the cast is entirely fictional.

Lastly, a special word of gratitude to everyone, including friends, curlers, libraries, and bookstores who took a chance on a new author and purchased *The Stones of Ailsa Craig*. Your support and kind words are the only reason for this book. Thank you so much.

David S. Florig
Ocean Park, Maine.

Chapter 1
No, Nae, Never

"Hugh," William Beveridge began, "I can't allow it to continue anymore. There have simply been too many complaints." William Beveridge was the President of the Musselburgh Curling Club, which had been founded in 1812, more than sixty years earlier. He was also a good friend of Hugh Maclaren, and took no pleasure in delivering the news to him. Hugh Maclaren's sin was in taking his twelve-year-old daughter onto the club's pond to teach her how to curl.

Hugh Maclaren was a noted and decorated curler, as well as the highly-respected Secretary of the Musselburgh Curling Club. In fact, he had played a substantial role in curling's rapid growth throughout Scotland in the latter part of the 1800s, often representing Musselburgh at meetings of the Royal Caledonian Curling Club. The Royal Caledonian Curling Club had been formed to standardize and govern curling throughout Scotland, where the sport was born in the 1500s. The Royal Caledonian Curling Club was not a curling club in the usual sense, but rather an umbrella organization for existing clubs. The Royal Club, initially named the *Grand* Caledonian Curling Club, was founded at the Waterloo Hotel in Edinburgh on July 25, 1838, by a group of forty-four curlers, each and every one of them a man. It was a woman, however, Her Majesty Queen Victoria, who bestowed the title of *Royal* Caledonian Curling Club on the club five years later. Queen Victoria had become fascinated by curling after watching a demonstration of the sport on the wooden floor of the Scone Palace in Perth.

"What is the problem, exactly, William?" Hugh asked. "We don't disturb anyone. We don't keep any of the members from the ice. Who made the complaints?" Hugh Maclaren had a very strong suspicion about who the most vociferous complainer might be.

"I'm not at liberty to say, Hugh," Beveridge answered. "You understand. But I simply can't permit it any further."

"Is it because she's a girl, William? Is that the objection?" Hugh asked. He knew the answer, of course. Girls weren't supposed to curl. Curling was, after all, considered to be "productive of health and *manly* disposition," according to one of the early books about curling, *Memorabilia Curliana Mabenensia,* published in 1830, and was deemed "the manly Scottish exercise" by both Robert Burns and Sir Walter Scott. Who knew where all of this might lead if it were allowed to continue?

"She's not a member of the club, Hugh. The pond is only for the use of our members. It's as simple as that," Beveridge answered. Beveridge knew otherwise. He knew that the complaints were precisely because Ailsa Maclaren was a girl. Hugh Maclaren knew it, too. Ailsa's father had committed the apparently egregious mistake of taking his daughter onto the club's pond a few times to begin teaching her the game.

"Would you reach the same conclusion if Ailsa were a boy?" Hugh asked. He was getting angry. Even though Beveridge was a friend, as president of the club, Beveridge should not be spoken to in such a manner.

"That's enough, Hugh," Beveridge said sternly. "The decision has been made. Let it be, please. I wish that it were otherwise."

———◆———

A few days later, when another deep frost had settled in over Musselburgh, Ailsa asked her father if he would again take her to the pond to teach her more about how to curl and to afford her another chance to practice. He knew that the question would come eventually. Hugh Maclaren sat down with his daughter and explained that the Musselburgh Curling Club would not permit anyone who was not a member of the club to curl on the club's pond. That wasn't the real reason, but it was the one he had been given. Ailsa started to cry. After only a few hours of learning the game, she had already come to love it, just as her father did. Now, she was being told that she wouldn't be allowed to play anymore.

"It's not fair!" Ailsa protested. "Some of the fathers take their sons curling. You told me so. I've even seen them! Why can't I play just like them?" She was right. Boys did sometimes take to the club's ice to learn the game from their fathers. No one at the club had ever raised any objection to that practice.

"I know, sweetheart. You're right. It isn't fair. But there's nothing I can do. Believe me, I tried," her father answered. Disappointing Ailsa was not something that Hugh Maclaren liked or was accustomed to. He was used to indulging her, pampering her, even. She was his only child. In the back of his mind, Hugh Maclaren thought that there just might be something that he *could* do. Until he was certain that it was possible, he would not reveal his idea to Ailsa.

Chapter 2
A Pond of Her Own

From the very first day that she sent curling stones rumbling down the ice of the Musselburgh Curling Club, under the tutelage of her father, Ailsa Maclaren was good. Very good, in fact. Destined to be great, perhaps, if only she were allowed to continue playing. For the rest of her life, she would remember and cherish that day as one of the best ever. It had been just she and her father, on a sparkling Scottish day, throwing stones down the ice. Each time that she ventured out onto the ice with her father – which only amounted to three before the club put an abrupt end to it – she was a better curler than the time before. If ever there was someone who appeared to have been born to curl, it was Ailsa Maclaren.

Ever since she was very young, Ailsa had gone with her mother to watch her father compete for the Musselburgh Curling Club at bonspiels. Sometimes he played with the married men against the bachelors, sometimes he played for the shaven against the unshaven, sometimes he played for his parish, and sometimes he competed in the Grand Match between the North and South of Scotland. The Grand Match was an annual bonspiel, first played in 1847, which was the most important bonspiel in the country. The Grand Match often involved upwards of a thousand curlers from all corners of Scotland. Ailsa watched her father compete in Grand Matches in Lochwinnoch and Carsebreck, marveling at the hundreds of rinks of competitors and the thousands of spectators crowded onto the ice. She was brazen enough, and still naive enough, to dream that some day people would gather to watch *her* play.

For the past few years, Ailsa had begged her father to take her curling with him and to teach her how to play. He had always refused, telling her that curling was not something that young lasses like her should engage in. Ailsa didn't understand why. If boys could do it, why couldn't she? Hugh Maclaren knew, however, that his resolve was weakening and was no match for Ailsa's. Few fathers can deny their daughters nor long resist their pleas, and Hugh Maclaren was most assuredly not one of the few who could.

By the time that Hugh Maclaren walked out onto the ice with his curling stones and his daughter for the first time on that glorious January day in 1880, Ailsa already knew almost all of the rules, and most of the traditions, terms, and tactics associated with the nearly 400-year-old game. She had watched her father play for years, and asked him questions about the rules and the strategy he employed after each match that he played. Ailsa often remembered more about the specific details of each game than her father did. She could recount nearly every situation and shot. She already understood so much about a game which she had never played. Her father was finally allowing her the chance. It would prove to be a life-changing occasion for Ailsa, but not just for her.

That January day, at barely twelve years old, alone on the ice with her father, learning how to throw curling stones and how to soop and guide them to their mark with a besom, was the most exhilarating day of Ailsa's young life. She was sure that no day ever could, or would, surpass it. It wasn't easy, though, for a girl her age to throw the thirty or forty-pound stones down the length of the ice, but Ailsa figured out a way. She almost always figured out a way. For Ailsa, it was equally a matter of will as it was one of strength. Hugh Maclaren recognized Ailsa's talent almost immediately. He had seen a lot of beginners, both men and boys, struggle to throw the stones far more than Ailsa did at first. To

Ailsa's disappointment and her father's indignation, Ailsa was only able to curl twice more that winter before being refused allowance to curl on the club's pond. Her father was determined to find a way for Ailsa to continue to play, with or without the blessing of the Musselburgh Curling Club.

Hugh Maclaren owned several curling stones – blue Ailsas. They were some of his most cherished possessions, fashioned from the blue hone granite and common green granite found only on the volcanic Scottish island of Ailsa Craig, ten miles west of the Scottish mainland. Some of the stones he had won as the skip of the winning rink at a bonspiel, some had been handed down by his father – also a dedicated curler – and others he had purchased. At the time when the Maclarens' daughter was born on New Year's Day in 1868, Ailsa Craig was becoming renowned as home to the best curling stone granite in the world. Ailsa Craig stones, referred to as "Ailsas," were quickly becoming the preferred curling stones in Scotland, as they already were in Canada, or at least in those parts of Canada where curling was played with stones. Other parts of Canada used "stones" made of iron or carved wooden blocks. Hugh and Mrs. Maclaren, but Hugh, mainly, decided to name their baby girl "Ailsa." Some day, when Ailsa was older, Hugh promised, he would take her to see the island of Ailsa Craig for herself. It was a promise which he fulfilled many years later.

Ailsa was an extraordinary girl in many ways, but what girl isn't? There was very little that she set her mind to that she wasn't able to accomplish. She grew up on a small farm in Musselburgh, a market town on the Firth of Forth, next to the River Esk, as an only child. She learned not only how to entertain herself, but also how to perform most of the chores required at a farm. She tended to the vegetables and to the animals – chickens, goats, horses, and sheep. She fed them, watered them, collected eggs, learned how to shear the sheep, and gathered and spread manure, which was her least favorite responsibility. When Ailsa was nine years old, her father presented her with a pony, which Ailsa named "Magic." Hugh Maclaren taught Ailsa how to ride, which she quickly and enthusiastically mastered. He sometimes took her to the magnificent Musselburgh Racecourse, not to gamble, of course, but to study and admire the horses.

Ailsa loved going to school, not only because she liked learning, but because she got to be with other children. Without brothers or sisters, it was her best chance to play in groups, rather than alone. Athletic and nearly fearless, Ailsa preferred to play with the boys, when she was allowed to. Usually she wasn't, unless the boys happened to need another player. The truth was, the boys didn't really want to play with a girl who was better than them at most of their games.

What Ailsa liked the most about school, though, was reading. At home, if she wasn't riding, or taking care of Magic, or performing her chores, Ailsa was reading. She especially enjoyed Lewis Carroll's *Alice's Adventures in Wonderland*, Robert Louis Stevenson's *Treasure Island*, and Anna Sewell's *Black Beauty*, which she read several times. Her teachers adored her, and Ailsa never once had to receive so much as even a mild strapping from the dreaded tawse.

⚬

Hugh Maclaren was not a man who was easily dissuaded once he set his mind on something. He had introduced Ailsa to curling, she loved it, and was very good at it. With or without the blessing of the Musselburgh Curling Club, Ailsa was going to continue curling. Her father would make sure of that. As the summertime approached, Hugh Maclaren devised a plan. He secured a copy of John Cairnie's *Essay on Curling and*

Artificial Pond Making and began reading and studying. He took note of the statement in the Preface that "the hot weather is by far the best for the formation of Artificial Ponds."

He kept reading and writing down notes:

> *run the water on the pond to a depth of 1/4 inch, which readily gives ice fit for Curling in one night's frost . . . another object to be attended to, in fixing the site, is to have it defended, if possible, against the wind . . . if the wind be moderate, the water is to be let in upon the rink in such a quantity as barely to cover the highest part . . . should the wind chance to blow hard, the coating must be put on differently; for from inattention to this, it is easily conceived that very much of the water will be driven to the end or side . . . to prevent this, we have watering-cans with roses, with one of which a man begins at one end throwing water out from the rose, across the pond, and walking backwards . . . in frosty weather, the water no sooner falls than it is frozen, and this prevents it from being driven by the wind . . .*

He made particular note of the dimensions: 55-60 yards in length, 5-6 yards in width, 8 inches deep, 4-5 inches of clay, 3-4 inches of riddled earth, sown with grass, beat down, levelled, with an outlet for excess water. He began thinking about where on the farm such a pond could be located.

Hugh Maclaren felt like it just might be possible. There was a low-lying section of the farm, less than a quarter of an acre, that might work well. It was bounded on one side by some trees, which would provide partial protection from wind and sun. There were several clay deposits on the farm, brick clay mostly, but that would do well-enough.

It would require about one-hundred cubic yards of clay, he calculated, which wouldn't present too much of a problem. Clay, he had. Water could be diverted from one of the small streams that traversed the property. He decided to try it, if Ailsa was willing to do some hard, dirty work.

One evening in May, Hugh Maclaren sat down with Ailsa. "Sweetheart, I have a question for you. Do you want to continue curling when winter arrives?"

Ailsa was confused. She had almost resigned herself to the fact that she would never again be allowed to play. "Yes, father, yes! How would it be possible? Is your club going to let me?"

"No, I'm afraid not, dear. They're a rather stubborn lot. Once a decision is made, they do not change their minds easily," her father answered. "But I thought that we might try to make our own little curling pond. Just for us. What would you think of that?"

"Really?!?" Ailsa exclaimed. "Yes, yes, let's build our own! We could play every day all winter. Where can we build it?" Ailsa had no idea how much work it would take, or that she would have to do most of it. Not yet, at least. She would come to learn that soon enough.

Hugh Maclaren had to laugh at his daughter's excitement, although it did not surprise him at all. Ailsa took on almost everything with a determination and enthusiasm that he admired. "I have an idea about that," he said. "Let's take a walk around the farm tomorrow and see what you think. Now, head on off to bed. We'll have a lot of work to do tomorrow."

The next morning, father and daughter headed out to take a look at the location that he had chosen. "I think that this spot would be perfect," Ailsa's father offered, standing on a relatively flat parcel to the northwest of a stand of birch trees.

"Why here, father? What makes this the best place?" Ailsa asked. Her father was very used to hearing those kinds of questions from Ailsa. He enjoyed answering them for her. He explained things to her as if she were an adult. It was one of the things that made him such a wonderful father and that made their relationship unusually close by nineteenth century father-daughter standards. Hugh Maclaren began his explanation.

"A couple of things, sweetheart." Ailsa liked when her father called her "sweetheart." "For one, those trees are to the west of us. Since most of our wind comes from the west, they will offer some protection from the wind. Wind would drive the water to one side of the pond and result in some very biased ice. And we wouldn't want biased ice, now, would we?" Ailsa shook her head. "For another, it is downhill from one of our streams, so diverting water here will be easier. And, as you can see, it's flat." They stood there in the warmth of the late spring day. Ailsa was already dreaming of curling there during the coming winter. Her father was thinking about how much work it would be. "Are you ready to get to work?" he asked.

"Yes, father, I'm ready," Ailsa answered excitedly. "Let's get to work."

Hugh Maclaren and his daughter walked up to the barn. He retrieved a mallet, four wooden stakes, and a big roll of string. "The first thing we'll have to do is make our measurements," he said. "We want it to be big enough, but not too big, because that would mean a lot more work. And it's already going to be work enough. We want it to be just the right size. Not too big, not too small, just right." Hugh Maclaren elongated the word "just." Ailsa understood her father's reference and laughed. "Yes," Ailsa said, "It has to be just right," also emphasizing "just." They carried everything down to the spot where they would try to build their private curling pond together.

Hugh Maclaren stood and surveyed the area. He had already visualized what it would look like as a curling pond. He walked to his chosen spot and drove the first stake into the ground, Ailsa following. He handed the end of the string to Ailsa and told her to hold it at the stake, which Ailsa did. Hugh then walked along what would be one long side of the pond a distance of fifty-five yards and stopped. He drove another wooden stake into the ground. At a right angle to the second stake, Hugh Maclaren measured six yards and drove another stake. He followed the same procedure to measure off the other side and the other end. There were now four wooden stakes in the ground defining a perfect rectangle which would be their curling pond. "That was the easiest part of the whole project, I'm afraid," he smiled to Ailsa. "Now the hard work begins. Are you ready to get dirty?" Father and daughter walked to the barn as Ailsa's father began to explain all of the hard, nasty work which would need to be done over the summer.

"The first thing we have to do is break up the soil. Right now, it's far too rocky and hard to work with. We need to plough it, first. Let's hook up the plough," the father said. Once the plough and horse were set up, they headed back to the appointed place. Ailsa's father explained that the plough would not only loosen the soil, but that it would also dig up lots and lots of rocks, which would all have to be removed by hand. For the next several days and weeks, Hugh said, that would be Ailsa's job, because all of the loose rocks would have to be removed before the base of the pond could be laid. Ailsa grossly underestimated the magnitude of the job ahead of her. Her father had to be exaggerating. She thought that she might even be able to finish it that very day, if she worked really hard. Her father knew otherwise.

Hugh explained that not only did the rocks have to be removed, but they also needed to be re-used. The rocks had to be piled all along the four sides of the pond to serve as the base of an embankment which would not only define the contours of the pond, but which would also help contain the water and provide some additional measure of protection from wind and debris, which would help to maintain a smooth surface as ice was forming. As her father began ploughing, he began churning up hundreds – thousands – of rocks, large and small. Each and every one of them would have to be removed. The enormity of the task started to set in with Ailsa. She realized that she would not finish the job that day. Probably not tomorrow, either. Or the next day. Ailsa knew that it would be worth it, but still . . .

As her father continued to plough, Ailsa donned heavy leather gloves and began removing rocks. Some were small, but others were quite large and heavy. Some, she had to roll because she could not carry them. She was still just twelve years old and slight, and the job was by no means either easy or fun, but she tackled it nonetheless. By the time the next winter rolled in, she would be nearly three inches taller and fifteen pounds heavier, almost all of it muscle.

When her father was finally finished ploughing, and Ailsa had removed a few dozen rocks, her father said to her, "Let's take the plough back to the barn and go inside for some lunch. You must be hungry and thirsty by now." Ailsa suddenly realized just how hungry she was. As they sat down to the lunch prepared by Mrs. Maclaren, Hugh asked Ailsa, "So, dear, do you think that you're going to be able to do it? Most of the hard work is going to be up to you, now." He knew better than to ask. Ailsa believed that she could do almost anything.

"Of course I can do it, father. Just watch me!" Ailsa answered. She wasn't quite as confident as she tried to sound. She was already tired and sore.

After finishing lunch, Ailsa ran back down to the site of the pond. She again put on her gloves and began removing rocks one-by-one and piling them along the perimeter. Some were so large and heavy that they required two hands to carry, others needed only one, and the biggest ones could only be rolled. After an hour, she sat down to rest. Ailsa was used to working around the farm, but not quite like this. Her father walked down from the house to check on her. She had cleared about three square yards out of more than 300. At this rate, her father calculated, it would take more than a hundred hours just to remove the rocks. If Ailsa worked hard for twenty hours a week, a formidable task for any twelve-year-old, it would take a month and a half. Hugh Maclaren wondered whether Ailsa would actually do it, although he strongly suspected that she would. Mrs. Maclaren worried that it might be too much to ask of such a young lass.

Ailsa soon settled into a routine for removing the rocks. Most days, she went to the site early in the morning, right after breakfast, when the temperatures were cooler, and worked for two or three hours. For the rest of the day, she tended to her chores and helped her mother with household work. She tried to take a nap most days, too. In the evenings, when it was again cooler, she spent another hour or two clearing rocks. She usually fell asleep early, an open book on her chest, and slept soundly.

Sundays and Mondays provided Ailsa with a respite. On Sundays, the Maclarens went to church and generally refrained from all but necessary work, like feeding the animals and tending the garden. Mondays meant that Ailsa would accompany her mother to market and wherever else Mrs. Maclaren needed to go in town. She liked to ride Magic on Sundays and Mondays, as well. She didn't want Magic to feel neglected. With that weekly routine, Ailsa was devoting around twenty hours a week to the unending work of clearing rocks. The mound of rocks around the periphery of the pond was growing steadily. Her father was pleased, yet not surprised.

By late June, the project was finished. Almost all of the rocks had been removed, although there were still a few stragglers that would be removed during the next phase. A ring of rocks, a foot or two high, encircled the site. Ailsa was proud of her work, especially after her father told her how impressed he was that she had worked so hard and seen the project through. She was excited, but a bit apprehensive about whatever would come next.

Ailsa's father explained what needed to happen now. The entire site had to be raked, excavated, leveled, and compacted. "What you need to do is rake the entire area with a bow rake to loosen more of the soil. You'll probably find some more rocks, too, which you will have to remove." Ailsa frowned. She didn't really want to hear about more rocks.

Ailsa retrieved the bow rake from the barn, slung it over her shoulder, and walked down to the site. She looked down the length of the would-be pond. It doesn't seem too awfully imposing, she thought. Raking couldn't possibly be as hard as picking rocks. She quickly learned differently. First of all, the bow rake dug three or four inches down into the loose earth, encountering far more rocks than anticipated, and each one had to be picked up and removed. Second, and far worse, were the blisters. Despite wearing heavy gloves, the rake's wooden handle rubbed and pressed Ailsa's fingers and hands, creating nasty, painful blisters. Ailsa's mother tended to them, but it set Ailsa back several days as they healed. When the blisters were finally gone, Ailsa resumed her raking, taking far more care about how she handled the rake.

With the last of the rocks all but gone and the soil sufficiently loosened, Ailsa's father explained the next step. The top eight inches of soil needed to be removed from the pond site and piled along the perimeter, on top of the ring of rocks. Once again, it didn't seem like a lot to Ailsa. After all, eight inches wasn't all that much. In reality, it meant shoveling more than 200 cubic yards of soil. Even with a wheelbarrow, which could only hold one-tenth of a cubic yard and still be manageable for the young lass, it meant that 2,000 loads had to be shoveled into the wheelbarrow and dumped. After about twenty-five loads, Ailsa seriously wondered for the first time if it was worth all of this sweaty, dirty work. She wasn't about to stop now, though, not after the rock-picking, raking, and blisters. Ailsa Maclaren was not a quitter.

Her father helped Ailsa as often as he could, especially with pushing the wheelbarrow, the task which Ailsa found the most difficult because of her short height. Wheelbarrows seemed like they had been designed for taller people. Sometimes, Ailsa's father even went alone to work on the pond for an hour or two. He didn't want Ailsa to have to do all of the work, but he did have his own work which needed to be done. He was able to make progress more quickly than Ailsa, being much bigger and stronger. By the time that late-August came, the necessary soil had been removed and stood in large mounds all around the pond. Three months had gone by, and they still hadn't started to actually construct the pond. Ailsa's father told her that they needed to take a week off, which came as most welcome news.

After a week's break, Ailsa's father took her back down to the site and explained the next step, which would be a much easier one, he assured her. Ailsa liked hearing that. Hugh Maclaren carried with him two wooden planks, each about two feet long, with leather staps that he had affixed to them. "What I need for you to do is to put these on your boots and walk. All you have to do is walk. Up and down, back and forth, over and over again, to tamp down the dirt. It has to be perfectly flat. Once it is, the horse can do the rest of the work. I'll come down with a level now and then to help us make it perfectly level and compact. If it isn't, I'm afraid we'll have ourselves some very biased ice. Biased ice won't do, now, will it?"

"No way!" Ailsa exclaimed. "I hate biased ice!"

For parts of the next two days, Ailsa donned the makeshift wooden planks and walked. It was a boring, but not very difficult, job, although her legs got tired from the exaggerated steps she had to take. Periodically, Ailsa's father checked to make sure that the ground was level. When he encountered low or high spots, he staked them off so that Ailsa could add or remove soil. After dozens of back-and-forths, the base no longer gave way under her feet and felt hard, compact, and, best of all, level. Ailsa announced to her father that she thought that she was finished. Her father inspected the area and agreed. "Tomorrow, we'll put the horse to work," he said. "Let's go inside and play a game of chess, shall we? We haven't played in a long, long time." Ailsa loved playing chess with her father, although she wished that she could win occasionally.

On Saturday morning, Hugh Maclaren went to the barn with Ailsa and attached a roller, weighing over 700 pounds, to the Shire horse, and led the enormous workhorse down to the pond, pulling the roller behind it. The horse seemed to barely notice that it was pulling something. Shires were born to pull things. Very heavy things. Hugh Maclaren led the horse onto the pond site and slowly walked up and down the length of the pond, the roller compacting the earth further with each pass. After two hours, satisfied with the condition of the area, man and beast stepped off of the perfectly flat rectangle and headed back up to the barn. The Shire wasn't even sweating. Hugh Maclaren was.

Although the hardest parts of the project were finished, there were still weeks of labor ahead. At least the weather was getting cooler. The process was almost the same as excavating the site, except in reverse. Hugh Maclaren delivered mounds of clay with his tractor, clay harvested from one of the clay deposits on the farm, and Ailsa spent her days covering the entire base of the pond with a four-inch layer. Ailsa's walking planks and then the workhorse again did the compacting. Finally, finally, a three-inch layer of riddled earth, taken from the soil which Ailsa had removed months ago, was put down over the base of clay and compacted. As November rolled in, there was nothing left for Ailsa to do except wait for winter.

⸺◆⸺

At the first sign of a coming frost, Ailsa and her father went down and cleared the leaves and sticks from their curling pond site, flooded it from a diverted stream to a depth of less than half-an-inch, and went inside for the night. At seven o'clock the next morning, Ailsa came bursting inside through the front door as her parents sat at the breakfast table. "There's ice! There's really ice! Hurry, father. Come and see it! It worked!"

Hugh Maclaren smiled at his wife, quickly retrieved his coat and hat, and followed Ailsa down to the pond. "By God, it *did* work," Hugh thought to himself. It was as keen and shiny and unbiased as any curling ice he had ever seen. They both stepped out onto the ice – their ice – which was solid and hard. "I'll go to the barn and bring the curling stones and crampit down with Magic. He could use the exercise," Ailsa finally offered. She hugged her father, told him, "Thank you," and ran off to the barn as fast as she could to retrieve the stones and crampit. Father and daughter spent the better part of a glorious day on their little pond. Hugh Maclaren wondered a couple of times what John Carswell, the member of the Musselburgh Curling Club complaining most about Ailsa curling, might think if he saw them. Not that he cared, he just wondered.

That winter, whenever his time, but more importantly, the frost, permitted, Hugh took Ailsa out onto their ice to practice and to receive further instruction. When he wasn't able, Ailsa went to the pond alone. Her father taught her the Fenwick Twist, or the turning of the wrist upon releasing the stone, so that the stone would curl on the ice to land in its desired spot or strike its intended target. Hugh Maclaren was a great teacher. He was patient, methodical, and willing to listen and to answer questions. He stacked one bit of learning on top of the prior one. Just like he had done in teaching Ailsa how to ride a horse or shear a sheep or construct their curling pond, he not only showed her how to do something, but also the reasoning and science behind it.

In the case of the Fenwick Twist, he explained that it allegedly originated in Fenwick, North Ayrshire, where curlers had discovered that by turning the wrist one way or the other when releasing the stone, it would rotate on its axis either clockwise or counterclockwise, thereby counteracting any bias, or slant, to the ice. Later, it was discovered that the twist could actually cause the stone to curl, or travel in an arc, making it possible for a stone to bend around other stones which might be in its path. Not everyone used the twist, but Hugh Maclaren knew just how important it was to a serious curler.

He remembered the day that he taught Ailsa the Fenwick twist. "It's a very subtle maneuver, Ailsa," he had told her. "You don't want to set the stone spinning down the ice like a top. That will do not good. You want to the stone to turn gently, so that it can grip the ice and curl. Just two or three revolutions down the length of the ice." Hugh Maclaren demonstrated for Ailsa, who soon mastered the twist, just as her father had.

Ailsa's father also taught her about wicking and guarding and running a port and ticking and tapping and cannoning. He placed stones at various positions on the ice and explained to Ailsa what shot should be played next and why. He showed her how to play aggressively and defensively, as the situation and score demanded. Ailsa learned quickly and began to master the many strategies, nuances, and subtleties of the game. She learned how to navigate both dull ice and keen ice, for outdoor curling required a mastery of both, sometimes on the same day. Ailsa never wanted to stop learning and practicing and improving. It was usually the setting of the sun or a thaw setting in which forced father and daughter from their ice.

As a young man, just eighteen years old, Hugh Maclaren volunteered to join the Scottish Army. He was a natural fit, with an innate self-discipline and extraordinary leadership skills. What he learned during his service time was to put individual interest aside and to focus only on what was best for the group collectively. Hugh Maclaren worked efficiently and collectively for the greater good and success of the unit, and he expected each of the other men to do his best to advance the goals of the team, as well. By the time that his service ended, he had assimilated all of those habits into his daily life, always thinking first of the interest of whatever group he was part of, whether family, work, the curling club, or country.

The most important lessons which Ailsa's father imparted to her were not about rules and strategy, or the intricacies of executing various curling shots, they were about leadership and teamwork. Were Ailsa ever to play on a curling team, she needed to understand that every single shot must be designed to advance the cause of the team, not to bring individual glory to whoever happened to be attempting it. A perfectly executed shot, while wonderful to make and to witness, would ultimately mean nothing if it didn't advance the aims of the entire rink. She would also need to learn how to draw the very best out of her teammates, not by criticizing or demeaning, but by encouraging and supporting. Ailsa understood, although she had never curled with a team.

When Hugh Maclaren met his future wife, she immediately recognized those traits and admired them. Throughout their courtship and early years of marriage, Hugh Maclaren dedicated himself to building the best life and future that they could have together. He worked hard, saved money, and purchased the small farm that Mrs. Maclaren believed would be perfect for starting and raising a family. Ailsa arrived soon thereafter.

Chapter 3
Girls Don't Curl

I n 1880s Scotland, during the latter part of the Victorian Era, curling was definitely not a sport in which the "weaker sex" were generally tolerated, much less welcomed. Nor were other sports, either. The sporting life was for men, who enthusiastically took to golf, archery, football, shinty, and, of course, curling.

Young Victorian girls and women, rather than wasting their time at sports, were expected to marry, bear children, maintain households, or work in the fishing, spinning, or weaving industries, if economically necessary. But Ailsa Maclaren was not of the "weaker sex," either in spirit or in body. No, she was strong, in both ways. And she was determined to be a curler. Not just any curler, either – she wanted to be the best.

That is not to say that women never curled in the eighteenth and nineteenth centuries, because they occasionally did. It was just that they were neither encouraged nor instructed in the art and the science of the game. By and large, it was just something that wasn't really an issue. Curling clubs had been opening throughout Scotland for more than 150 years, and not one of them had a single woman member. A few curling clubs or societies did expressly forbid women from joining, although that hardly seemed necessary. For example, the Auchterarder Curling Club, founded in 1830, was open to "all the *male* inhabitants of the parish." At almost all other clubs, it was simply understood and went without the necessity and trouble of being memorialized in writing.

There were those scattered times, however, when women dared to venture out onto the frozen board to try their hands at "the Roarin' Game," but those times were very much the exceptions that proved the rule. As far back as 1740, a curling match between the married and unmarried women of Tinron was reported in the *Ipswich Journal*:

> *A famous Curling Match was lately play'd on the Water of Skarr in Nithfdale, between the married Wives and the young Girls of the Parifh of Tinron, the Maids fhew'd a good deal of dexterity in handling the Stones, and will, no doubt, be very expert in Time...*

After first admonishing that, "Ladies do not curl – on the ice," a rather curious phrase, curling historian the Reverend John Kerr made note of women's "dexterity" when they were permitted to curl. He wrote about an 1800s bonspiel between the "maidens" of Capenoch and those of Waterside:

> *[S]kips of acknowledged skill presided over them. An enormous concourse of spectators assembled, and the sun in honour of the occasion shown out brightly upon the scene. The ice was bad, and ... the maidens had to play the match 'fetlock-deep in water;' but great skill was displayed on both sides, the curling-broom being handled as dexterously as the domestic one..." History of Curling – Scotland's Ain Game (John Kerr 1890).*

Of particular note in Kerr's account are the facts that the women were "presided over" by men who served as skips, or directors, for the women, who were apparently presumed to be incapable of skipping their own teams, and that their skill at the game was compared to their skills at performing household chores. Perhaps the women would have been better off skipping their own matches, based on this account of an 1841 match in Buittle:

> *On 10th February 1841, the married ladies of Buittle challenged the unmarried, and the match came off at Loch-bill, twenty ladies a side, and a gentleman skipping each team. So novel a scene attracted such a crowd that the players were compelled to shift the rink several times. The game was carried out with the determination peculiar to the sex, and resulted in the defeat of the married party, who declared that there had been treachery in their camp. That they had some ground for their suspicion was proved by the fact that soon afterwards the skip of the married ladies was united to a young widow who had played on the unmarried side, and had cast sheep's eyes over the hog score all the time of the match. History of Curling – Scotland's Ain Game (John Kerr 1890).*

The Reverend Kerr does not elaborate on what he meant by the "determination peculiar to the sex." Perhaps it was intended as a compliment, perhaps not. In any case, the women of Tinron and Buittle were mimicking a practice which was quite ubiquitous in the early days of curling – matches between bachelors and married men – matches which Hugn Maclaren himself had participated in. Nearly every curling club held such competitions.

More than a century after the wives and maidens met to curl in Tinron in 1740, another ladies' curling match was held between rival parishes. The account is less-than-flattering, although the reporter may have believed otherwise:

> *The game was, however, played on several strips of water which collected in hollows in some of the fields round the town. In one . . . a notable game was played between the wives of Sanquhar and Crawick Mill, who were directed by men. The game was, we understand, played with all the spirit and determination which usually characterise female fights. The Channel-Stane or Sweeping Frae the Rinks (First Series 1883).*

It was quite apparent that the men who wrote the reports about the adventurous Victorian ladies who braved trying their hands at curling had a significant level of difficulty handing out real compliments. They always seemed to be backhanded, at best.

That is not to say, however, that women weren't permitted, or even encouraged, to *watch* as the men curled, because they most certainly were. Women, as spectators at curling matches, were often noticed and commented upon by the presumably male reporters covering the events. As reported by the *Caledonian Mercury* on January 24, 1820:

> *A curling match took place on the 21st inst. on the river Carron . . . between the curlers of the parish of Falkirk and the best and most distinguished curlers of the parishes of Larbert, Dunnipace, Denny, and St. Ninians . . . The hostile (or rather the friendly) parties numbered on each side 36. This keen contest, and manly amusement, was witnessed by all the beauty and fashion of the surrounding neighbourhood.*

The "beauty and fashion of the surrounding neighbourhood" no doubt referred to the many women who came out adorned in their finest winter garb to watch as their sons, husbands, beaus, and fathers played the game. An Annual from the Royal Caledonian Curling Club contains this account of a bonspiel played before a large crowd, which included "a large number of ladies, who, wrapped in furs, flitted about on skates in the vicinity of the particular rink in which a father, brother, or probably some one as dear was playing his part in the roarin' game."

At a bonspiel held at Tibbermore on January 12, 1843, it was reported that: "Persons of every grade in society were engaged in the play. Ladies of high quality stood among the observers and admirers." *Curling - The Ancient Scottish Game (James Taylor 2d ed. 1887)*. Yes, the women were certainly more than welcome to watch, presumably provided that they had completed all of their duties and chores at home. "Ladies of high quality" were especially welcome.

The curling men were often emboldened in playing their games by the married, but more likely by the unmarried, women who came out to witness a bonspiel. As reported by the *Illustrated Berwick Journal* on March 20, 1858:

> *So very intense has the frost been for some time, that the Whitadder was completely frozen over on Thursday last, when a number of gentlemen met for a day's curling. After a few preliminary arrangements the sport commenced, and was carried on for a considerable time, with great and spirited competition. The day being excellent, several ladies came out to witness the games, which contributed not a little to fire the courage of the players, as well as to add a charm to the whole scene.*

Had the game been anything other than curling, which induces such a passion and fervor in its devotees as to allow for no distractions, the men could have easily lost focus on their matches due to the presence of the several charming ladies. No keen, experienced skip, however, would ever allow his men to lose their concentration over so trifling a thing, as reflected in this account of the Grand Match at Carsebreck on February 12, 1873:

> *A number of skaters . . . had accompanied the curlers, and were gliding over the loch in all directions, some executing all kinds of fancy 'figures,' while others contented themselves with plain straight-forward skating. Not the least skilful, and decidedly the most graceful, among them were a few daring spirits of the gentler sex, whose evolutions might well have distracted the attention of the players themselves had any game less fascinating than curling been on the tapis. Curling – The Ancient Scottish Game (James Taylor 2d ed. 1887).*

Although women did not often get the opportunity to curl themselves, they did not always serve merely as spectators, either. They played other very significant roles, as well. Roles to which they were presumably much better suited. Roles which served the needs of their men. Wives were often expected, or required, to help their husbands prepare for a day on the ice, or to provide food and drink to the men during the matches, so that the men could play their best and enjoy their well-deserved fellowship with their brethren. An excerpt from *Curling – The Ancient Scottish Game,* reveals what was much more commonly the Scottish woman's role in curling in the 1700s and 1800s:

It may be doubted, however, whether any of these acts of self-denial deserve so well to be had in remembrance as the exploit of the wife of a noted curler in the Upper Ward of Lanarkshire about the beginning of the present century. The veteran 'knight of the channel-stane' had acquired great celebrity as a skilful and sagacious skip, but age crept on 'wi' stealthy pace,' and infirmity followed in its train. The announcement of a parish bonspeil fired the spirit of the veteran curler, but his failing strength made it impossible for him to carry his curling stone over a rough worn track two long miles to the scene of action. 'I'm no able,' he was often heard to mutter on the evening before the match and on the morning of the eventful day. The burden of the old man's song was, 'I needna try't, I canna carry't.' 'Could you do ony gude gin ye were there?' inquired his wife, who was several years younger than her husband. 'Ay, that could I,' was his ready rejoinder. 'My certie, ye's be there then,' was her prompt reply; and forthwith putting the curling stone into a bag, the faithful matron heaved it on her shoulder, and followed by her husband she halted not till she had deposited her load on the ice at the loch where the match was to be played. 'There, my bonnie man,' she said, 'play ye're part, and gif ye win, my faith ye's got something gude and warm to ye're supper the nicht,' and home the courageous dame wended her way.

Not only did the "gude wife" carry her husband's curling stone two miles to the ice (and walk back alone), but she also made sure to have a hot supper waiting for him when he finished playing.

No, rather than being encouraged, or in most cases even allowed, to join in the curling fun with the men, women, young and old, single and married, far more often served as spectators, beasts of burden, cooks, or even as mere props for the male curlers:

> *Whilst last, not least, the peerless maidens, 'busked braw,' coming to draw water, coyly submit to those delightful abductions which their swains impose - and, seated upon their water-cans, are hurled over the ice amidst the shouts and emulation of their numerous attendants . . . Memorabilia Curliana Mabenensia (1830).*

Boys and young men, on the other hand, were invited and welcomed into the world of curling at a young age. Many learned the game and its intricacies from their fathers, who proudly instructed them and initiated them into "the mysteries of the game."

So obsessed and consumed with curling were some men when old John Frost came calling that many of the abandoned wives developed a healthy resentment of their husbands' days spent curling and neglecting their work and other worldly responsibilities. They believed that their husbands would be far better off working than playing, and they were probably right. Some wives even took a measure of revenge on their wayward, derelict spouses:

> *The curling mania that winter [1829-30] was felt by many a weaver very severely, and also by his dearly beloved spouse, who so testified by her thin chafts and by the blae color of her face. A craftsman of this sort in this village uttered his complaints to his helpmate one night, and gave many a weary look to her tume ambrie (empty cupboard). But she*

assumed a blythe countenance and bade him keep his spirits up till she should present him with a substantial supper. She bustled, set a table before him, and laid a knife and a fork; when the supper came – lo! it was a curling stane. Curling – The Ancient Scottish Game (James Taylor 2d ed. 1887).

The man's "helpmate" delivered a simple, yet undeniably brilliant, message. Some other curling widows were so anxious to see their husbands attend to their employments, rather than spend their time on the ice, that they eagerly volunteered to assist the wayward men in attending to their avocations. Women took to helping their husbands by wielding sledgehammers for blacksmiths, ploughing for farmers, and chiseling for stonemasons.

The curling-obsessed husbands, of course, did not and could not understand their spouses' ill-feelings toward their favourite game. Some quite deeply resented their wives' intolerance for their hard-earned and well-deserved curling time. Even a funeral might not be enough to keep the men from curling, especially if the ice was keen:

Another of these enthusiastic Kilmarnock curlers was even 'mair left to himsel" in his absorbing pursuit of this bewitching game, for he expressed his earnest hope that his wife, who was unwell, 'wadna dee till there cam' a thaw, for otherwise he wadna be able to attend her burial.' Curling – The Ancient Scottish Game (James Taylor 2d ed. 1887).

Yes, in 1700s and 1800s Scotland, curling was decidedly, and almost exclusively, a man's game. It was played by men, governed by men, and its clubs were solely for men. Surely, women played their part, although rarely as curlers. They came out to watch, provided food and drink to the needy men, sometimes lugged the men's curling stones for them, and made sure that a hot meal awaited them when they returned from their play. Even if there were no express prohibitions on women participating in the games, it was considered something that women or girls should neither want to do nor be encouraged to do. Who knew where it might lead? Partly, it was considered to be "unladylike;" partly, women weren't thought to be strong enough to play; and partly, no doubt, the men preferred that *someone* be at home to have a meal prepared when they returned from their hard day of ice-playing. Roles were roles. The men had theirs and the women had theirs.

Illustrative of the extent of male domination of the sport were the annual Grand Matches between the North and South of Scotland. The Grand Matches were the highlight of every curling season, at least when they could be held. The Grand Matches were supposed to be annual events, but in reality they were held less frequently due to want of sufficient ice. When they were held, however, they were a sight to behold, capturing the imagination and attention of the whole country. They were played for the honour of the North and South. Nonetheless, the Grand Matches were exclusively men's events. At the Grand Match on Linlithgow Loch on January 25, 1848, there were reported to be 680 curlers, all of them men. At the Grand Match at Lochwinnoch on January 11, 1850, there were reported to be 1,100 curlers, again nothing but men. It was into this world that young Ailsa Maclaren, aided considerably by her father, would venture.

Chapter 4

Recruitment and Resistance

Hugh Maclaren quickly came to understand that Ailsa could only continue her curling development by actually playing in matches, with a team, not simply by practicing shots with him on their private pond. He knew that he had to find some way for Ailsa to play competitively, to play on a team. It wasn't going to be easy in 1880s Scotland. There simply weren't any ladies' teams. Certainly, Ailsa would never be admitted into the Musselburgh Curling Club, nor would she be allowed to play in any bonspiels, or even in some less formal, "friendly" matches. Those were for men, and *only* for men. Hugh Maclaren knew much better than to even broach that subject at the club.

After two winters of practicing and playing with his daughter on their own pond, Ailsa's father came up with an idea. Ailsa was too good to be held back simply by a lack of opportunity. Even at only fifteen years old, Ailsa by now could more than hold her own in a "points game" against him. Points games were designed to let curlers play one against another and did not require teams. Each curler attempted eight different kinds of shots, from guarding to wicking to striking to drawing, and received a point for each successful shot. Ailsa and her father played points games against each other. After Ailsa actually bested him in a points game, Hugh Maclaren decided that he simply had to find some way for Ailsa to compete on a team.

Several members of the Musselburgh Curling Club had daughters close in age to Ailsa, who attended the same school or church. Ailsa's father discretely approached them individually about the possibility of introducing their daughters to the game. Most of them immediately and summarily refused – some with varying degrees of hostility and disdain – to approve of any such thing for their daughters. Some were of the very strong opinion that it was simply improper for girls to curl, some were fearful of the disapproval of other club members, and others said that their daughter would have no interest in giving it a try, without even bothering to ask. Ailsa's father had anticipated many of those responses. Hugh Maclaren, though, was persistent, persuasive, and charming. That was, after all, how he had long-ago won over Mrs. Maclaren. He was not dissuaded in his quest to find people, girls in particular, for Ailsa to curl with.

Eventually, Hugh Maclaren found three fathers who were bold enough to permit, and even encourage, their daughters to try curling. They were not in the least bit concerned by what others might think and thought that their daughters might enjoy playing. The three girls knew who Ailsa Maclaren was, and they liked and admired her. Their fathers likewise admired and respected Hugh. So Hugh Maclaren arranged to meet Effie Lawrie, Sheenagh Gillie, and Kirsty Barnett, together with their curling fathers, on the Maclarens' private curling pond one cold January morning in 1883. The girls had all seen their fathers play, but none of the three had ever thought to ask if they could try it for themselves, unlike Ailsa. Now, their fathers were asking *them* to give it a try.

Ailsa and the four fathers set about the task of teaching the three novices how to curl. It wasn't easy, but it was certainly fun, especially for Effie and Kirsty, who had been friends for years. They loved to tease each other, almost nonstop. When Effie tried to throw her first stone, she drew her arm back and proceeded to drop the heavy stone.

"Oops. I don't think that's the way to do it," Kirsty chuckled.

"Shut yer geggie," Effie responded, retrieving the stone and trying again. This time, Effie managed to hold onto the stone and sent it down the ice, although only fifteen feet or so.

"That's much better," Kirsty said sarcastically, but in good fun. Her turn would come next.

Kirsty picked up a stone and stepped onto the crampit. Effie watched, ready to pounce. Kirsty drew the stone back. Just as she started to bring it forward, she dropped it straight down onto the crampit, missing her toes by mere inches.

"Oops. I don't think that's the way to do it,"Effie said in sing-song, copycat fashion.

"Shut *yer* geggie," Kirsty shot back. Most of the day went like that for Effie and Kirsty, trading barbs and laughing with each other. Their fathers had seen it countless times before.

"You'll get used to it," Kirsty's father said to Hugh Maclaren.

Like Ailsa had at first, each of the lassies found it difficult to send the heavy stones all the way down the ice. And, just like Ailsa had done, they each eventually figured out a way. Ailsa was ecstatic at actually curling with other girls and introducing them to the intricacies and mysteries of the game. Ailsa was a natural teacher and a natural leader for the girls, skills which had been passed on by her father. Encouragement, not criticism, was the way to teach.

Teaching the girls the game was a slow, deliberate process, just like it had been when Ailsa was first learning. First, how to grip the handle, how to stand in the crampit, then how to slide the stone down the ice, then how to control the distance the stone was meant to slide, then how to guide the stone with sweeping, and so on through all of the nuances and different manner of shots necessary during the course of a game.

Sweeping was the hardest thing, at least physically. It required some stooping, balancing, and exertion which the new curlers weren't used to.

"I'm fair puckled!" Sheenagh announced after a few sweeping sessions, breathing hard.

After three hours on the ice, the girls were tired. They were using muscles which they didn't ordinarily use. Hugh Maclaren suggested that the fathers and daughters head inside. "If you practice when you're tired, you develop bad habits. We wouldn't want that, would we?" he asked. As much fun as they were having, the girls were ready to stop for the day.

Once inside, the fathers and daughters sat together around the fireplace. Ailsa's father asked the girls first, and then their fathers, whether they wanted to continue their instruction in the game. Each of the girls enthusiastically said that they did. It had been fun! The fathers concurred. "If that be the case," Maclaren said, "we'll need a lot more time to practice."

Each of the girls was a willing, quick, and voracious learner, Sheenagh Gillie in particular. Sheenagh was more athletic than Effie or Kirsty, and more competitive. In those ways, she was more like Ailsa. With their fathers' encouragement, and recognizing how good Ailsa had quickly become, they continued to learn and to try to master the game. They met on the Maclarens' pond at every opportunity to practice. Just as importantly, they were becoming friends. Effie and Kirsty continued with their nonstop chatter whenever they practiced. Ailsa and Sheenagh mostly just listened and laughed.

With no one else to play against, the girls settled into playing points games among themselves and competing against their bigger, stronger, and vastly more experienced fathers when they could. Finally, it happened. One winter day, when Ailsa was sixteen years old, her rink, with Kirsty Barnett leading, Effie Lawrie playing second, Sheenagh Gillie serving as vice, and Ailsa skipping, defeated their fathers for the first time. It was not an insignificant victory, since the fathers were among the better curlers in the Musselburgh Curling Club. Ailsa was so proud, so excited, to have actually won. She made her father promise that he had not intentionally let her win. He assured her that he had not. Her father was perhaps even prouder than Ailsa was.

The four girls continued to practice, practice, and practice some more. They were actually curling more than their fathers were. When the winter was over, much too soon for the girls' liking, they sometimes met off of the ice to study strategy and tactics. They even set up imaginary games on the floor using pebbles. Naturally, with their new common bond, they also grew as friends. Sheenagh and Ailsa, in particular, developed a close relationship. The lassies were beginning to grow restless, though, with no one other than their fathers to play against. They needed to test their skills against other people, other rinks, perhaps even other girls.

———◦◦◦———

Hugh Maclaren was generally held in very high esteem throughout the Musselburgh Curling Club. He served as an officer of the club as well as its representative at meetings of the Royal Caledonian Curling Club. On the ice, his rink won several district medals for the club at bonspiels. He had played in three Grand Matches for the South of Scotland. Each time, the South had won. He was honourable and respectful of the game and its traditions. Hugh Maclaren was not only respected, he was genuinely liked.

There was one thing, though, about Hugh Maclaren which a few members of the club didn't much care for or approve of. Hugh Maclaren not only taught Ailsa how to curl, but he actually encouraged her to curl. He had even built a curling pond for her, they muttered, although the truth was that Ailsa herself had done most of the building. Now, he had the audacity to involve some other girls, as well. It just didn't sit well with everyone. One member in particular.

The Maclarens' curling pond sparked a lot of curiosity and interest among the members of the Musselburgh Curling Club. Some of the members had passed by the site during its construction and wondered what Maclaren was doing. Several asked about the more technical aspects of constructing an artificial curling pond, which Hugh Maclaren was happy to share with them. Some were particularly jealous that the pond offered better and more frequent ice than the club's natural pond did. Still others felt that if Hugh Maclaren wanted to build a curling pond, he should build it for the club, not for himself. A few hinted that they would welcome the chance to come and try it out for themselves sometime. A couple even asked explicitly. None received an invitation to do so. The club had its own pond and the Maclarens had theirs.

Not everyone at the club was opposed to what Maclaren was doing in introducing the girls to curling. Some inquired about Ailsa's progress. "I've never seen a young lad Ailsa's age who could best her," he sometimes said to a fellow club member. "She's really quite remarkable. Effie, Kirsty, and Sheenagh are, too." It was exactly what a proud father should say. Many clubs members, however, did not approve of Hugh Maclaren's daughter curling, nor of the amount of time he was devoting to teaching her and her friends the game. Even if not stated explicitly, they thought that it was understood that curling was for men, and one of their officers and most respected players was flagrantly breaching that understanding.

One of the members, a rather loud and unpopular chap named John Carswell, eventually felt the need to speak up. John Carswell almost always felt the need to speak up. And he always believed that he was speaking on behalf of the club. Carswell approached Hugh Maclaren one day. "I've been needing to talk to you, Hugh," Carswell began. Being approached by John Carswell was rarely a pleasant thing. Maclaren braced himself for what he knew was coming. "It's not right how you've been doin' so much ice playin' w' your daughter. She's a bonnie young lass, I ken, but yer missus should be teachin' her the necessaries, rather than you teachin' her curlin'." Neither Carswell himself, nor his words in particular, sat well with Maclaren. What Hugh Maclaren did with his daughter was none of Carswell's concern.

"John," Hugh responded, as calmly, yet emphatically, as he could, "Ailsa is my daughter and the missus and I will raise her just as we see fit. If I want to take her out onto the ice on my own land, that's none of your concern."

"Hugh . . ." Carswell began to respond.

Maclaren cut him off, saying, "That's enough, John. You've said your piece. Ailsa is *my* daughter and I need no help in raisin' her from you. She's a keen curler and we're doin' no harm to anyone. Let it go, John."

Maclaren seriously doubted that Carswell *would* let it go. And he turned out to be right.

Chapter 5
Curling Court

Naturally, word that Ailsa, Sheenagh, Effie, and Kirsty had defeated their fathers, all very good curlers, reached and circulated through the Musselburgh Curling Club. Loudmouth John Carswell, in particular, took great pleasure in circulating the news. There was a good deal of speculation that the fathers had conspired to let their girls win, which was not true. So, after the next club dinner, the club's Curling Court convened, as it normally did, and imposed a fine on each of the fathers for the twin offenses of teaching their daughters to curl and then losing a match to them. The fathers didn't mind, though. They were proud of their girls, so they played along with good humour, as did the rest of the club . . . for the most part.

—◆—

Curling itself, of course, was the most important thing to the men who played and who devoted so much of their time and energy to it. Nearly as important, though, was the increasingly social aspect of the game. Following most bonspiels and club meetings, curlers shared in a traditional curling dinner of "beef and greens." Those dinners, attended by both the victorious and vanquished teams, were an important element in creating what came to be known as "the spirit of curling." They served to bring together, on relatively equal footing, at least for a few hours, differing classes and social ranks. The poor partook with the wealthy, the barons with the laborers. "On the turf, as under it, all men are equal," was the old adage, honoured throughout history mostly in the breach. But with curling, it was largely true. Whisky, toddy, and ale were always present in ample amounts, which may partially explain why there was always such "hearty fellowship and kindly feeling" at the beef and greens dinners.

On some ocasions, the "fellowship" amongst the men curlers went a wee bit overboard, though, as recorded in *Curling – The Ancient Scottish Game*. The national beverage of Scotland no doubt played a significant role.

One time, after an apparent defeat, a party of Sanquhar curlers had ensconced themselves in an upper room of one of the public-houses of the place, and were engaged comforting themselves over their bad luck, and seeking to drown their grief in 'a wee drappie o't,' when a messenger opened the door and announced the welcome news that Sanquhar was victorious by two shots. The announcement acted like magic on the entire company; several mounted the table and danced thereon; while others rushed to the stair head, and, seizing a row of flower-pots which adorned the window, in the very wantonness of delight sent them down with a clash to the foot of the stair.

There are precious few things which define "hearty fellowship" amongst men than dancing on tables, smashing flower pots, and a wee drappie.

In most Scottish curling clubs there were constituted what were known as "Curling Courts." Where and when Curling Courts first came into being remains a mystery, but nearly every curling club had one. They were originally designed to initiate new members into the "mysteries" of the game, including "the Word and the Grip," and to enforce club rules against offenses such as swearing while on the ice and gambling on matches. Both prohibitions appeared in the constitutions and rules of almost all curling clubs, perhaps due to the significant early role played by the clergy in expanding the popularity of the sport. Swearing and gambling were considered serious violations, and most clubs attempted to strictly enforce rules prohibiting such conduct. As early as 1739, the Rules and Statutes of the Society of Curlers in Muthill provided, "That there shall be no wagers, cursing or swearing, during the course of game under the penalty of Two Shillings Scots for each oath, and the fines for wagers to be at the discretion of the Preces and the other members present, and the wagers in themselves void and null."

Curling Courts usually sat during club meetings and after dinners and were a source of great entertainment and hilarity among the men. Eventually, and all too predictably, Curling Courts ventured far beyond enforcing club rules and began imposing fines for all manner of offenses, large and trivial, both real and imagined, not just for swearing and gambling. Their judgments weren't confined to offenses against the club or curling, either. The judgments spilled over into real life. Having a baby was an oft-punished offense. More than one young father found himself paying tribute to the Curling Court:

> *The birth of a 'young curler' is another [offense, and the member] pled guilty to the charge of his lady having presented him with a young curler without the sanction of the club; he was fined one shilling, having promised not to repeat the misdemeanour without the full concurrence of*

> *the club, &c. Curling – The Ancient Scottish Game. (James Taylor 2d ed. 1887).*

Both being "presented with a young curler" and getting married were events which were supposed to be approved in advance by the club. What started as a simple means of enforcing club rules continued to devolve into something else altogether. Without any women around to harness their manly impulses, the men took Curling Courts to places where they were never intended to go. There seemed to be no limit to the trespasses for which a club member could be held to account. One can only imagine the charges being aired and the rebuttals being offered. Finally, the decision would be handed down by "My Lord." And the decision of "My Lord," the presiding officer of the Curling Court, was absolute. There was no appeal from his judgment. Appealing, in and of itself, would inspire an additional fine.

Among the violations for which punishment was imposed by a Curling Court over the years were:

Marrying an Heiress;
Weighing a lady;
Dancing on one's potato pits;
Taking away the club's officer to spread dung;
Coming out of a train at the wrong station;
Allowing oneself to be made a town councillor;
Having a queer-looking coat;
Being the first member of the club who had condescended to the use of chloroform in having a tooth extracted;
Bringing a dog to the ice;
Being unwell;
Singing inaccurately;

Having, to the great danger of the digestion and bodily health of the members present, supplied hard, tough beef for dinner;

Playing with another's stones;

Putting in a bow window;

Falling and breaking an arm;

Drinking a neighbor's toddy;

Buying a ship;

Combing one's hair;

Not having a beard;

Not having one's beard in order;

Having been "best man" six times;

Keeping a noisy fowl;

Keeping a rookery;

Shooting at a hare in her seat, the offence being aggravated by the fact that the hare had been dead for some days previous;

Not having been fined;

Publishing a book;

Getting on a gown and thereby obtaining admittance to the Court in Edinburgh (a grave misdemeanor);

Saying that one knew the market would fall, but not having told before it did so;

A reverend for having his Fast day on the same day as the club dinner;

Appearing on the ice in full canonicals.

Fortunately, there was at least one factor which may have helped, just a little bit, in tempering the men's impulses. Most of the men's curling clubs counted clergy amongst their members. Most even appointed a club chaplain. The approval and promotion of curling by the clergy early on in the sport's growth certainly helped it to gain a foothold and widespread acceptance. Curiously, when ladies' curling clubs were finally formed, and they *were* called "ladies'" clubs, most did not feel the need to appoint a chaplain, believing that chaplains "were only necessary in men's clubs."

Yes, curling was fully and almost unconditionally a man's game throughout most of its history. It was played by men and governed by men, its rules were written by men, its clubs were exclusively for men, its frozen domain was for men, and its history was written by men. Eventually, that would begin to change, thanks, in no small part, to Ailsa and Hugh Maclaren.

Chapter 6
Challenge Match

After the meal was finished and the Curling Court at the Musselburgh Curling Club adjourned, the curlers began to slowly disband. The evening was growing later, and the good humour was starting to wane, particularly for the increasingly belligerent John Carswell, inexplicably still a member of the club. The man who four years earlier had first confronted Hugh Maclaren about teaching Ailsa to curl. Carswell's vitriol had continued almost nonstop and unchecked over the years. He mocked Hugh Maclaren, and Sheenagh, Kirsty, and Effie's fathers, too, for teaching their daughters to curl and then having lost a match to them. Carswell was particularly critical of the fact that Hugh Maclaren had built a curling pond for the girls. Had he wanted to build a pond, why not one for the club which the men could enjoy? The fathers politely advised Carswell to stop, as they had repeatedly done, but, inspired partly by the whisky and partly by his braggadocio and his disdain for the notion of girls taking to the ice, he kept it up at every opportunity. Finally, Hugh Maclaren, normally a man of nearly boundless patience, had heard enough. "Ye know, John, those girls would make easy work of your rink, should you ever be bold enough to play them, which everyone here knows ye are not." He said it loudly enough for others to hear.

Carswell hadn't anticipated this response. An argument, certainly, or even a fight, but not a challenge. Carswell looked around to see who might be listening. "I ain't curlin' against no girls," he spit. "And it has nothin' to do with bein' bold enough, either. I just won't do it."

"No, I didn't suspect that you would," Hugh replied matter-of-factly. "I didn't suspect that you would." With that, Hugh turned and walked away before things had a chance to escalate. He returned to his table and the fathers of the curling lasses. Maybe Carswell would finally be quiet about the girls curling, although all four fathers doubted that. For his part, Carswell had to decide how to keep what there was of his honour intact without actually having to play against girls. Avoiding a challenge without seeming to be afraid would require some finessing, not one of Carswell's strong suits. He dreaded the thought of having to back up his mouth with action. For the rest of the night, Carswell stayed silent, to almost everyone's delight. He finally thought up a plan which would enable him to avoid having to meet the challenge and curl against Ailsa's rink.

Three days later, the cold had produced some capital ice on the club's pond, and most members of the Musselburgh Curling Club were again on the ice for the better part of the day. As the sun set, the men adjourned to the upper room of a local inn. Maclaren was sitting with the three fathers of the curling lassies, chatting quietly, when he felt a tap on his shoulder. It was Carswell, which was an unwelcome and unpleasant intrusion. "Hugh," he began. "Me and my rink have talked about your challenge, and we're willing to play the girls, so long as you're willing to make it worth our while. Something to fire our interest." Carswell leaned closer and whispered, "You know, a little wager to make it worth our time." Carswell knew full well that Hugh Maclaren would never agree to gambling on curling, even more so if it involved Ailsa. Carswell mistakenly thought that his proposal would put an end to the issue, or at least he hoped that it would.

"Absolutely not," Maclaren replied, exactly as Carswell knew that he would. "You know the club forbids wagering on matches. Besides, I'll not be having Ailsa and her friends treated like racing ponies. You can either accept the challenge and play them or not. It doesn't really matter to me. But we all know what refusing to meet a challenge means, don't we, John? It means exactly what everyone here knows it means." Carswell quickly scanned the room. More than a few people were trying to catch some of the conversation.

Maclaren was right. The club did strictly forbid gambling on matches. And the club members surely knew what it meant to decline a challenge. Hugh Maclaren also knew that Carswell would be looking for any excuse to avoid playing the girls. In fact, Maclaren had anticipated that Carswell might try precisely this gambit. Carswell was known to make a wager now and then. He had even been fined on several occasions by the Curling Court. Maclaren reached into his pocket and withdrew a piece of paper which he had been carrying with him in anticipation of this exact situation. He handed it to Carswell. "Read this, John," Maclaren said.

One circumstance which has contributed not a little to the success and permanence of curling as a national game, and to the high estimate in which it is held, has been the firm determination to put down peremptorily every attempt to make bonspiels the subject of gambling and betting. Our venerable friend, Mr. Charles Cowan, a keen and skilful curler, relates in his 'Reminiscences' an interesting anecdote illustrative of this resolution. 'Few of the existing curlers,' he says, 'can now remember a true and keen curler of the last century, and a perfect gentleman, who lived in Gilmore Place, Edinburgh, who I have heard, I think from his own lips, played in a bonspiel . . . more than a hundred years ago. Mr. MacGeorge told me once that in a very keen

*game when he was skip of his rink both sides were equal,
and MacGeorge had to play the last stone, when some one
said, 'Take care, MacGeorge, there's a guinea on that shot.'
MacGeorge could not and would not play his stone; and
it is a game where everything of the nature of betting is
discouraged and detested as destructive to the enjoyment of
the pastime. The game is in itself sufficiently exciting, and
needs no such artificial allurements to keep alive its interest.*

Carswell was in a bad spot, and he knew it. There would be no wager. Hugh Maclaren would never agree to one, and the club would never allow it, anyway. The Curling Court might even fine him for refusing the challenge, or, worse yet, laugh at him for being too timid to meet it. The word throughout the club would be that Carswell was too frightened to curl against the teenage lassies. How humiliating would that be? Most of the club members would be delighted to spread that bit of news. Carswell would never again be able to chastise anyone for allowing their daughter to curl. He would look both a coward and a fool, and he didn't know which was worse. Carswell despised the thought of being considered either. There were only two courses for Carswell, and only one of them was acceptable – he could either get the club to forbid such a match, which he hoped it would do, or he would have to accept the challenge, which he hoped never to have to do.

"I'll need the approval of the President," Carswell offered, in an attempt to find a different way out. "Which I very much doubt that he will provide." Challenge matches were not at all uncommon at curling clubs. They kept interest high, and winning one was a source of great pride for the victors. This rink would challenge that rink, this profession would challenge that profession, or those who lived on the north of some line would challenge those who lived to the south of it, or vice versa.

Most challenges were issued purely for fun and almost all were played for a donation of coal or meal for the poor. This challenge was of a different character. It was made out of true animous.

"Why don't we see what the club says about it, then," said Maclaren. "President Beveridge is a wise and reasonable fellow. I'm sure he'll make a fair decision. He's sitting in the chair right now. Let's go and see what he says, shall we?" Carswell was certain that President Beveridge would not permit such a thing. After all, the girls weren't even club members. And he was praying that Beveridge wouldn't allow it, too.

Hugh Maclaren had anticipated Carswell's maneuver. He had already raised the idea of a match between Ailsa's rink and Carswell's privately with his friend Beveridge. Beveridge had initially been cool to the notion, but the club's general dislike of the coarse and mouthy Carswell led President Beveridge to reconsider, and he began to warm to the idea. A chance to humiliate Carswell held a good deal of appeal. He told Maclaren that he would consent to the contest, but only under certain strict conditions. There was to be absolutely no wagering. None. No spectators would be permitted other than the club's officers and the girls' fathers. The match would consist of eight ends and Royal Caledonian Curling Club rules would apply. Beveridge himself would serve as umpire, since he could think of no more fair and impartial man. Hugh Maclaren immediately agreed to all of the conditions and thanked Beveridge for his consideration.

Maclaren and Carswell approached the President and presented their situation to him. Beveridge looked pensive, as if he were deep in thought as he considered the issue, even though he already knew what his answer would be. Carswell's look virtually begged for Beveridge to forbid the match. Finally, Beveridge spoke. "Gentlemen, I shall allow the match to proceed." He then recited the list of conditions to both men and secured their assent. Carswell considered arguing against Beveridge's decision, but that would appear weak. "It shall proceed on Friday next at nine o'clock a.m. provided the ice is suitable," Beveridge announced. Maclaren smiled. Carswell frowned and seemed a little more pale than usual. His mouth was dry. For once, Carswell had nothing to say. "I'll see you on Friday morning then, John," Maclaren said as he returned to his table.

The three other fathers had all eagerly agreed to the match. They were anxious to see how the girls would fare in a real competition. They also were hopeful of seeing John Carswell humiliated. Now, Maclaren would have to tell Ailsa and the girls what he had done and secure their agreement. There was never a doubt what their answers would be.

⸺◆⸺

Ailsa, of course, was ecstatic over the prospect of finally playing in a real match. She didn't care at all who it might happen to be against. She had never even heard of John Carswell. Sheenagh, Effie, and Kirsty were equally excited about the prospect. Carswell and his rink most definitely were not. Carwell's mouth had landed his rink in a very awkward spot. My God, what if they lost? His rink had a few unflattering words for him. Words like "eejit," "choob," "roaster," and "scabby bassa."

For the first time, after playing only amongst themselves and against their fathers, Ailsa's rink was getting the chance to play against some different people in a real curling match. Ailsa didn't particularly care whether they were men, boys, ladies, or other girls, although playing against other girls would have been the most fun. To her, Carswell and his rink were just curlers. In telling Ailsa and her friends about the match, her father had not let on that it was a challenge match, nor had he revealed anything about the bad blood between the fathers and Carswell. The girls needn't worry about that detail. They would be nervous enough.

By eight-thirty on Friday morning, Ailsa, Sheenagh, Effie, Kirsty, their fathers, the Musselburgh Curling Club officers, and John Carswell's rink were all at the club's frozen pond preparing for the match. The girls' fathers swept the ice, while the club's officers made the necessary measurements and marked the ice. President Beveridge ordered a few of the more curious club members who had come to watch the spectacle to leave. Unfortunately for Carswell, old John Frost had produced a perfectly fine sheet of ice. Carswell would have much preferred a good thaw and unplayable ice. His last possible excuse for not playing the match was gone. He cursed the weather, while his rink cursed him.

The only people who didn't really want to be there were the four men who would have to face off against Ailsa's rink. All of the others were excited to see if the girls could actually play the game well enough to compete. As much as they loved curling, each member of Carswell's rink could think of many places where they would prefer to be. It wasn't as if they were afraid of losing, because they honestly weren't. They knew that they would win. It was that they just didn't want to be playing against girls at all. Carswell's rink muttered some additional silent oaths about him and his perpetually loud mouth. If Carswell weren't such a good curler, they just might form their own rink without him.

After Beveridge reminded everyone of the rules for the match, Ailsa's rink and Carswell's rink took their positions. Ailsa lost the toss, and her rink would throw the first stone in the first end and Carswell's would throw the last, a distinct advantage for Carswell to be holding "the hammer." Kirsty Barnett, Ailsa's lead, prepared to throw her first stone ever in a real match. She was very nervous. It was a disaster, the stone not even reaching the hog-score, and therefore, the stone was a hog and removed from play. Carswell smirked, intentionally, for all to see, which did not go unnoticed by Kirsty's father, who took a step forward before Ailsa's father stopped him. For her next shot, Kirsty overcompensated, and her stone rumbled ten feet past the tee. Carswell was relieved to know that this was going to be easy, and he seemed to be right. All of the girls played poorly at the outset, from nerves more so than lack of ability. It fell to Ailsa, as their skip and leader, to help them recover. Ailsa summoned the advice which she had long-ago read and committed to memory:

> *A word, en passant, upon display of temper in skips. Nothing is weaker, or more defective in tact, than to discover irascibility or peevishness at any of your party if they are not in good play. This serves no other purpose than to damp their spirits and increase their nervousness. Be certain that they will ever endeavour to do their best. Where the will then is not awanting, it is folly to find fault. Patience is no where a greater virtue than upon the ice. To humour and encourage your [wo]men is half the battle in every spiel.*

By the time that the third end was over, Ailsa's rink trailed Carswell's 5-0, although they were beginning to calm down and play better. By now, Carswell's rink was confident – cocky, even. They began laughing and joking amongst themselves, loudly enough for Ailsa's rink, the club's officers, and the girls' fathers to hear. President Beveridge heard them, too. He directed a stern look to Carswell. Carswell's men allowed themselves to lose some of their focus, and it cost them, as Ailsa's rink pounced on each opportunity. Ailsa's rink scored their first point in the fourth end, another in the fifth, and two more in the sixth to make the score 5-4 with two ends left to play. Carswell's rink grew much quieter as they tried to recapture their focus. Not a single person on the scene was rooting for them.

In the seventh end, Carswell played a brilliant inwick with his final stone to take two points and virtually seal the match. Whatever else there was to say about John Carswell, and there was much to say, he was an excellent player. Ailsa's rink tried valiantly to find a way to score at least three points in the final end, a difficult feat even with the hammer, but only managed to score a lone point, and they lost the match 7-5. The girls were devastated. They had lost the first real match that they ever played. Carswell gave a disdainful look at the fathers when the match ended, but said nothing. President Beveridge and the other club officers congratulated the eight players on a splendid match, spending more time with the girls than with the men. Why would anyone elect to spend more time with John Carswell than absolutely necessary?

The four fathers walked off the pond with their disappointed daughters. The fathers could not have been any prouder. Of course, they were hoping that the girls would win, especially given the circumstances, but that would have been a lot to expect. While the girls could have lost all hope and fallen apart after playing so poorly at the beginning, they didn't. They kept their composure, worked together, and came up just short against their far, far, more experienced opponents. Yes, they had lost, but they had also learned, and those lessons would serve them well in the future.

Later that night, in their parlor at home, Ailsa and her father recounted the match, almost shot-for-shot. Hugh Maclaren had taken some notes during the game. They placed buttons on the table and used them to re-create the game in explicit detail. Ailsa had called shots and directed her rink almost exactly as he would have, her father told her. Her strategy was nearly flawless. He also told her that she may have won but for the poor start to the game, which was completely understandable. He told her how proud he was of her, and that she should be very proud of herself and her rink. If the girls could make a game of it against a rink of very experienced and able curlers, they could compete against anyone. As for himself, Hugh Maclaren was fairly certain that he would no longer be bothered by John Carswell, who had indeed won a battle, but lost a war.

Chapter 7
Other Ladies

Following Ailsa's loss to John Carswell's rink, Hugh Maclaren embarked on a discreet mission. Unbeknownst to Ailsa, Sheenagh, Effie, Kirsty, or to their fathers, even, Hugh Maclaren began contacting curling clubs throughout Scotland, inquiring as to whether they had any ladies' rinks. He assumed that they didn't, because he had never heard of any, but he wanted to know for sure. Most were quite adamant that they had no ladies among their curlers, nor would there likely ever be any. Some took offense that he would even ask. To Maclaren's surprise, however, the Hercules Curling Club, Balyarrow, Cambo, Kinross, and Orwell each responded that they did, in fact, have a few lady curlers – not as club members, of course – who had recently taken to the game. Some even commented on how surprisingly good their ladies were. With the winter of 1884-85 coming to an end, Hugh Maclaren began making arrangements for the next season, one which he thought that Ailsa, Sheenagh, Effie, and Kirsty might very much enjoy.

In the springtime, Maclaren invited the three girls and their fathers to the Maclaren home. After the girls had come back inside from visiting the horses, and the men had emptied their tumblers, Ailsa's father asked everyone to convene around the dining room table. "You're probably wondering why I've invited you all here when there's no curling to be done. The first reason is that Ailsa and I have missed you all and wanted to see you. The second is this – I've been in contact with several other curling clubs, and it seems that you, young lassies, are not alone in your love of the roarin' game. I have learned that there are a few other ladies' rinks who play the game, too. Not many, mind you, but a few," Maclaren began. The girls looked both surprised and excited. Their fathers seemed to be, as well. It was unexpected news to all of them.

"Where, father? Where do they play?" Ailsa blurted.

"Well, I've learned of ladies' rinks at Hercules, Balyarrow, Cambo, Kinross, and Orwell. There may be some others, as well," her father replied. It took a moment for everyone to process the information.

"Can we play against them?" Ailsa asked. "Can we?" Everyone looked at Hugh Maclaren, eager for the answer.

"That's what I've asked you all here for," Maclaren offered. "To see whether or not you might be interested in doing just that, if it could even be arranged." The girls looked at each other, smiling, not having dared to imagine this happening. They were already beginning to picture it.

"Yes, yes, yes, yes!" came the four answers, almost simultaneously. "When? When can we do it?!" Ailsa pleaded.

Ailsa's father knew that he had to temper the girls' excitement. He didn't like doing it, but he needed to be honest. "I'm not saying that you *can*, or that it could even be arranged. I'm just asking whether that is something that you would like to do. It would take quite a commitment from everyone. But since it clearly is something that you would like to do, and I believe that it is with your fathers, as well, I shall inquire and see if arrangements might possibly be made." Each of the fathers nodded. The notion of playing against other girls and ladies had been inconceivable before this. Who even knew that there were others?

Over the spring and summer of 1885, Hugh Maclaren busied himself with correspondence between the various clubs where there were lady curlers. His hope was to arrange for a modest bonspiel in early 1886 at a time and place convenient for everyone. It was the Boghead ladies who took the initiative to actually arrange the event. In October, Hugh Maclaren received a formal invitation from the Boghead ladies for Ailsa's rink to play against other women's rinks in January, ice permitting, of course. As January approached, Maclaren learned that six women's rinks would be playing – one from Hercules, one each from Kinross, Orwell, and Boghead, and a rink skipped by Henrietta Gilmour from Lundin and Montrave, along with Ailsa's. The bonspiel would be played on Boghead Loch at Bathgate. It would not, however, be played under the auspices of the Royal Caledonian Curling Club, which declined to even consider sanctioning the event. That was still a bridge way, way too far for the mother club.

The four lassies practiced on the Maclarens' private curling pond as often as the weather permitted. They practiced with a renewed and sharpened focus created by the upcoming ladies' bonspiel in Bathgate. Their fathers continued to coach them and to instruct them further in some of the nuances of the game, reviewing some of the potential situations that they might encounter at a bonspiel. They discussed some of the subtleties involved in playing lead, second, vice, and skip. The young ladies, now in their later teenage years, absorbed the lessons and worked hard on their individual and collective skills. They settled on their final lineup of Kirsty as lead, Effie as second, Sheenagh as vice, with Ailsa skipping.

The anxiety leading up to the ladies bonspiel was almost overwhelming for Ailsa and her teammates. None of them had ever so much as seen any other women curlers, let alone played against any, and they had no idea how they would fare against them. Would they be able to compete with the other women? Would they be humiliated? *Soutered* even? There was no possible way to know what they might be up against, although they had more than held their own against John Carswell. The wait was excruciating.

The day arrived at long last, with the four fathers and their daughters arriving at Boghead Loch for the nine o'clock start of the day-long ladies' bonspiel. Even Mrs. Maclaren made the trip to watch her daughter and her friends play. Word that the ladies were taking to the ice for their own bonspiel had spread throughout the area, and a steady stream of curious onlookers, curlers and non-curlers alike, were making their way to the loch. None had ever witnessed such a thing. Lots were drawn to divide the six teams into two groups of three. Within each group, each team would play each of the other two teams. The teams with the best record within each group would meet for the championship.

In the morning, when the bonspiel began, the ice was hard and fast. As the sun climbed higher into the sky and the temperature rose, the ice became softer and slower. Changing tactics and style of play to deal with drug ice was one test of a rink's skill. Even though each of the other rinks had women who were at least ten years older than those that comprised Ailsa's rink, the younger curlers adapted to the changing ice conditions more quickly and smoothly than their opponents.

Whether the ice was fast or slow, hard or dull, it didn't really matter to Ailsa's rink. They dominated their first two games, winning each by a lopsided score. They defeated the Hercules ladies in the first game and the Orwell ladies in the second. The championship game against Henrietta Gilmour's rink from Lundin and Montrave would present a much more difficult challenge.

Henrietta Gilmour's rink had been curling together for longer than the barely three years that Ailsa's rink had. Gilmour's rink was very accomplished – Henrietta Gilmour, particularly – and it took until the final end of the championship game for Ailsa's rink to secure an 8-6 victory. Although very competitive, Gilmour's more enduring interest was in growing ladies' curling. She was amazed at how good Ailsa's rink was, and studied Ailsa's play in particular. As Ailsa prepared to throw her final stone to secure the championship, Gilmour actually found herself rooting for Ailsa.

Kirsty, Effie, Sheenagh, and Ailsa were presented with a small silver medal, inscribed with the date January 23, 1886, commissioned by the host women. No one knows for certain, but it may have been the first ladies' bonspiel in curling history. It was certainly the first one in Scotland. And Ailsa Maclaren's rink had won it. After the presentation, Henrietta Gilmour approached Ailsa. "Ailsa, you are the finest lady curler I have seen. I am honoured to have played against you. You must continue playing, not only for yourself, but for all of the lady curlers in Scotland. If you do, you will surely be remembered for what you have done. I hope to meet you on the ice many more times."

"Thank you so much, Mrs. Gilmour. It was so much fun playing against other ladies. We had never done it before. We didn't even know that there were others until very recently," Ailsa explained. The two women, of different ages and social classes, stood and talked for some time. They couldn't be certain at the time, but they would, in fact, meet on the ice again.

The day was notable for another reason. The bonspiel was contested in front of a large crowd of spectators, who had differing motivations for attending. Young men came to watch, for obvious reasons. Seasoned curlers came to see whether ladies, with their "delicate arms," could actually play the game. A few came to scoff. Girls and women came to cheer on the pioneers. Nearly everyone left impressed, especially by the four young lassie curlers from Musselburgh led by Ailsa Maclaren. The ladies' bonspiel on Boghead Loch would lead to a rapid growth in the number of women and girls trying their hands at "the manly Scottish exercise."

Ailsa's rink didn't have any more opportunities to play against other ladies that winter. In fact, they didn't have any more opportunities to play against anyone at all. The balance of the winter was largely mild, the ice, when there was any, dull and drug, much to the dismay of every true curler throughout Auld Scotia.

Two weeks after winning the women's bonspiel on Boghead Loch, Ailsa received a letter postmarked from Glasgow. It was just one of many, but for some reason it stood out to her. The letter read:

Dear Ailsa,

My name is Darcie Gilday. I am 19 years old and live in Glasgow. I watched you curling on Boghead Loch with your friends on Saturday last against the other ladies. As we appear to be nearly of the same age, I was very much hoping that your rink would carry the day. It was so wonderful to see that you were able to prevail. I am extremely proud of you, as I hope that you are of yourselves. It was a glorious day for the girls and ladies of Scotland, and for Scotland herself. I am so glad that I was able to watch.

As you probably know, not everyone amongst the spectators was keen on seeing ladies taking to the ice. I heard some of their criticisms as I watched. I wish that I were brave enough to have responded to them, but I was not. I heard many others, though, who offered that it was a most special day for Scotland, seeing her daughters able to finally participate in our national game. You and your friends are an inspiration to the girls and ladies who will surely follow.

I write to let you know how honoured I feel to have witnessed the bonspiel and how proud I am of you and your friends for winning. Please convey to each of them my sincerest congratulations. I hope to one day see you again on the ice, and to perhaps meet you in person.

Most truly yours,

Darcie Gilday

Ailsa hadn't yet taken the time to truly reflect on the ramifications of the women's bonspiel or on those of winning it. Those things would become clearer in time. The pioneering ladies who participated in it, as well as those who witnessed it, set off an explosion of interest among girls and ladies who wanted to play. It now seemed like it was proper and acceptable. Ailsa immediately replied to Darcie's letter with one of her own. If someone took the time to write to her, especially someone who apparently was not a curler, Ailsa was certainly going to give the courtesy of a response. And she had a feeling about Darcie Gilday's letter in particular. Ailsa wrote:

Dear Darcie,

Thank you for your kind letter. I have shown it to Sheenagh, Effie, and Kirsty, the other girls in my rink. They wish for me to tell you how much they appreciate your kindness in writing to us and coming to watch us play. We only wish that you had spoken to us in person that day, so that we could have met you in person. My hope is that one day we shall.

We had so much fun playing against the other ladies. Until recently, we did not even know that there were ladies other than us who played. We all agreed that it would be wonderful to have another ladies' bonspiel next year, if possible. Perhaps there will be many more ladies who will want to play! Maybe you yourself!

My horse, Magic, is anxious for my attention, so I must go now. He has been feeling ignored and lonely these recent days. I think that he wants to be saddled up and taken out. I would love to hear more about you and your life in Glasgow. Please write soon.

Sincerely yours,

Ailsa Maclaren

Those letters began a friendship that both young women would come to cherish. They continued to exchange letters, and shared their hopes and dreams. Even though they had never met, each sensed a connection, a bond, a sense that their friendship was meant to be. They began thinking about plans to meet each other one day.

Chapter 8
Meeting Lucas Plotcok

He appeared from seemingly out of nowhere, walking toward the frozen loch with an air of confidence and purpose. Ailsa took notice of him immediately. How could she not? She had never seen such a handsome and well-dressed young man at a bonspiel, or perhaps anywhere else that she could recall, for that matter. And Ailsa had attended a fair number of her father's bonspiels. It had been just two weeks since Ailsa's rink had won the first ladies' championship.

Ailsa was standing on the edge of the loch, watching her father's rink doing battle against another rink of men, and the match was going well. Her father, of course, was the skip of his rink, now comprised of the four fathers from the Musselburgh Curling Club who had introduced their daughters to curling. He was once again expertly directing his team, simultaneously strategizing while offering praise and encouragement. The men responded well to his calm and steady leadership. Whether they were playing well or playing poorly, Hugh Maclaren's demeanor on the ice never changed. It was a lesson which he had imparted to Ailsa, and which she had learned well.

"Good morning, Ailsa," the debonair young man said. "What an absolutely beautiful day for curling." At first, Ailsa didn't even notice that the man had used her name, so captivated was she by his striking appearance. She caught herself unintentionally staring at him. "Which one is your father?," the young man asked, as if he didn't already know.

"He's the skip of the Musselburgh rink," Ailsa managed to get out. "The tall man with the black tam standing at the tee." Ailsa tried to regain her composure.

"Ah, yes," the man replied. "I can certainly see the resemblance. It's quite apparent, even from a distance." It was true. Ailsa did share many of her father's features.

"Excuse me, sir, but have we met before?" Ailsa asked, suddenly wondering why the man knew her name.

"Oh, no," the man said. "We haven't met until just now, I can assure you of that. I would most certainly remember if we had. You are really quite beautiful. A man surely would not forget meeting you. My name is Lucas, by the way. Lucas Plotcok." Ailsa certainly would have remembered, too, whether they had met before.

"Then how did you know my name?" Ailsa asked.

"I make it my business to know people's names. Especially someone so stunning and skilled as yourself," Lucas replied. Ailsa accepted the second compliment about her beauty, but was curious about why he had added "skilled."

"I don't know what you mean by 'skilled'," Ailsa inquired. She was still largely unaware of her rapidly growing fame.

"No need to be so modest, Ailsa," Lucas answered. "You've earned quite a reputation in these parts recently. I think that almost everyone knows about Ailsa Maclaren and her rink. They say that no other ladies' rink can compare to yours. You seem to have proven that recently." It was true. Ailsa, at just eighteen years old, had become what everyone now agreed was the best woman curler in the parish, or in all of Scotland, most likely. Her rink of four young lasses was thought to be the best, too, and would likely be having more opportunities to prove it. It was one of the fortunate byproducts of the women's bonspiel. Ladies' curling was destined to become more popular and accepted, which would lead to more and more opportunities for Ailsa to play.

"Well, yes. We've done very well, thank you." Ailsa was becoming infatuated with the dashing, well-spoken, polite young man, whom she guessed was a few years older than herself, maybe twenty-three or twenty-four. She wasn't flirting with him, exactly, or maybe she was, but she was certainly intrigued, and wanted the conversation to continue. "Do you live nearby?" Ailsa asked, curious to learn more about the stunningly handsome Lucas Plotcok. It would be a good thing if he did, Ailsa thought. Since Lucas knew some things about her already, it seemed only fair that she should learn some things about him. "I don't remember ever seeing you before."

"No, I do not live nearby," Lucas answered. "I travel quite a bit. My work often requires it. But at the present time, I'm staying in Edinburgh. I'll be staying there until I conclude some important business that I wish to attend to. I was free today, and it seemed like a glorious day to enjoy some of the local charm, although I'm not terribly fond of the cold."

"What type of business is that?" Ailsa inquired. "If I may ask."

"Of course you may. A man should be proud of his work. If I had to put a name to it, I would probably say that I'm an 'investor.' I look for properties which are of particular interest to me, and then see whether I can strike a deal with the owner. Sometimes, it's quite easy, and takes only a few minutes. Other times, it's a difficult and protracted process. Some people are far more attached to their possessions than others – too attached, in my opinion – while some are quick to strike a bargain which they think will be of some benefit. Others mainly enjoy the haggling and have no real interest in consummating a deal. I don't particularly enjoy that part of the business, but it's often necessary. Usually, though, it's simply a matter of finding the right opportunity with the right person at just the right time," Lucas explained. He then asked, "And what of yourself? What do you do when not curling?" Lucas was far more interested in learning more about Ailsa than he was in talking about himself.

"I do lots of things. First, I finished my schooling. I live on a farm near town with my mother and father. Mostly, I help my mother with the household duties, go to market, and tend to the gardens and to the animals. On Saturdays, I like to read books and ride my horse, and on Sundays, we always attend services. Of course, in the wintertime, when the ice is bearing, I'm often practicing my curling or watching father play. Father and I built our own curling pond." There was silence for a few moments as Ailsa and Lucas returned their attention to the bonspiel playing out before them. Ailsa's thoughts were racing. She wished that her father's match had taken a little longer to afford her more time with Lucas. Unfortunately for Ailsa, Hugh Maclaren's rink was wrapping up their lopsided win and walking off of the ice.

"Do you curl, Lucas?" Ailsa asked. "Is that why you're here watching?"

"Oh, no, I've never had the chance to give it a try, unfortunately. I would like to, if I ever get the opportunity," Lucas answered. "Perhaps someday I will." Ailsa hoped that Lucas was hinting at something. She tried to convince herself that he was. Ailsa's father was approaching, all too quickly.

"It was a true pleasure to meet you, Ailsa. My good fortune," Lucas said, before Ailsa's father drew too near. "One more thing, if I may be so bold as to ask – do you have a suitor? A boyfriend?" It was a rather bold question by Victorian Scotland standards, since they had only first met moments earlier. Ailsa lowered her head a bit, embarrassed, yet pleasantly surprised, by the question. She was very happy that Lucas had asked. The question could only mean one thing.

"No," she finally answered. The truth was that Ailsa had never had a real suitor or boyfriend, although there were no doubt quite a few young men in Musselburgh who would have been more than willing to court Ailsa Maclaren. Ailsa was, after all, smart, quick-witted, funny, quite pretty, and very athletic. When young men came out to watch the lady curlers on those infrequent occasions when women took to "the Roarin'

Game," most of them gathered around Ailsa's rink, not only because they were the best, but also because they enjoyed looking at Ailsa. Very few had ever been bold enough to approach her. Lucas was the very welcome exception.

"Well then, Ailsa, may I call on you sometime soon?" Lucas asked. "I would certainly like to learn more about you." It was the question which Ailsa most feared, but most wanted him to ask. Lucas, who did not lack for self-confidence, was certain of the answer before Ailsa even gave it. Ailsa would gladly accept a visit from Lucas Plotcok, although the decision would not be hers alone to make.

"I would enjoy that, but you would have to ask my father," Ailsa answered. She hoped that her father would approve. As far as Ailsa knew, no man had ever asked Hugh Maclaren for permission to call on his daughter. Hugh Maclaren shook hands heartily with his mates, and bade them farewell. He walked up to his daughter and said, "Hello, sweetheart. The ice was the keenest it's been here in a few years." At first, he didn't even take notice of Lucas.

"Hello, father. Your rink played very well today. Those poor devils from Linlithgow never had much of a chance against you," Ailsa said, as her father gave her a warm hug. Lucas grinned ever so slightly and studied both father and daughter. It was obvious that they were very close. Lucas waited politely for Ailsa to make the introductions.

As Hugh Maclaren released his hug, he noticed the impeccably groomed and sharply-dressed young man standing next to Ailsa. It was a bit out of the ordinary for a man to dress so nattily just to observe a bonspiel. Ailsa looked at her father and said, "Father, this is Lucas Plotcok. Lucas, this is my father, Hugh Maclaren. Lucas and I have been watching your match and talking." Hugh Maclaren eyed Lucas warily, as fathers universally do when first meeting a daughter's suitor. At first glance, Lucas appeared to be quite respectable. First impressions were important to Lucas, and he always tried his best to make a good one. He knew that bad ones could be difficult to overcome.

"A pleasure and an honour to meet you, sir," Lucas offered, extending his right hand even before Ailsa's father could. Hugh extended his own, and the two men shook hands. Lucas's grip was firm and confident. "A young man with a proper handshake is becoming harder to find these days," Hugh said, with a sense of approval. So far, Lucas was doing very well for himself. A bad first impression with Ailsa's father would not bode well for either Ailsa or Lucas.

"Are you a curler, Lucas?" Hugh asked. "I don't recall ever seeing you on the ice."

"Nae," Lucas answered. "I've never been in one place long enough to join a club or to take it up. I've become quite interested in it of late, though. A fascinating game, full of foresight and strategy. It reminds me a bit of chess in that way." Lucas made the reference to chess intentionally. Being a chess player conveyed a message of sophistication and refinement, which he guessed would be noticed by Ailsa's father.

"A very apt observation, Lucas. The difference is that curling challenges both the mind *and* the body, unlike chess. As you said, it requires foresight and planning, almost like preparing for battle, as well as steady nerves and strength. Ailsa has become quite adept at it, if you didn't know," Maclaren offered. "She's nearly as good at it as I am. Perhaps better." He exchanged smiles with Ailsa.

"Yes, I know," Lucas responded. "She has begun to make a name for herself."

"It's too bad that you don't play," Ailsa's father offered. "We could use more young men like you joining the ranks. Perhaps Ailsa and I could teach you, if you have an interest." Ailsa was surprised. Very pleasantly surprised. It was not the kind of thing that Ailsa expected to hear from her father. It seemed that he, too, was impressed by Lucas.

"If the opportunity arises, I would be honoured to learn the game from you," Lucas told him, smiling at Ailsa, as well. "Why not learn from the best?" Flattery, in sincere and measured amounts, always worked well.

Hugh Maclaren finally turned to his daughter and said, "Alright now, Ailsa. I think that it's time for us to head home to your mother. She probably has some pots on the stove waiting for us." Ailsa looked at Lucas, waiting – hoping – that he would ask her father if he could call on her. "Ask, Lucas," she thought. "Ask." He did.

"Mr. Maclaren, sir. I would be honoured if you were to allow me to call on Ailsa sometime soon. She's quite a remarkable young lady." It would have been unthinkable for Lucas to ask permission to see Ailsa alone. In 1880s Scotland, there was always a chaperone when a young couple began a proper courtship. The first step would be to see each other under a very close and watchful pair of eyes. Lucas understood the process, cumbersome and inconvenient though it might be.

Ailsa's father stopped and once again eyed Lucas up and down. He looked at Ailsa, whose expression virtually begged him to say "yes." Hugh Maclaren thought on the matter for a moment. There was no reason to say "no" – a firm handshake, fine clothing, impeccable grooming, well-mannered, a chess player, even. "You may," Ailsa's father announced. "Tuesday at two-thirty. I'll ask Mrs. Maclaren to prepare some tea." With that, Ailsa's father turned away, taking Ailsa's hand in his and walking up from the pond. Ailsa looked back over her shoulder, flashed a brilliant smile, and said, "G'bye, Lucas! I'll see you on Tuesday!" She tossed her hair for effect. Lucas couldn't believe his good fortune, although fortune does favor the bold. He had met Ailsa and her father on the same day, and it seemed that he had secured the approval of both of them, most importantly, Ailsa.

Ailsa longed for Tuesday to come, and quickly, although it was three long, long days away. All of her thoughts were on Lucas. She found it rather unsettling how much she thought about him, even though she had just met him. Unsettling, but not in the least unpleasant. What should she wear? How should she arrange her hair? What would they talk about? It was hard for her to concentrate on anything else, nor did she really want to concentrate on anything else. Daydreaming about Lucas Plotcok was just fine with her. Still, the rest of Saturday dragged on and on. Tuesday seemed so far away.

On Sunday morning, Ailsa and her parents went to church in Musselburgh, as they always did. Ailsa enjoyed going to church, and especially enjoyed listening to the scriptures, but today, she was preoccupied with thoughts about Tuesday and simply couldn't concentrate. She looked around the sanctuary a few times, on the off-chance, and hope, that she might see Lucas there. She didn't.

The rest of Sunday passed ponderously. After taking a ride on Magic, Ailsa spent a good deal of the day in her room reading. Her reading was interrupted again and again by images of Lucas which repeatedly popped into her head. Ailsa didn't mind the intrusions at all. Late in the afternoon, she helped her mother prepare supper, which helped to pass some of the time. An evening game of chess with her father helped, too.

Monday was a little bit easier, because Ailsa had things to do which kept her busy. Mondays were when Ailsa went into town to go to market for her mother. Ailsa bought the necessities which her mother required for the home, and occasionally picked up a special indulgence for the small family. On this day, just as she had done in church the day before, Ailsa periodically scanned the street in the hope that she might spy Lucas. Once again, she was disappointed. The anticipation of Lucas's impending visit made it difficult to sleep that night. But at least it would finally happen tomorrow.

The first part of Tuesday was the worst wait of all. The anticipation was wonderful, yet stressful. Time inched forward slowly. Why hadn't her father suggested that Lucas call at ten o'clock rather than at two-thirty? At least he had granted permission for Lucas to call on her, though, and that was the most important thing. Finally, finally, there came a knock on the door. Ailsa flinched when she heard it. Mrs. Maclaren smiled at Ailsa as the older woman went to answer the door. She remembered exactly what it was like when she had received her first gentleman caller. It was an important event in the life a young lass. When Ailsa's mother opened the door, she was certainly not disappointed. She had heard a lot about Lucas over the past three days, and, at first blush, everything that she had heard seemed to be absolutely true.

"Good afternoon, ma'am," Lucas said, removing his hat and bowing ever so slightly. Simple acts of respect were important to Ailsa's mother. Lucas suspected that they would be well-received. "It's a pleasure to meet you. I'm Lucas. Lucas Plotcok. I believe that you and Ailsa are expecting me."

"It's a pleasure to meet you, Mr. Plotcok," Mrs. Maclaren offered. "Please come in." Lucas stepped into the Maclaren home.

As he had been on Saturday, Lucas was impeccably dressed and immaculately groomed. His black leather boots were polished and buffed, his suit tailored and crisp, his topcoat made of fine wool. Every single hair was in place and his face was freshly shaved. His cologne smelled expensive – French, perhaps. His dark eyes sparkled. Mrs. Maclaren took silent, approving inventory of all of those things. Lucas was precisely as he had been described. Perhaps even more perfect than described, if that were possible. If conclusions about a person can be reached in an instant, Ailsa's mother had done so.

"Ailsa, dear, Mr. Plotcok is here," Mrs. Maclaren called out to her daughter, as if Ailsa didn't already know. Mrs. Maclaren collected Lucas's topcoat and hat and hung them carefully on the coat stand.

Ailsa appeared from the parlor where she had been waiting and waiting. Her hair had been meticulously braided by her mother and hung down her back between her shoulder blades. She wore a simple cotton dress with an ivory brooch in the shape of a flower and a thin silver necklace bearing a small cross pendant. The necklace had once been her maternal grandmother's. Ailsa was nearly as beautiful as Lucas was handsome. If they were ever to be a couple, a possibility which Ailsa had already dared to consider, they would make a most striking one.

Mrs. Maclaren escorted them into the parlor, where they sat across from each other in matching Queen Anne wingback chairs, a table conveniently sitting between them. "Would you care for some tea, Mr. Plotcok?" Mrs. Maclaren asked.

"Yes, ma'am, if it's not an imposition. Thank you. But please, call me Lucas," Lucas answered.

"Ailsa?" Mrs. Maclaren asked. Ailsa's mother could see her daughter's nervousness and excitement. She now understood it, as well.

"Yes, please, mother. Thank you," Ailsa answered. Mrs. Maclaren turned and headed for the kitchen, leaving Ailsa and Lucas alone.

"It's very nice to see you again, Ailsa," Lucas offered after Ailsa's mother had left the parlor."I've been very much looking forward to this day."

"As have I," Ailsa responded. She doubted that Lucas knew how much.

By the time that Mrs. Maclaren returned with their tea, Lucas and Ailsa were already deep in conversation, sometimes smiling, sometimes laughing. Knowing virtually nothing about each other, everything they revealed was new and interesting and exciting. The time flew by for Ailsa as she told Lucas about her childhood, her schooling, her family, her friends, her horse, her books, and about her life as a curler, which Lucas seemed to be the most interested in. He listened intently as Ailsa shared her life story. He asked a lot of questions. Lucas, on the other hand, shared little about himself, content to listen to Ailsa and to learn all that he could about her. After two hours, though, Lucas unfortunately announced that it was time for him to excuse himself. Ailsa couldn't believe how quickly the time had gone by. She was a bit embarrassed by how much she had talked. Ailsa's mother, who had been keeping a watchful, but discreet, eye on the conversation, retrieved Lucas's hat and coat.

As Lucas was leaving, he said to Mrs. Maclaren, "Thank you for your graciousness in allowing me to visit with Ailsa. She's really quite the charming and enchanting young lady. You and Mr. Maclaren must be very proud of her. It was a pleasure." He made sure that Ailsa heard.

"And it was a pleasure to meet you, too, sir," Mrs. Maclaren replied.

"If I may, and if Ailsa approves, I would be delighted to visit with her again, Mrs. Maclaren," Lucas said. Mrs. Maclaren looked to her daughter, who smiled and nodded. It wasn't as if Ailsa's mother really needed to check. She already knew what her daughter's answer would be. "Would Thursday at two-thirty be agreeable? Perhaps Ailsa and Mr. Maclaren could give me an introduction to curling, if they don't mind instructing a novice."

"I believe that Thursday would be fine. Ailsa?" Mrs. Maclaren asked. By now, Mrs. Maclaren was nearly as enchanted by Lucas Plotcok as her daughter was. His manners and bearing were impeccable, and most endearing.

"Yes. Thursday at two-thirty would be fine. I'll ask father about curling," Ailsa answered. Mrs. Maclaren nodded in agreement. With that, Lucas left. Ailsa looked at her mother, wanting to see her reaction. For a moment, they looked at each other before bursting into smiles.

"He seems like a very fine young man, dear," Mrs. Maclaren said. Then she added, almost in a whisper, "I think that your father approves of him, too."

Ailsa nearly floated off to her room, fell down onto her bed, closed her eyes, and thought of nothing but Thursday and another afternoon with Lucas.

At supper that night, Ailsa's father asked how the visit with Lucas had gone. The look on his daughter's face said everything that he needed to know, but he asked anyway. Ailsa was radiant, beaming. There was no denying that the visit had gone very well, indeed. He recognized the look of a young woman who believed that she was falling in love. He could also tell that Mrs. Maclaren was impressed.

"He is a perfectly charming and well-mannered young man, Hugh. He and Ailsa sat in the parlor and chatted all afternoon. Ailsa couldn't stop talking. He seems to be as smitten by her as she is by him," Mrs. Maclaren offered. "'Charming and enchanting' were the exact words he used to describe her, if I'm not mistaken." Ailsa was blushing, because she knew it was true. She had heard him say it.

"Mother!" Ailsa exclaimed.

"Now, now, dear. Mothers can tell these things. I've seen the look before. I had more than a few gentlemen callers myself, you know, including your father. Lucas was looking at you just like your father used to look at me when he first came calling." Hugh smiled, recalling those times, trying so hard to pass muster with both Mrs. Maclaren and her parents.

"It seems that you both approve, then?" Ailsa's father asked.

Looking at each other and smiling, both women replied, "We do."

"He's going to visit again on Thursday," Mrs. Maclaren announced. "He's hoping that you and Ailsa might take him down to the pond and introduce him to the game."

Chapter 9
Thursday

Just as he had done two days earlier, Lucas arrived at the Maclarens' home at precisely two-thirty. For Ailsa, the wait and anticipation had once again seemed interminable, even though it had only been two days. She could now add punctuality to the rapidly growing list of Lucas's admirable qualities. Once again, he looked dapper and displayed perfect manners. By this time, even Ailsa's mother was more than a little taken by Lucas Plotcok. During this visit, Ailsa and Lucas were afforded a little bit more freedom from Mrs. Maclaren's watchful eye. Not too much, but a little more.

Ailsa first showed Lucas to the barn and introduced him to her horse, Magic, as well as to her father's horse, Blaze. Lucas explained that animals, especially dogs and horses, seemed to take a cautious approach with him, for reasons he didn't quite understand. They often acted disturbed and anxious around him. Magic and Blaze were the same. Magic laid his ears back, Blaze backed away and fluttered his eyes. Ailsa was particularly disappointed that Magic seemed skittish and reticent with Lucas. Magic usually enjoyed being visited by people and welcomed the attention. Ailsa had assumed that everyone and every creature would naturally like Lucas. When Ailsa and Lucas returned to the house after a few minutes, they were welcomed back with fresh cups of hot tea, courtesy of Ailsa's mother. Once again, they were seated across from each other in the parlor.

Lucas glanced across the room at the chessboard. The pieces, which appeared to Lucas to be made of rosewood, were in place and at the ready. He had noted it on Tuesday, but hadn't mentioned it. "Do you play, Ailsa?" he asked, gesturing at the board.

"Oh, yes. Father taught me how to play when I was quite young. I think he was wishing that I were a boy back then. He's gotten over it, though," she answered playfully. "Would you like to try a game?"

"Absolutely! It's been quite some time since I've had occasion to play, and I thoroughly enjoy the game. I find that it stimulates the mind and the nerves," Lucas replied. Ailsa's competitive spirit immediately awakened. "I don't often get the opportunity to play, so I'm probably a little rusty," Lucas continued. "You'll be easy on me, won't you, Ailsa?" The mutual flirtation was beginning.

"Not a chance!" Ailsa responded. She was growing more and more comfortable with him.

Ailsa and Lucas were both good players. Ailsa, employing the King's Gambit, won the first game. They didn't talk much during the game, concentrating on their play and content to simply be doing something that they both enjoyed together. "Well-played, Ailsa. You seem to be as adept on the chessboard as you are on the frozen board," Lucas congratulated her. "But now that I've refreshed myself about the game, perhaps we can play again."

"If you dare," Ailsa answered mischievously. It surprised Ailsa a bit how easy it was being with Lucas. Almost all of her nervousness was gone.

This time, Lucas launched an attack which Ailsa had never encountered before. Confused, she miscalculated her response. Before she knew it, she was checkmated. "I've not seen that tactic before," Ailsa said. "What's it called?"

"It's a rather uncommon one called the Devil's Gambit. It used to be quite popular, but has fallen into disfavour over the years, because once someone has encountered it, they usually learn rather quickly how to defend against it. It's a risky play, creating some vulnerabilities, but it can be quite effective against someone who hasn't seen it before," Lucas stated.

"Someone like me, you mean?" Ailsa asked.

"Someone like you," he answered. For a few moments they sat silently, staring at the chessboard, thoroughly enjoying their growing bond. They returned the pieces to their proper places, got up from the chessboard, and returned to their seats.

The budding friendship – perhaps it would grow to be more, Ailsa hoped – led to an easy, flowing conversation, much more so than two days earlier, when Ailsa had dominated the talking. Lucas revealed more about himself this day than he had on Tuesday. His childhood, he said, had been rather challenging, since his family had moved around a lot, which left Lucas with no enduring, close friendships. His mother had died while giving birth to her fourth child, Lucas's sister, when Lucas was only eight years old. Lucas was forced to grow up quickly, bearing much of the responsibility for taking care of his younger siblings as his father moved from place to place looking for work. Perhaps that was why Lucas himself was moving about constantly, he offered. If he were to find the right situation, he confided, he would very much like to settle down and have a complete family. He missed his mother dearly, he said. Ailsa liked him even more.

It was exactly what Ailsa wanted, too. She wanted a family of her own, with a husband, children, perhaps a small farm like her parents owned, lots of animals – especially horses – and maybe even a pond suited to curling in the wintertime, where she could teach the game to her children. She confided that she had no interest in building another one herself, though. Once was quite enough. She could still remember the blisters and the aching muscles. Ailsa was beginning to picture all of this happening with Lucas, even though she had met him just five days earlier. They were fanciful thoughts, but Ailsa was already starting to imagine them coming true. If only she could know what Lucas was thinking.

Just then, Ailsa's father appeared in the entranceway to the parlor. "Hello, sweetheart," he said to Ailsa. "Good afternoon, Lucas. Are you still interested in trying your hand at curling? The ice and weather are perfect."

"Hello, sir," Lucas replied. "If it's not a bother, I would be delighted to receive some instruction from you and Ailsa. But only if it's not an inconvenience." Lucas wasn't really all that interested in learning how to curl, but he was very interested in endearing himself to Ailsa and her father. Spending some time on the ice with them, learning their favorite game, seemed like a sure way to do that. Curling was, after all, what Ailsa most loved doing, and why Lucas had become interested in her in the first place.

"Not at all. Our game needs more young men joining the ranks," Mr. Maclaren answered. "I think that you'll enjoy it. Let's head down and give it a try, shall we?"

The three of them donned their coats, hats, and gloves and began walking down toward the pond. As they walked, Hugh Maclaren began his instruction. "Well, Lucas, you've already watched some games, so I suppose that you have a little understanding of the basics."

"Yes, sir. I know a little bit about the game. Ailsa explained some of it to me while we were watching you play," Lucas answered.

"Good," Maclaren answered. "I believe you'll find playing to be quite a bit different from simply watching, though." All three smiled.

"Anyone can watch," Ailsa said.

Hugh Maclaren, Ailsa, and Lucas stepped onto the frozen surface of the small pond. Lucas slipped and almost fell. He looked sheepishly at Ailsa. Ailsa laughed. Ailsa's father led Lucas's instruction. He introduced Lucas to the equipment and to the set-up of the ice. First, he showed

Lucas the crampit. The crampit was a flat, rectangular board which the curler stood upon when throwing the curling stone down the ice, so as not to have the curler's feet slipping on the ice, Mr. Maclaren explained. Ailsa looked at Lucas and giggled again. Her father gave her a disapproving glance. Some clubs used footholds carved into the ice, called "hacks," but they were much less common than crampits, at least in Scotland, Maclaren explained. Besides, the thin layer of ice on the artificial pond wasn't suited to carving hacks.

The student and teachers next walked down the sheet to a line etched in the ice. "This line is the hog-score," Maclaren explained. "If you throw a stone which does not pass the hog-score, the stone is a hog and must immediately be removed from the ice. Never fail to get your stone past the hog-score."

"I'll try my best, sir," Lucas responded.

"We'll soon see whether you are strong enough to throw a stone past the hog-score," Ailsa smiled, looking at Lucas. "I can do it, so perhaps you will be able, too." They continued walking down the ice to a small mark in the center of two concentric circles etched into the ice. "This is the tee," Hugh Maclaren said. "The stone closest to the tee gains the point. In very basic terms, the object is to get your team's stones closer to the tee than your antagonists' stones." The trio walked back to the crampit.

Hugh Maclaren first showed Lucas how to grip the stone's handle, then how to position himself on the crampit. The feet should be positioned just so, Maclaren demonstrated. "The most important thing is to keep your eyes on the target, not on the stone. The eyes will dictate where you throw it. Looking at the stone as you throw it will be bad for your balance and will guarantee a poor result. Eyes constantly fixed on the target. Understand?" Whenever Hugh Maclaren instructed anyone on something, curling or otherwise, he always sought confirmation that his student understood.

"Yes, sir, I understand," Lucas acknowledged.

"Good," Ailsa's father replied. "First, you will draw your arm back with the stone, then come forward with it. At the exact moment when the sole of the stone meets the ice, release your grip. The sole should be perfectly flat on the ice, or else the stone will rock and wobble. You want the stone to slide perfectly flat down the ice. It requires a good deal of practice and a deft touch to release it at the precise time," Maclaren explained. "Watch me." Maclaren stepped onto the crampit and demonstrated. It didn't seem so difficult to Lucas.

"I see," said Lucas, watching his instructor's stone glide smoothly down the ice to the tee.

"Now you give it a try," Maclaren said to Lucas.

Lucas picked up a stone and gripped it just as he had been shown. He stepped onto the crampit, Ailsa and her father watching his technique closely. Mr. Maclaren had Lucas adjust the width of his stance and the position of his feet. Lucas drew the stone back slowly, his eyes fixed on the target, although his natural instinct told him to watch the stone. He pulled his arm and the stone forward and set the stone down on the ice as he released it. Lucas didn't get it exactly right, and the stone bounced and wobbled a bit as it began its journey, greatly diminishing its momentum. It stopped well short of the hog-score. Ailsa looked at Lucas, smiling. "Perhaps you're just not strong enough," she teased.

"Not bad at all," Mr. Maclaren said to Lucas. "Try another one."

Lucas picked up another stone and repeated the process. This time, he swung his arm back and forward with a bit more force so that the stone would travel farther. Once again, Lucas didn't set the stone down perfectly, and it again wobbled, but at least it managed to make it past the hog-score, if not anywhere near the tee.

"Much better, Lucas," Mr. Maclaren offered. "It will take some practice to learn how hard you need to deliver the stone and how to set it down properly, but that will come. Repetition is the only way to get it right. Try another one."

Lucas picked up another stone and again sent it down the ice. And then another. And another. The closest stone to the tee was more than eight feet away. Satisfied that Lucas understood the technique, Maclaren said, "Ailsa, why don't you let Lucas try a few more and then come back inside." Ailsa's father headed back to the house. Ailsa immediately noticed that her father was allowing her a few moments alone with Lucas, which was a very good sign. And it was clearly intentional. Hugh Maclaren didn't do many things without intent. Lucas took notice, too.

After Lucas threw a few more stones, Ailsa and Lucas left the ice and began walking back to the house. It was a slow, leisurely stroll. "You did very well for your first time," Ailsa said. "You have some things to work on, but you did very well. Much better than I did the first time. And at least we now know that you are not too weak." They both found that funny.

"Thank you," Lucas answered. "It's not as easy as one might suppose, but I did have two very good teachers."

"I trust that you want to continue learning," Ailsa said, hopefully. "You might find that you really enjoy it."

"Perhaps I will. I would love to try it again, should the opportunity arise," Lucas answered. Ailsa hoped that it would.

All too soon, shortly after returning inside, Lucas announced that it was time for him to take his leave. As he headed out the door, he asked, "Will you be attending your father's bonspiel this Saturday?"

"I certainly hope to," Ailsa answered. "I try never to miss one of them when father is playing nearby."

"Then I shall hope to see you there," Lucas said. "G'day, Ailsa." And with that, Lucas left.

Ailsa was falling in love with Lucas. She knew it. Each time that she had seen him, it was better than the time before. She sensed that he felt the same, although she couldn't be certain. Now, he had confessed to wanting to have a home and a family. Ailsa knew that Lucas was talking about them and their future together. And he had even curled with her! Best of all, he wanted to see her again.

Chapter 10

Away on Business

The frost which had settled over Scotland more than a week earlier persisted into Saturday, driving nearly every curler around the country to neglect his labor and household duties in favor of Scotland's favorite winter game. Bonspiels, or simply just friendly games, had been arranged on nearly every curling pond, loch, and river with sufficient ice, enough room, and enough curlers, for matches to be played. Scotland wasn't often blessed with such a sustained frost, and its curlers were in a celebratory way.

Hugh Maclaren was once again leading his rink into friendly battle in the bonspiel on Duddingston Loch for a Royal Caledonian Curling Club district medal. The sun shone throughout the entire day, although not enough to thaw the ice in the face of temperatures not venturing above twenty-four degrees. It was a perfect day both for playing and for watching. Ailsa arrived early with her father, and she very much looked forward to watching him and to absorbing what more she could learn about strategy and teamwork from him. He was a brilliant strategist and tactician when it came to Scotland's truly scientific game, as the masters called it. As much as she loved her father and watching him curl, though, her excitement was really at the thought of seeing Lucas again. Two days was way too long a time to be away from Lucas.

The gun fired at 9:00 a.m. to signal the start of the bonspiel. Ailsa watched, but mostly waited, as the clock crept to 9:30, then to 9:45, then to 10:00, and then roundabout again to almost 11:00. She looked around, scanning the small crowd, trying not to appear conspicuous or frantic in her search, but she didn't see Lucas anywhere. She was crushed, nearly to the point of tears, but she fought them back. What had she done? What had she said that could cause him to abandon her like this? The thoughts and feelings were horrible. The very last thing that he had said to her on Thursday was that he hoped to see her today. "Then I shall hope to see you there," were his exact words to her when he had left. She had memorized the words, savored them. "Hope" meant that he wanted to see her. Perhaps as much as she wanted to see him again, but that might just be too wishful, and now it seemed like a mere fantasy. Everything had been perfect just two days earlier. Now, it seemed that she may have lost him.

Try as she might, Ailsa simply couldn't concentrate on her father's match. She heard the huzzas for shots well made, and the groans when stones failed to fulfill what was intended as their destiny, but she paid them little mind. And then, Lucas appeared, again seemingly out of nowhere, and was standing right beside her. Not as close as Ailsa would have liked, but beside her nonetheless. "G'morning, Ailsa. A glorious day for a bonspiel, wouldn't you agree?" Ailsa's heart began beating faster, and louder as well. She could hear it pounding. Lucas might even hear it! Lucas's belated appearance was carefully calculated and timed, and it had produced its intended effect.

"Good morning, Lucas. Yes, 'tis a glorious morn'." And for Ailsa Maclaren, it had suddenly become much, much better. She was trying to appear nonchalant, although she felt that her heart and face must be betraying that foolish attempt. Lucas certainly had the power to bring her senses and feelings to life. "Father's rink is right there," she said, pointing towards her father. They're playing quite well." Lucas spotted him.

"Yes, I see him," Lucas said. He turned to Ailsa and looked right at her. Somehow, Lucas had become even more handsome than he was on

Thursday. Ailsa noticed how dark, dark brown his eyes were. "I've missed you, Ailsa, " he finally said, even though it had been just two days. Ailsa's heart pounded even harder. All of her doubts and fears melted away upon hearing those words. If she needed reassurance about Lucas, she had just gotten it. Everything felt right again.

"I've missed you, too," she said, surprised that she had the courage to say the words aloud. It seemed so intimate, but Lucas made it seem so easy. They stood in contented silence for minutes, happy to be back together, but for quite different reasons. Ailsa was the one who interrupted the silence with her news. "Did you hear that the the Royal Caledonian Curling Club is going to allow a ladies' bonspiel next year, with the winners pronounced the 'Queens o' Curling' in Scotland? Father somehow convinced them to do it. I've dreamt of it, but I thought that this day would never come to pass." Ailsa's excitement was abundantly evident to Lucas, and it pleased him greatly. She was absolutely radiant with the thought of becoming the Royal Club's first ladies' champion.

"And will you be playing, Ailsa?" Lucas asked, although he was certain of the answer. There was absolutely no chance that Ailsa would not be playing.

"We'll be playing and we'll be winning, too," she answered, with conviction and without hesitation. Although she intended for it to sound light and matter-of-fact, she was deadly serious.

"How can you be so sure?" Lucas asked.

"Because we're the best ladies' rink from the Highlands to England," came Ailsa's quick and confident reply. Lucas admired the young woman's resolve and determination. She believed in herself and she believed in her rink. "And because I would do anything to make sure that we win." They were the words that Lucas needed to hear. He had heard them many, many times before. They were like familiar music to his ears. "I would do anything . . ."

"*Anything*?" Lucas asked, his eyes twinkling, a mischievous smile forming. Ailsa hesitated, fearing that perhaps she was sounding a little too aggressive, too brash, too . . . *unladylike*. She most assuredly did not want to seem unladylike to Lucas Plotcok. Quite the opposite. So she backed up.

"Well, *almost* anything," she answered, with much less bravado and more coyly. Finally, Ailsa worked up the nerve to say, "I hope that you will come and watch us play." Those words carried so many meanings. They obviously meant that Ailsa liked Lucas. That was no longer something that she could hide or that she wanted to hide. They also meant that she wanted to see him again. They meant that Ailsa wanted their relationship to continue for a long time, because the ladies' championship was nearly a full year away. Ailsa was hoping that Lucas felt the same.

"If I can put everything in proper order ahead of the date, I most certainly will. I most certainly will." That was all that Ailsa needed to hear. As if she needed any extra motivation, the thought of playing in front of Lucas provided it.

⋅◦⋅

They stood side-by-side in the cold for a long time, still watching Hugh Maclaren's rink, but they both had their minds on other things. Ailsa, having known Lucas for only a week, nevertheless was thinking that perhaps they might be beginning a life together. Lucas was thinking about how he would break his own news, which he knew that Ailsa wouldn't like, to her.

Lucas turned toward Ailsa and took her hand. Ailsa's heart, which had finally returned to a normal rhythm, immediately raced again. It was the first time that he had actually touched her. She felt a jolt. "I'm afraid that I have some rather unfortunate news, Ailsa," he began. With just those few words, Lucas sent so many thoughts rumbling through her mind.

Was he leaving her? Was there someone else? Had she done something wrong? Was he ill? The last thing that Ailsa wanted to hear right now was bad news. She wanted to simply bask in the pure joy of being with Lucas. She braced herself for whatever it might be.

"Please understand, Ailsa," Lucas continued. "I wish that it weren't like this, believe me, I do. I've grown very fond of you over these past weeks and hope that we can continue on our wonderful journey together. We have something very special together, don't you agree? More special than I could have dared to imagine." She was gripped with fear over what might be coming next.

Ailsa was feeling frantic. "I do. Yes, I do," Ailsa answered. "But what is wrong, Lucas? Please tell me."

Lucas looked down. He didn't like telling her what he was about to tell her, or so it seemed to Ailsa. He broke the news. "I'm afraid that I must be leaving for some time. My business demands that I be away from quite a while. Several months, perhaps. It will even take me away from Scotland."

Ailsa was devastated. There were far worse things that Lucas could have told her, she knew, but it hurt anyway. No sooner had she met him than he was leaving her. "When will you be leaving?" she asked. Perhaps they would at least have a few more days together before he left. Days filled with memories to sustain her.

"I must be going tomorrow morning. I'm afraid it's unavoidable. I wish that it were not so, but there are some matters that simply cannot wait," Lucas answered. It was the worst answer Ailsa could have heard. Tomorrow morning? She wondered whether she would ever see him again.

"Ailsa, dear, I hope that you understand. I've come to enjoy your company very much and hope that one day it won't be like this. This has all taken me by a bit of a surprise. But I knew right away, when we first met. I look forward to a possible future with you, if you feel the same," Lucas told her.

"I do. I hope that we might have a future together," Ailsa said. "But this is so sudden and it feels like so long for you to be away."

"It will be long," Lucas said, "and I will miss you each and every day. But I will think of you constantly and write to you faithfully. And I will return as soon as I possibly can. Believe me. I promise you." Ailsa desperately wanted to believe him. She needed to believe him.

The truth was that Lucas didn't have to go anywhere, really. He was free to make his own schedule and work on his own time, however and whenever he saw fit. He was in complete control of his travel and timetable. He could have stayed in Musselburgh for as long as he pleased to continue their courtship. Instead, he decided that this was a better way. He would allow Ailsa lots of time to miss him, to long for his return, to dream about being with him. He would write to her faithfully, prove to her that he was true to his word, and then return to her, just as he promised. He believed that his absence truly would make Ailsa's heart grow fonder. If it worked as planned, Ailsa would be his forever.

He had sensed that Ailsa's feelings for him were growing each time that they had been together. He had planted his seeds carefully and nurtured them tenderly along the way. He had chosen his words deliberately and with forethought, and had delivered them at precisely the right time. Everything he had done, he had done to win her. When he returned, he would collect his reward. Looking into her eyes, he was quite certain that it had all worked perfectly.

When the bonspiel was ending, Lucas turned to Ailsa and said, "It's time now, Ailsa. I must go. I will write to you very soon." They embraced and held each other until Lucas finally let go. It took Ailsa a little longer to let go of Lucas. Lucas saw that she was crying. "Please don't be sad, Ailsa. Everything will be fine. Trust me." Ailsa nodded. Lucas turned and walked away. Ailsa watched until he was gone.

The only real risk to Lucas was that Ailsa might not wait for him. He calculated that the risk was a small and acceptable one. He was confident that he had done his best and that everything was in perfect order. Yes, it was possible that someone else might try to woo her while he was away, but Lucas would do all that he could to keep himself front of heart and mind. He wouldn't allow anyone else to take that which was rightfully his.

Chapter 11
Belief and Trust

It had been more than nine months since Ailsa had last seen Lucas. Nine excruciating months of worrying, hoping, and wondering. Where was he? When was he coming back? *Was* he coming back? When would she see him again? Would everything be different? There was no way for Ailsa to know.

Lucas thought that it was the perfect amount of time for him to be gone. Now, it was time for him to make his return.

Lucas had been extremely faithful in writing to Ailsa while he was away, just as he had promised. What better way to build her trust in him? To prove his fidelity to her? It seemed that a new letter from Lucas arrived every week, each one warmer and more intimate than the last. Sometimes, two would arrive during the same week. They were all written on Lucas's fine, engraved, monogrammed stationery. The letters were addressed from different and distant locales – Ireland, Wales, England – and some even arrived from the continent, France and Belgium, in particular. Ailsa read each of them over and over, imagining Lucas's adventures in such exotic places without her. She longed to be there with him. She was hopelessly in love. Someday, Lucas wrote, he hoped to visit some of the places with her. Yes, he was planning on a future together.

When Lucas knew what his itinerary would be, he sent Ailsa an address where she could write to him. She would tell Lucas about spring and summer on the farm; about her parents and the horses; and about

Sheenagh, Effie, and Kirsty, even though he was yet to meet them. Ailsa was certain that Lucas would like them, and that they would be enchanted by him, too. Ailsa's letters were long and leisurely, and yet somehow urgent, recounting everything that was happening in her life. Lucas read them carefully to see if there were any signs that Ailsa's feelings toward him were changing. He detected none.

Lucas's letters were shorter, but were filled with great warmth and intimacy. He told her how much he missed her and and how often he thought about her. He wrote that he had purchased some gifts for her along the way, which he was anxious to give her. One in particular which he thought she would especially like.

The last letter that Ailsa received arrived in October, postmarked from Paris. It was the one which she had been waiting for, longing for, and daring to dream of. It was the letter in which Lucas first confessed to being in love with her. Ailsa spent the rest of the day and night composing her own letter in response. She told Lucas that she, too, was in love and begged him to return from his travels to be with her. Ailsa placed the letter in the post the next morning.

For two months she waited for a reply. Two months of elation and dismay. Elation at the knowledge that Lucas indeed loved her and dismay that she had heard nothing in response to her last letter. She lived in dread that something may have happened to Lucas. Two weeks without a letter from Lucas had never passed before, much less two months. She asked her father to make inquiries, but no one knew anything about Lucas Plotcok, last known to be in France on business.

⚬

On a cold, blustery December morning, Ailsa was standing alone outside, once again consigned to being a mere spectator as her father played in a large bonspiel. It was a tense and even match between long-time rivals, and for one of the few times in weeks, Ailsa was concentrating on what she was doing rather than thinking about Lucas. There was a whisper in her ear that startled her.

"Hello, Ailsa. Remember me?" She turned and looked. It was him!

Ailsa flung her arms around Lucas's neck and squeezed as hard as she could, tears cascading. He looked as perfect as ever, perhaps even better, if that were possible. He even smelled good and familiar. Then she kissed him, impulsively, something that she had never done before. It was wonderful, although she probably shouldn't have done it quite so publicly. Lucas was elated by Ailsa's greeting.

"It seems that you do remember," Lucas grinned. "I'm glad. It's been far, far too long. I have missed you dearly."

Nothing that had happened over the past year was either by accident or coincidence. Lucas had arrived in Musselburgh for the express purpose of meeting Ailsa, courting her, and hopefully having her fall in love with him. The manners, the dress, the grooming, it was all important and meticulously calculated to achieve its purpose. Impressing both of Ailsa's parents, and receiving curling instruction was also part of the plan. So was leaving abruptly for nine long months. It was the part of the plan with the greatest risk, but also a great potential reward. Writing faithfully, just as he promised he would do, and lastly confessing his love, those were the final pieces. Lucas needed for Ailsa to like him, love him, believe him when he spoke, and trust him unconditionally at his word. It all seemed to have worked according to plan, and Lucas was quite impressed with how perfectly everything had turned out.

"I've been so worried, Lucas. I haven't heard from you for nearly two months. Where have you been? Why didn't you write?" Ailsa asked. "I thought that something terrible had happened to you." Lucas's disappearance had produced its intended effect.

"I'm so sorry to have worried you," Lucas apologized. "I've been on the continent. Several times it seemed like I would be returning to Scotland imminently, but obstacles kept presenting themselves. I didn't want to write and tell you that I would be returning shortly, only to have my plans change. I knew that you would worry greatly if I didn't return according to plan. When I was finally able, I headed straight for Musselburgh, as quickly as I could. To be with you," Lucas declared.

There was not an overabundance of truth in Lucas's explanation. He knew exactly when he would be returning to Musselburgh – he had known it for nine months – but he wanted Ailsa to worry over him and obsess over him. It would make his return far more dramatic and emotional. If anything, Ailsa would be more in love with him now than when he had left. That was Lucas's calculation. Ailsa didn't really care much about the explanation. All that mattered was that Lucas was back. And he had come back to be with her.

"I have something for you," Lucas announced. "I think that you will like it." He reached into his pocket and withdrew a small black box. He handed the box to Ailsa. She looked at Lucas. "Go ahead, open it," he said.

Ailsa slowly lifted the lid and carefully removed a thin, elegant, gold necklace. A gold pendant, fashioned in the shape of a curling stone, hung from the chain. On the back, the pendant was inscribed, "To Ailsa, from Lucas. 1886." It was beautiful. "I had it specially made for you in Paris," Lucas told her. Ailsa blushed. It wasn't really made in Paris, but it sounded so convincingly romantic.

Ailsa put the necklace on and turned to let Lucas fix the clasp. "It's beautiful, Thank you so much, Lucas," Ailsa said. "I love it." She kissed him again.

They stood side-by-side in the cold, Ailsa leaning her head on Lucas's shoulder. Everything was perfect, and Ailsa was ready to begin a life with Lucas Plotcok. There would be plans to make, of course, but those could wait. Today was for reveling in the pure, unbounded joy of Lucas's return.

***

Lucas and Ailsa spent almost all of the next two weeks together, mostly at the Maclarens' home. They walked the farm when the weather was nice, played chess, and Ailsa even tried to get Magic and Blaze to warm to Lucas, with only minimal success. Twice, they went into town together, unchaperoned. They also attended another of Hugh Maclaren's bonspiels together. It was at that bonspiel when Lucas took the next step. The most important step. The one that everything else had led them to. He took hold of her hands and looked directly at her.

"Ailsa," Lucas said, sensing that the time was at long last right. "Do you trust me?" It was an odd question, coming seemingly from out of nowhere. Of course she trusted him. He had written to her faithfully while he was gone, just as he had promised. He had returned to her, just as he had promised. He had even been the first to confess his love. No, there was no reason not to trust him. She would probably have walked across hot coals in her bare feet for Lucas Plotcok, had he asked.

"Of course I do," Ailsa answered, "although I'm very curious why you ask. What do you mean and why do you ask?" She thought that perhaps Lucas was just being flirtatious, conspiratorial, mysterious, playing a game with her. Intrigue was certainly one of Lucas's more interesting and charming traits.

"I ask because what I shall tell you, you surely will not believe, at least not at first," Lucas stated. He was very accustomed to doubt and disbelief. He encountered those reactions all the time. But, right now, he wanted and needed for Ailsa to trust him. She said that she did.

"I'm getting a little nervous," Ailsa said. "But please tell me, and we'll then see whether I believe you or not," Ailsa responded, enjoying the little verbal game they seemed to be playing.

"As you wish," said Lucas, convinced that Ailsa, after a year of painstaking grooming, was indeed ready. He looked into Ailsa's face so that he could guage her response. She didn't seem frightened. She seemed expectant. "You see, Ailsa, I'm not really Lucas Plotcok, although for present purposes that has sufficed."

Ailsa, of course, was confused. His words made no sense. First, he had asked if she trusted him, and next, he announced that he had lied to her. She had no idea what to think. "What do you mean?" Ailsa asked, pulling back slightly. "If you're not Lucas Plotcok, then who are you?" She was confused and discomfited about being lied to, but was at least willing to listen to an explanation. She was, after all, totally invested in Lucas already. She was in love with him, and he with her.

"Why, I'm the Devil, of course. Satan, Lucifer, Old Clootie, the Deil, Beelzebub, Mephistopheles, Iblis, El Diablo, Shaitan, Baphomet, Moloch, Maara, Perdition, the Prince of Darkness . . . People have come up with all manner of silly names for me. You may continue to call me 'Lucas,' though." Lucas stopped and waited for Ailsa's response. Ailsa remained composed for a few seconds, then finally broke out into laughter. She felt a sense of relief that Lucas was only joking. This was fun! She decided that she would play along.

"If you're the Devil, then where are your horns and tail and hooves?" Ailsa smiled, eyeing Lucas up and down. "Tucked beneath your coat and hat and inside of your boots?" She knew that Lucas was joking, having fun with her, teasing. Isn't that what young people falling in love did?

"It's a most unflattering portrait which people have created of me. I've never had horns or hooves or a tail in my entire being," Lucas protested. He actually seemed offended by the notion. "And you can clearly see that I don't have them now. I would look grotesque. Do I look grotesque to you, Ailsa?" Lucas didn't look grotesque. He looked beautiful. "However, I can grow some for you, if you'd like."

"Yes, please!" Ailsa answered enthusiastically. "Grow them for me right now! Big, pointy horns and a forked tail!" She was having even more fun now, not having seen Lucas in this playful light before. She was enjoying playing this game.

Lucas looked at Ailsa, suddenly with a much more somber, portentous look on his face. "Ailsa, look at me," he commanded. There was a sharpness in Lucas's voice which she had not heard before. Ailsa abandoned her smile and looked directly at Lucas. She suddenly noticed how cold she felt and how stern Lucas looked. His graceful features had hardened. "This is not a joke or a trick, Ailsa. I am the Devil and I have sought you out very intentionally. I arrived in Musselburgh with the sole intention of meeting you and hopefully striking a mutually beneficial bargain with you. One which I believe you will very much approve of." Lucas paused to let his words sink in. He continued. "Remember when I told you that I was an 'investor'? That is precisely what I am, and I want to invest in you. I like you, Ailsa, and I think that we could work very well together. Very well, indeed."

Ailsa was frightened by Lucas's abrupt change in tone and countenance. He was no longer warm, charming, and friendly. He wasn't threatening or menacing in any way, just solemn, strict, and, most disturbingly, apparently quite serious. Against her will, she found herself beginning to believe him, almost. Convincing people that he was who he claimed to be was his extraordinary gift.

"I don't believe you. I don't understand. What have I done wrong to be visited by the Devil?" Ailsa asked. It was another common question which Lucas was used to answering.

"Oh, Ailsa, dear, you've done nothing wrong. Absolutely nothing wrong at all. In fact, you've lived quite the exemplary life so far, I must say. But people have been mistakenly led to assume that I am only interested in terrible people, the worst of the worst. The pagans and blasphemers, thieves and swindlers. The truth is quite the opposite, of course. For sure, I deal with all manner of those people, but those are not the ones who most interest and excite me. I am far more interested in those who are strong, who are clever, who are smart, who have the kind of discipline and leadership qualities which I can put to good use. People just like you, Ailsa. I seek out people just like you. People who might very badly want something which I am very willing and happy to provide." Lucas stopped, anticipating the questions which were sure to come.

"Seek out people for what?" Ailsa asked. Her thoughts were awash with confusion. There was nothing that Ailsa really wanted except to embark on a life together with Lucas Plotcok. She was surprised to even be asking the question, for it assumed that Lucas actually *was* the Devil.

"When you deal largely with the kinds of people that I deal with, you know, the rogues and scoundrels and reprobates, it is quite a challenge to keep them all in line," Lucas began. "Most of them are not at all keen on rules and responsibilities and in doing what is expected of them. They prefer to make their own rules. They've lived their lives that way, and now they're being asked to change. People don't like to change. They are now required to listen and obey. It's not easy for me to impart any sense of discipline in them, especially spending so much of my time on the road. So I seek out people who can be – how can I state this? – my field marshalls, supervisors, group leaders, if you will. People that they will listen to and follow. Like I said, people very much like you."

"You can't be wanting me," Ailsa protested. "I go to church every Sunday and say my prayers for salvation. When the roll is called, my name shall be on it."

"Perhaps it will, perhaps it won't," Lucas offered. "I have no real say in such a thing." He stopped to look at Ailsa, to try to ascertain her reaction. She hadn't turned and run away, as many people did, which was a hopeful start. She was apparently willing to hear more, which was always a good sign to Lucas. His persuasive powers were quite strong, even to skeptics like Ailsa. He saved the most mysterious, enigmatic part of his tale for last. He shared this part with very few people. Conspiratorially, he asked, "Would you like to know how it *really* works, Ailsa?"

"How what works?" she asked in return.

"Why, the afterlife, of course. The journey that everyone takes eventually. The rich and the poor, the good and the evil, saints and sinners, the powerful and the powerless. Everyone. Would you like to know what *really* happens? Everyone is curious to know, but most people never hear the true story. They only hear what the churches, priests, ministers, and charlatans, even, are interested in telling them. Would you like to know, Ailsa? I can tell you if you'd like to know, but it's probably not at all what you would suspect," Lucas or Satan or Beelzebub or El Diablo or *Whoever He Was*, asked. How could she not want to know the answer to the eternal mystery?

Still very confused, but also captivated, Ailsa simply said, "Go on." There was no harm in listening. She had completely forgotten about her father's bonspiel being played before her. She was becoming lost in the tale Lucas was spinning.

"It works like this," *Whoever He Was* began. "But I must warn you that it is probably not anything like you've been led to believe. The churches have gotten quite a few things wrong, I must tell you, despite each and every one of them proclaiming to be the sole purveyors of Truth," Lucas explained. "But I can tell you the Truth. Here is the Truth – when a person leaves these earthly shackles behind, my 'Counterpart', if you will, gets the first opportunity to take possession of their soul. Each and every time. It's not really fair, in my opinion, but those are the rules that I am burdened with. My Counterpart does have seniority, though, so I cannot protest too vehemently, I suppose. I have no doubt that my protestations would be unfavorably received, anyway.

"Nonetheless, should my Counterpart pass on the opportunity to collect a particular soul, I then have the opportunity to do so. Just because a soul becomes available to me does not at all mean that they were a bad person or an evil person, or a heathen, even. It simply means that they don't fully measure up to my Counterpart's rather lofty and exacting standards. Very few actually pass His muster. You have no doubt heard about the 'eye of the needle' analogy from the pulpit. So I always have quite a large selection to choose from. Most are of little interest to me, though. Fortunately, no one is forced upon me.

"Well, I have my standards, too. Just because a soul doesn't gain entry into what you might call 'Paradise' or 'Heaven' doesn't mean that I wish to be stuck with them. With some, of course, I really have no choice. Their time on earth earned them their time with me, so I welcome them in. Other than those, I mostly take only those who I believe will work out well and fit my vision. A lot of pretty nasty, unpleasant sorts of characters. Not easy folks to keep in line, as you might imagine." Lucas paused, mostly for effect. He continued, "It may surprise you to learn that only a rather small sampling are actually chosen by either of us. Most simply go unclaimed."

Ailsa was now rapt. Whether fictitious or not, she was mesmerized by the tale. Lucas certainly was a grand storyteller. And a very good liar, of course. "What happens to everyone who goes unchosen by either of you? What about them?" Ailsa asked. Lucas was very pleased that Ailsa was asking these questions.

"That's a rather sad story. Not much at all happens, really. They spend their time doing virtually nothing, feeling virtually nothing. It's like a waiting room. Yes, that's what they do, they wait and they wait to receive an assignment which will not be coming. Those decisions have already been made, I'm afraid. My Counterpart and I are both quite disciplined in that way. Decisions are final and are never changed. So they simply wait. You might have heard something akin to it called 'purgatory,' although it's not at all like what is sometimes taught."

"How long must they wait? Forever?" Ailsa asked. She continued to ask questions as if any of this were actually true. She had forgotten that it was just a silly tale. At least she hoped that it was.

"No," Lucas answered. "Eventually they simply give up, accept their fate, and vanish into nothingness. Like a bird that you can no longer see as it approaches the horizon. Some abandon hope very quickly. For others, giving up can be a slow process. But sooner or later, they all give up." Lucas paused. "There is one exception, and only one exception, to my Counterpart getting first crack at a newly departed, though. A very important exception that may apply to you, Ailsa, should you choose to avail yourself of it. Would you like to hear it?" Ailsa nodded weakly.

"Wonderful!" Lucas exclaimed. "The exception is this. If I enter into a legally binding contract prior to a person's earthly demise, entitling me to possession of their soul, my Counterpart will honour it. My suspicion is that He has concluded that He really wouldn't want to claim anyone who would do business with me, anyway, even though I am very honourable in all of my dealings. It is the only situation in which I get the first option on a dearly departed one's soul. The only one. And that's where my business with you begins, Ailsa."

Ailsa found herself increasingly spellbound, listening intently, almost getting caught up in believing Lucas's silly story. It was not remotely like anything she had been taught in church. Suddenly, the crowd erupted in a large cheer for one of the rinks which had just won its match, and Ailsa snapped out of her entrancement. "Lucas, stop. I don't want to hear any more o' this talk. It's dangerous. The Devil doesn't take kindly to being made fun of."

"I don't, that's true. But I've grown accustomed to it. People think that if they make fun of me, put up a false bravado, it hides the fact that they're really quite afraid of me. I really don't mind all that much. In the end, I can have the last laugh if I choose to," Lucas explained. "You're not afraid of me, are you, Ailsa?"

"That's enough. Stop this Devil talk now, Lucas. Please. You're frightening me," Ailsa pleaded. "You've gone too far."

"We have some business to discuss first, Ailsa," Lucas continued. "Some business which I think you will be very interested in and happy about," Lucas responded. "I've come a long way and waited very patiently to make you my offer. But you need to believe me when I tell you that I am the Devil Himself before we can discuss my offer. You said that you trusted me."

"Well, I don't trust you anymore, Lucas Plotcok, or whoever you are. How am I to know that you're the Devil Himse'f? It's ridiculous. All of your talk is just that."

Lucas chuckled. "It's the most common question of all. Everyone I deal with asks the same things – How do I know? How can I trust you? Prove it to me! It's really quite sad, the lack of trust that abounds in the world today. No one ever believes me . . . at least not at first. You're going to want me to do something to prove to you that I am who I say I am, right, Ailsa, even though down inside you already know? You're going to require some kind of miracle or parlor trick or sleight-of-hand? Irrefutable proof?"

"You would have to prove it, yes, which we know you cannot do," Ailsa answered. Lucas was wrong. Ailsa wasn't certain about who he really was. Not just yet.

"I can do that for you if I must, Ailsa. I can certainly do something to convince you. I have to do it each and every single time. I wish that I didn't have to do it for you, though, Ailsa. I had hoped that you would believe me," Lucas responded. It was an old, tiring part of his negotiations. Everyone wanted proof, not trusting their instincts to discern the truth. "It saddens me, after all that we've experienced together. I had hoped that you trusted me by now."

Proving himself was not always an easy matter. Each situation was different. Some people wanted enormous, earth-changing events which interfered with the natural order of things on earth. Some wanted foes or rivals killed. Some greedily asked for earthly riches. The Devil refused all of those demands. He understood that his Counterpart would not tolerate such shenanigans for very long. Smaller things, harmless things, usually worked just as well in convincing skeptics. What Lucas proposed was simple proof, something beyond a magician or conjuror's ability, something rather benign, but unassailably proof of his true identity and powers. Lucas pondered over what might work with Ailsa.

"What if I were to make your father a hero today?" Lucas finally proposed. "Would that convince you?"

Ailsa didn't know what to say, or even what to think or feel. Everything she hoped for with Lucas was now different, wrong. Whoever he was, whatever he wanted from her, it was all askew. Lucas wasn't who he said he was, or what Ailsa wanted him to be, regardless of whether he was actually the Devil or not. "Father is already a hero," Ailsa snapped. Lucas stood perfectly still and silent.

"Why don't we take a moment to let you think about what I've revealed to you, Ailsa. I know that this is a lot for you, and probably very confusing," Lucas offered. He was right, of course. Ailsa again thought of running away, but what would that do? Lucas would surely be able to find her. He had been to her home. So they stood silently as Ailsa thought about what all of this could possibly mean.

Suddenly, while Ailsa was lost in her thoughts, there was a commotion on the ice near where her father was playing. A young boy, only nine or ten years old, had somehow fallen through the ice and disappeared. Hugh Maclaren was the first one to jump into the frigid water after him.

Ailsa raced to the edge of the pond and watched as her father pulled the terrified, screeching young boy from the water. She now knew – if she didn't already – who "Lucas" was. Yes, indeed! – he was the *Devil Himself*. And he was standing right beside her. There was no way that it was a coincidence. Lucas had made it happen. Ailsa stared at Lucas, after watching her father climb back onto the ice with the boy, her mouth agape and her face betraying shock and fear. It was the first time that she actually feared him. If she *were* going to turn and run, this was surely the time.

With that necessary demonstration out of the way, Lucas asked, "Would you like to hear my proposition now, Ailsa? Now that your father has finished his heroics? After all, it's the entire reason behind our getting to know one another." When they first met, Ailsa had hoped that they would come to know each other in a much different way. Her parents had even approved of Lucas. That notion was in tatters amidst a whirlwind of shock, betrayal, and fear.

Ailsa had no idea what Lucas was going to propose, but she knew that she wouldn't like it. She shouldn't even be doing any of this. Merely talking to Lucas now seemed fraught with danger. She was afraid to even listen, but also felt powerless to resist. "If I listen, I'm not bound to consider it or accept it, am I? You can't make me do anything, can you?"

"Of course not, my dear lass. You are always free to reject a proposal, tell me to be gone, and be done with me. I will not presume to require you to either accept or reject my proposition. That decision is yours, and yours alone. Of course, I certainly hope that you will choose to accept it. It wouldn't be a fair bargain if one party were coerced into disagreeable terms. And despite my unwarranted reputation, I pride myself on being extremely fair. Plus, I think that you will be quite pleased with my offer.

I stand prepared to provide you with that which you most desire. That which you want above all else. That which you told me you would do anything for. All that you need to do is say 'Yes'."

"And if I were to accept your offer, whatever it may be, how do I know that I can trust you to live up to the bargain?" Ailsa inquired. "You claim, after all, to be the Devil – *the Deceiver* – and really cannot be trusted. You make people believe lies."

"Another very common question, although I must take umbrage at being called 'the Deceiver'. Your question, though, is an extremely difficult and complex one to answer. There is simply no way for me to make you trust that I will fulfill my part of the bargain. You either conclude that you do or you conclude that you do not. I can assure you of my trustworthiness, vouch for my own *bona fides*, as it were, but that would do little to sway you. You must decide for yourself, no matter how much I assure you of my trustworthiness. The difficulty lies in the unfortunate truth that you don't conclusively learn the answer until you enter into the next realm.

"Faith, or belief, or trust, if you will, is invisible, ephemeral. It is a belief in something that you can neither see nor touch. Yet, you believe it nonetheless. I believe that your Bible calls it, '*the substance of things hoped for and the evidence of things not seen.*'" Ailsa was surprised that Lucas could recite from the Scriptures. She knew the verse from *Hebrews 11*. "You either believe something, rationally or not, or you do not. I'm assuring you that you can trust me, but only you can decide whether you do or not."

"Why do you want to tempt me?" Ailsa pleaded.

"Oh, Ailsa, I don't want to tempt you. That's not at all how I conduct my business. There is no need for me to do that. I don't make it my business to place temptation before people. There are so many temptations abounding that I surely do not need to add to them. People desire so many things and succumb to so many poor choices in trying to attain them – stealing, adultery, trickery, for example – that I don't need to add to them," Lucas explained. "Although I often receive the blame."

"Then why are you trying to tempt me?" Ailsa asked again.

"I most assuredly am not," Lucas answered. "I am merely offering you only what you yourself said that you would do anything for. I am not the least bit interested in placing some other temptation before you. In fact, I suspect that you could easily resist one, even if I did." Lucas smiled at her.

"But you gave Jesus three temptations after He fasted in the desert. You said that you don't do such things," Ailsa rebutted. "Which makes you a liar!"

"It makes me no such thing," Lucas replied, indignantly. "Despite what you have been taught and what you might even believe, I did not provide those temptations. I do not offer things that people have expressed no desire for. Whoever concocted that story had a fanciful imagination. As I told you, I see no point in adding to the multitude of temptations presented to people all the time. What I offer instead is an opportunity for them to obtain what they have already decided that they want. Nothing more, nothing less. I am simply telling you that I can assure that you receive that which you most desire."

Chapter 12
The Bargain

Ailsa tried to make sense out of everything that Lucas was telling her. It seemed as though he might be telling the truth, although Ailsa understood that that was his special talent. As far as she could tell, he hadn't placed any temptations before her. "Let me hear your proposition, then, Lucas," Ailsa finally said, although she now feared that Lucas was really not his name.

"Perfect!" said Lucas. "I think that you'll be quite pleased. It's quite simple, really. Something you badly want for something I likewise want. I've made similar offers thousands upon thousands of times since the dawn of time, with only the slightest variations. The only real difference is what I provide. What I get in return never varies. You would be quite surprised to learn the names of some of those I've consummated deals with, if I were at liberty to say. Confidentiality, you know."

"And exactly what do you propose to provide to me?" Ailsa asked. There wasn't anything that Ailsa wanted from the Devil.

"Precisely the thing that you most want in this world right now – to win the Royal Club's Ladies' Championship. I am more than willing and able, and in fact would be very honoured, to assure that you are victorious." Lucas was all but certain that Ailsa would accept his proposal. The championship meant everything to her.

"And what do you expect from me in return?" Ailsa asked.

"I believe that you already know the answer to that, don't you, Ailsa?" the Devil replied. Ailsa feared that she did. She had heard of stories like this. "You know what I want. Your soul, of course. Simply your soul. I insure that you win, you consign your soul to me – when your natural time comes, of course. I am very patient in that way. You get what you desire and I get what I desire."

Ailsa didn't have to think very long at all on the Devil's offer. He was completely wrong about what Ailsa most wanted. He knew nothing about her. She didn't want to be handed the championship. Where was the challenge in that? What would that prove? She wanted to *win* it, to *earn* it, to actually skip the best ladies' rink in all of Scotland. What Lucas was offering amounted to cheating, to thievery. Ailsa wanted no part of it.

"No deal, Lucas," Ailsa said emphatically. "I am not interested in being handed the championship. I am going to earn it and win it. It seems that you don't know anything about me. I'm surprised that you think I would even consider such a thing. So you've wasted all of your time." It was not the answer Lucas expected to hear. Most of his clients gladly accepted their bounty. "Now b'gone," Ailsa said.

Lucas suddenly found himself on precarious ground. One of the details which he had conveniently and intentionally neglected to mention in his recitation of his arrangement with his Counterpart was that if one of his potential clients told him to "begone" three times, he was obligated to honour that command. Once someone made it clear that they were no longer interested in working out a deal, it would place unwanted pressure on the person, and the bargain would no longer be a truly voluntary one, should the Devil persist after being repeatedly asked to leave. So once he was commanded to "begone" three times, the Devil was required to leave. Ailsa had now said it once.

Lucas was surprised, to say the least, at Ailsa's refusal. He thought that this would be yet another simple, straightforward, rather routine, transaction. This for that, quid pro quo. He had consummated thousands upon thousands of them. A person shortsightedly trading eternity for a fleeting, earthly pleasure. Most of his proposals were eagerly accepted and closed without the need for much negotiation. He had been sure that Ailsa would accept this one. Now, he ran the risk of losing her, which he surely did not want to do. Were he to successfully negotiate for her soul, Ailsa Maclaren would be one of his most treasured prizes.

"I said b'gone now, Lucas, or whoever you are," Ailsa repeated. "You've no further business here with me."

Twice now Ailsa had said it. Once more and Lucas would have to leave forever. That simply would not do. Ailsa returned her attention to the bonspiel, where her father, after his heroics, was dominating the action. Whether the young man standing next to her was Lucas or Lucifer or whomever, Ailsa wished him gone, a notion which had been inconceivable to her earlier that day.

"So then," Lucas began, "You want to try to win with no help from me? That is quite interesting and noble. Are you really so certain that you can do it?"

"I am," answered Ailsa. "I don't need the Devil to help us win. We will do it by ourselves. Without cheating." Lucas thought that he detected a vulnerability that could be exploited. Her confidence, Lucas realized in that moment, could be leveraged against her. He really wanted to strike a deal. It was usually the other party who was most anxious to get what they wanted, but this time, it was Lucas who found himself in that spot. Ailsa was a very valuable commodity to him, particularly with the increased number of women now joining his legion, and Lucas had now invested a considerable amount of time in the pursuit. He was also on the brink of losing Ailsa forever if she gave the command one more time.

"Then I shall make you this offer, instead – If you lose, your soul shall be mine when your natural time comes," Lucas said.

"And if I win, without any help from you?" Ailsa asked. She didn't really know what she wanted if she won, because winning the Ladies' Championship on her own was enough.

"What would you *like* if you won?" Lucas asked. "Great wealth? A bonnie husband? Influence and power? I am quite open to whatever you may suggest. Within reason, of course. There must be a host of things that would please you."

Ailsa was silent for a moment, before finally blurting out, "I'll tell you what would please me, Lucas. It would please me greatly if you never again set foot in Scotland. For all eternity. You leave Scotland alone for all time. That's what I want and those are my terms. Nothing less. I win, and you are gone from this place forever. Never again will you take the soul of a Scot." Ailsa really hadn't thought too much about what she wanted, it just came out. A wildly outlandish proposal that Lucas would never agree to. She just wanted Lucas gone. He would immediately reject her terms and leave her alone for good. This time, it was Ailsa who miscalculated. She underestimated how much Lucas wanted her.

The Devil didn't like Ailsa's proposal. After all, Scotland had proven to be a fertile and abundant source of souls to be bargained-for. Back home, he had cabinets full of contracts with Scots and counted innumerable Scottish souls amongst his bounty. He certainly did not want to abandon Scotland, but he very, very much wanted Ailsa, once she became available. And his Counterpart was sure to claim her before Lucas ever got the chance. In time, and with proper guidance, he thought, she might even make a very able second-in-command. Was it worth the risk of losing out on thousands of Scottish souls in order to secure just this one? Lucas concluded that it was.

"You drive quite the bargain, Ailsa. And a very righteous one, if I may say. So selfless. Nonetheless, I accept your terms," Lucas announced. Ailsa was shocked by Lucas's answer. She was certain that he would summarily reject such an outrageous proposal and would simply be moving on to his next mark.

"There is one more thing, though," Lucas added.

Ailsa knew that the Devil was not to be trusted and that he was going to attempt to change their deal. "I knew it!" she said, "You cannot be trusted even for one minute!"

"Oh, no, my dear, you misunderstand. Our deal is agreed to," Lucas replied. "It's just that I am required to compile some documentation and to immortalize our agreement, so to speak. It's a safeguard for both of us, really, ironing out the finer points. The devil is always in the details." Lucas smiled at his little joke.

Chapter 13
The Contract

Even though Ailsa and Lucas had reached a verbal agreement, there remained many details to be worked out. Details which were of the utmost importance to both parties. There was language to be parsed, terms to be defined, and contingencies to be planned for and hashed out.

Ailsa had been thinking quite a bit about her agreement with Lucas. That is a gross understatement. It was *all* that she had been thinking about. The stakes were, after all, enormous and eternal. Most often, she thought that there was simply no chance that Lucas Plotcok was truly the *Devil Himself*. She had allowed herself to be seduced by a smooth-talking, conniving shyster, captivated by his looks, charm, and elaborate yarn. She felt embarrassed that she had fallen for it. Lucas may have been a crook or a con-man or a magician or a charlatan, but the *Devil*? Highly unlikely. Virtually impossible, although her father *had* rescued that boy.

If that were the case – if Lucas was simply some kind of prankster, or maybe even deranged – Ailsa had nothing at all to be fearful about. He had no dominion over her or over her soul, and their supposed agreement meant nothing, not worth the paper that it would soon be written on. He could not claim her soul and she could not banish him from Scotland for all time. Ironing out the details and entering into a contact in that case meant absolutely nothing. It would prove a ridiculous waste of time that would simply make her look and feel foolish.

On the other hand . . .

If he truly *was* who he professed to be, Ailsa had to be ready and could afford the *Liar* no possible means of breaching or cheating on their deal. Every possibility had to be considered, every possible maneuver around the bargain had to be foreclosed, every *i* had to be dotted and every *t* had to be crossed. The deal had to be locked in. Airtight. There could be no loopholes for Lucas to seize upon and exploit. Ailsa tried to think of every possibility and contingency ahead of time. She made notes of everything that would have to be included in the contract. It would have to be ironclad.

After Lucas had made Hugh Maclaren a hero, Lucas and Ailsa had agreed to meet with a solicitor to work out the precise details of their contract. It was Ailsa who insisted on having the contract drawn by a solicitor, not really trusting Lucas and what he had initially presented to her as his standard, boilerplate contract. This contract was much more complex. Besides, Lucas was correct about one thing – the devil *is* in the details. They settled on an attorney in Edinburgh, Mr. Pickering Paine. Pickering Paine wasn't the most successful attorney in town, but he was reputed to be most thorough, and was also known to do 'most anything that was legal for a fee. He was also known for being very discreet in his dealings.

Pickering Paine – friends and colleagues called him "Pick" – was a rather short, rotund fellow who wore his several indulgences about his middle. He had long ago abandoned the employment of a belt to keep his trousers at a respectable height, now relying on braces to meet the challenge. He moved himself about with short, shuffling steps, seemingly unsure of exactly where his center of gravity might be at any given time. He wore round, wire spectacles, which he obsessively removed and cleaned upwards of two or three dozen times each day.

The solicitor's office featured a constant pillow of blue-grey smoke hovering just below the ceiling. His meerschaum pipe was his omnipresent companion, and for ten hours a day it maintained the cloud. The smell of fresh pipe tobacco smoke mingled with the stale, permeating everything, including Paine himself. Lucas didn't mind the presence of the smoke. Ailsa found it nauseating.

After being escorted into Solicitor Paine's office, Ailsa and Lucas took their seats on opposite sides of the large oak table, Paine sitting at its head. It hadn't been easy for Ailsa to sneak away to meet with the solicitor, and she dreaded the thought of being sighted entering his office. That would take some explaining, which she was not currently of a mind to offer. It was Monday, Ailsa's usual day to go to market, so her mother expected her to be gone for some time – just not for most of the day. So Ailsa lied to her mother, something that she hated doing and had only very, very rarely done, usually what might be called a "teeny white lie." Ailsa told her mother that she would be seeing her curling teammate, Sheenagh Gillie, to plan for the upcoming Ladies' Championship. Ailsa slipped into Solicitor Paine's office wearing a hat, with a scarf covering most of her face. She wore a coat which she had not worn in a very long time.

Solicitor Paine immediately got down to business. He wasn't one for small talk. "I understand that you two have a contract of some kind which you need drawn up, is that correct?" Paine began.

"It is," Ailsa answered. She tried to hide her nervousness. It was the first time that she had ever met a solicitor, much less employed one. She projected confidence as best she could. "But we need to discuss some matters first. Things that are a bit unusual and outside of the realm of the kind of work you normally do and the kinds of contracts which you normally write. You can then decide whether or not you want to help us." Paine was slightly puzzled, but also intrigued. He was not one of those solicitors who enjoyed performing the same tasks, over and over again. He enjoyed meeting the challenge of doing something different. "Go on," he said.

"First things first, Mr. Paine," Ailsa began. "Could you please explain to us about confidentiality and how it applies to this meeting. Your discretion is vitally important to both of us."

"Of course," Paine began. "I am both legally and honourably bound not to disclose to anyone any of our communications without your consent. In this particular case, because both of you are clients, I would need explicit consent from each of you to disclose our communications to anyone. That obligation attaches from this moment forward to eternity. The only pertinent exception would be if you were to disclose to me that your intent was to commit a crime. In that limited instance, I would be permitted to disclose such information as to prevent the commission of said crime." Solicitor Paine stopped and looked at Ailsa and Lucas to make sure that they understood. They didn't appear to him to be criminals.

"I can assure you that there is no crime involved," Lucas offered, chuckling. Ailsa wasn't quite as certain about that.

"Very well, then. I also need to inform each of you at this stage that you have the right to have separate counsel in this matter. If your interests are adverse, or potentially adverse, I would recommend that you each retain your own counsel," Paine advised.

Lucas again offered a slight chuckle, and explained, "I believe that when you learn what we have in mind, you will see that we have no interest other than to reflect in writing our existing agreement, which we are both thoroughly pleased with. We have reached a 'meeting of the minds,' I believe your profession calls it. Reducing our agreement to writing is a formality, but a very necessary and important one. We are simply interested in a contract which precisely details our mutual responsibilities and obligations, one to the other."

"If that be the case," Paine said, "why don't you tell me what your agreement is and we will proceed from there." It was Ailsa who began.

"My name is Ailsa Maclaren. I live in Musselburgh. I am presently nineteen years old and unmarried. Also, I should tell you, and as you can plainly see, I am of perfectly sound mind and body, although you will perchance question that after I explain my deal with Mr. Plotcok to you. Nevertheless, it is true." Pickering Paine was now quite intrigued and waited for Ailsa to continue. He had no reason just yet to question her mental and cognitive condition. She was perfectly lucid and erudite thus far.

"Ever since I was a child, my father would take me out onto the ice in the wintertime, John Frost willing, to teach me about our great national winter sport of curling. He taught me of wicking and guarding and drawing and chipping. All of the things necessary to master the game. It was not generally something that girls were encouraged to do, but my father is a keen, keen curler, and wanted me to love the game as much as he did. Plus, I am an only child, so he had no son to teach. He even built a curling pond for us on our farm. As it turns out, I've become quite good at it, and can beat almost any man, given the chance, which I generally am not." Paine knew a bit about curling, but his main sporting interest was golf. He now remembered why he recognized Ailsa's name.

"Now, at long last, my father has convinced the Royal Caledonian Curling Club to allow ladies to compete for their own curling crown in Scotland, but only against other ladies, of course. I fully intend for my rink to become the first Scottish ladies' champions. The competition will be held in two weeks on Carsebreck Loch. Mr. Plotcok here would prefer that we not win." Paine shot a disapproving look at Lucas.

Ailsa stopped talking, waiting for the wise counselor to offer some response, ask some question. Finally, Paine asked, "What is my role in this? What is Mr. Plotcok's place in all of this? And why would he prefer that you not win the competition?" Lucas was more than happy to let Ailsa continue to do all of the explaining. The more that she was convinced that it was *her* deal, the more invested in it she would be.

"Those are much more complicated questions than you might realize, Mr. Paine," Ailsa answered. Lucas remained silent, content to let Ailsa press the issue. "You see, Mr. Plotcok is not exactly like you and I. In fact, he is not at all like you and I."

"Is that so? In what regard?" asked Paine, warily eyeing Lucas.

"Well," Ailsa replied, "in many regards, actually. First of all, I'm not sure that his name really is Lucas Plotcok, or even if he has a name in the same sense as you and I do. But he has gone by any number of monikers around the world and through the centuries."

"Around the world? Through the centuries?" Paine asked, not having any inkling what Ailsa was talking about. He thought that she might be playing him for the fool, and he didn't like it.

"Yes, through the centuries," Ailsa responded. "You see, sir, Lucas is quite a bit older than you and I. And much, much older than he appears." The solicitor once again looked hard at Lucas Plotcok, estimating that he couldn't have been more than twenty-five, possibly thirty, years old at most. Paine removed his spectacles and cleaned the lenses, something he always did when trying to think. It was a habit he had developed when he wanted to buy some time.

"As to his name," Ailsa continued, "he has been called many things – Lucifer, Satan, Beelzebub, Mephistopheles, Old Clootie, Moloch, Shaytan, Maara, Pluto, Loki, the Prince of Darkness. Many different things by many different people all over the world. But I met him and know him as Lucas Plotcok."

"But those are all names for the devil!" Paine blurted out. He was both angry and confused.

"Exactly," Ailsa confirmed. Lucas shrugged at Paine.

"Always pleased to make a solicitor's acquaintance," smiled Lucas. "I know quite a few folks who are in your line of work. An extraordinary number, actually."

"I'm not sure what you two are trying to pull on me, exactly," Paine stated. "But I don't take kindly to having jokes played on me, and I have other matters to attend to." Nonetheless, Paine snuck a look at Lucas's forehead, instinctively checking for horns. There were none.

"This is not a joke, Mr. Paine," Lucas began. The solicitor noticed a sudden seriousness. "I am the *Devil Himself*. Whether you believe it or not, it really doesn't matter to me, nor to Ailsa, either, I presume. What you believe about me is of little consequence to this transaction. Allow me to offer an example, if I may. Suppose that a farmer and a miller want to enter into a contract for the farmer to sell the miller ten bushels of corn. Do you make it your concern whether you believe that the farmer can actually deliver the ten bushels or whether you believe that the miller can pay the agreed-upon price? No, you simply draw up their contract for them. Ailsa and I merely need for you to memorialize our duties and obligations into a written contract, for which you will be compensated at a rate above your normal one, I might add, understanding that this is a far-from-routine matter for you. If you choose not to do this for us, we will excuse ourselves and find another solicitor who will."

Solicitor Paine wasn't thrilled about what was going on, but the two potential clients were paying, and hearing them out wouldn't hurt anyone. He made a mental note to collect his fee in advance. Besides, there wasn't a line of clients outside anxiously awaiting the solicitor's wise counsel. "What are these terms that you are talking about?" he finally asked.

"The basic agreement is this," Ailsa began. "I and my rink will play in the Royal Caledonian Curling Club's Scottish Ladies' Championship in two weeks – January 29th, to be precise. The frost permitting, of course. If we lose, Mr. Plotcok, the Devil, takes my soul when my natural life is over, which he specifically agrees not to hasten, I might add." She gave a stern look at Lucas. "If we win, he never again sets foot or hoof in Scotland, in his present, or in any other, form. And he is to be forever barred from claiming the soul of any Scot. *Forever*." Ailsa looked at Paine, who was feverishly making notes, small droplets of sweat beginning to form on his forehead. He considered removing Lucas and Ailsa from his office. Lucas bristled at the "hoof" remark.

"Further," Ailsa continued, "Mr. Plotcok, or whatever he is to be called, will in no manner, shape, or form interfere with or influence the outcome of the championship. He will neither help us win nor will he help us lose. He will have no involvement of any kind in determining the outcome of the match. Those are the basic terms of our deal. We need for you to put them into writing and to account for any and all contingencies. Is that something that you are able and willing to do?"

Paine looked at Lucas. "Do you agree that the terms are as Miss Maclaren has stated them?" he asked.

"Yes," replied Lucas. "They are precisely as Miss Maclaren has stated."

"Miss Maclaren," Paine began. "If I may ask, how is it that you believe that Mr. Plotcok is actually Old Clootie himself?" Paine stopped abruptly and looked at Lucas. "My apologies, Mr. Plotcok, no disrespect intended. Just an old habit."

"I understand," Lucas smiled. "I've been called far worse things. I'm quite used to it. But I'd prefer to be called Lucas Plotcok, if you please."

Ailsa spoke. "Mr. Paine, I will simply tell you that I asked the exact same question of Mr. Plotcok. And I can assure you that he has demonstrated who he is to my complete satisfaction." Lucas was very happy to hear that.

Paine thought for a moment as he wrote more notes. "Well, then," he began, "if you really want to go through with this, I am willing and able to draw up the contract you desire. I must advise you of three things, however. First, in my considered judgment, such a contract would be unenforceable in the courts of Scotland. Contracts in the nature of gambling or wagering, which your contract could be deemed to be, although not in any traditional sense, are simply not enforceable.

Second, even were we to assume that you are both who you claim to be," Paine continued, eyeing Lucas, "a court would have no viable means of enforcing these terms. How could a court exercise jurisdiction over the Devil? And how could a court ensure that the Devil never returned to Scotland or claimed a Scottish soul? So our courts would be powerless to provide a remedy."

Lucas interrupted. "We understand completely. We do not expect the courts to intervene. Abiding by the terms will be a matter for Ailsa and I, as well as for an unnamed third-party." Ailsa understood the reference to Lucas's Counterpart, although Paine wasn't quite sure.

"You said that you must advise us about three things. What would the third one be?" Lucas asked.

"Because of the unusual nature of this work, I shall expect the entirety of my fee to be paid in advance," Paine answered, and announced his fee.

"Of course," Lucas replied. "I expected that you would. You can't be too careful these days." Lucas reached into his pocket and withdrew the precise amount of the charge, proferring it to Solicitor Paine, who examined the currency. It was real, as best he could tell. He would visit the bank that afternoon, just in case. Pickering Paine scheduled an appointment for his new clients to return the following Monday, and escorted them out of his office. Leaving the building, Ailsa turned right and Lucas turned left. Neither one said "goodbye" to the other.

⸻ ◆ ⸻

Back in his office, Paine chuckled to himself. He had already made the same mental calculation that Ailsa had made. If Lucas Plotcok was not the Devil, which was the only rational possibility, then this contract that he was charged with writing would mean nothing. If Lucas Plotcok and Ailsa wanted to pay him to write a worthless, utterly unenforceable contract, who was he to argue? Their money was as good as anyone else's. He had examined it once again after sitting down and cleaning his spectacles.

But if Lucas *was* who he and Ailsa said he was, Paine surmised that it was in his best interest to do a thorough job. The hardest part of the whole exercise would be not telling his fellow brethren at the bar that he was working on a contract for Old Clootie himself. Regardless of who the clients were, Paine was required to keep their secrets, preposterous though they may be. Besides, who would believe him, anyway? And it wouldn't be good for business if word got out that Pickering Paine was the solicitor for the Devil.

The first order of business for Solicitor Paine would be deciding how, exactly, to identify the parties to the contract, particularly Lucas Plotcok. How do you adequately describe and memorialize the Devil? After considering that tricky issue, Paine gave it a try:

> *The Party of the First Part, Lucas Plotcok [hereinafter "Lucas Plotcok"], being the Devil Himself, also known as, including, but not limited thereto, inter alia, Satan, Lucifer, the Deil, Beelzebub, Mephistopheles, Moloch, Shayton, Pluto, Loki, Old Clootie, Old Nick, the Prince of Darkness, Perdition, Baphomet, Iblis, El Diablo, and/or Lucas Plotcok, enters into this binding Agreement of his own free will and volition, and without reservation, intending to be forever bound by its terms, with no intent of evasion or deception, and covenants to be bound by its terms, conditions, duties, rights, and/or obligations for all time, from this day forward.*

The Party of the Second Part, Ailsa Maclaren [hereinafter "Ailsa Maclaren"], an unmarried adult woman currently residing in Musselburgh, Scotland, enters into this binding Agreement of her own free will and volition, and without reservation, intending to be forever bound by its terms, with no intent of evasion or deception, and covenants to be bound by its terms, conditions, duties, rights, and/or obligations for all time, from this day forward.

After making a few additions, deletions, and alterations, Paine was satisfied with his identification of the parties.

Solicitor Paine then decided to first set forth the parties' understanding and obligations in the event that Ailsa won the World Championship, since that was his certain preference:

First. Ailsa Maclaren and her rink, consisting of herself, Sheenagh Gillie, Effie Lawrie, and Kirsty Barnett [hereinafter "Maclaren's Rink"], intend to compete for the 1887 Royal Caledonian Curling Club's Ladies' Championship on Saturday, January 29, 1887, at Carsebreck Loch, Scotland. Despite their names being set forth herein, for the sole purpose of identifying Maclaren's Rink, the said Sheenagh Gillie, Effie Lawrie, and Kirsty Barnett are not parties to this Agreement, and do not in any manner or form whatsoever assume any burdens, duties, benefits, rights, and/or obligations hereunder.

Second. In the event that Maclaren's Rink wins the said 1887 Royal Caledonian Curling Club's Ladies'

Championship on Saturday, January 29, 1887, at Carsebreck Loch, Scotland, the said Party of the Second Part, Ailsa Maclaren, shall have no further burdens, duties, obligations, and/or debts of any kind or nature whatsoever, forever and always, to the said Party of the First Part, Lucas Plotcok, known by whatever name and/or in whatever form, as he may appear and/or be known.

Third. In the event that Maclaren's Rink wins the said 1887 Royal Caledonian Curling Club's Ladies' Championship on Saturday, January 29, 1887, at Carsebreck Loch, Scotland, the said Party of the First Part, Lucas Plotcok, known by whatever name and/or in whatever form as he may appear and/or be known, shall forever and always be barred from, and shall for all time, from that day forward, refrain from entering, manifesting, residing, and/or appearing anywhere and at any place and/or places, in the Country of Scotland.

Fourth. In the event that Maclaren's Rink wins the said 1887 Royal Caledonian Curling Club's Ladies' Championship on Saturday, January 29, 1887, at Carsebreck Loch, Scotland, the said Party of the First Part, Lucas Plotcok, known by whatever name and/or in whatever form as he may appear and/or be known, shall forever and always be barred from, and shall for all time, refrain from taking, harvesting, collecting, claiming, securing, and/or in any other manner of any nature whatsoever, the soul, essence, spirit, and/or any other afterlife incarnation of any Scotsman, whether man, woman, or child, including, but not limited to, that of the said Party of the Second Part, Ailsa Maclaren.

The solicitor was satisfied that he had set forth all of the repercussions and consequences in the event that Ailsa's rink won. He then tackled the issues of Lucas's interference in the match and the dire consequences should Ailsa's rink lose:

Fifth. The said Party of the First Part, Lucas Plotcok, known by whatever name and/or in whatever form as he may appear and/or be known, shall refrain from, and shall in no way, form, shape, or manner whatsoever, interfere with, influence, effect, impact, alter, and/or manipulate the playing or outcome of the said 1887 Royal Caledonian Curling Club's Ladies' Championship on Saturday, January 29, 1887, at Carsebreck Loch, Scotland, nor shall the said Party of the First Part, Lucas Plotcok, cause, aid, and/or abet another party, in any way, form, shape, or manner whatsoever, to interfere with the playing, contesting, and/or outcome of the said 1887 Royal Caledonian Curling Club's Ladies' Championship.

Sixth. In the event that Maclaren's Rink fails to win the said 1887 Royal Caledonian Curling Club's Ladies' Championship on Saturday, January 29, 1887, at Carsebreck Loch, Scotland, the said Party of the Second Part, Ailsa Maclaren, agrees and covenants that at the conclusion of her natural life and upon her death, which the said Party of the First Part, Lucas Plotcok, agrees and covenants that he will in no way, form, shape, and/or manner whatsoever either cause, hasten, accelerate, or precipitate, that the said Party of the First Part, Lucas Plotcok, shall take possession and control of her soul, essence, spirit, and/or any other afterlife incarnation, to possess and exercise full dominion over at his sole pleasure, to have and to hold from that day forward.

Seventh. In the event that the 1887 Royal Caledonian Curling Club's Ladies' Championship fails to be contested on Saturday, January 29, 1887, at Carsebreck Loch, Scotland, fails to be completed, or fails to produce a winner as certified by the Royal Caledonian Curling Club, or in the event that Maclaren's Rink, as defined in Paragraph First herein, is unable or does not for any reason or cause whatsoever, enter and compete in the said 1887 Royal Caledonian Curling Club's Ladies' Championship, this Agreement shall be void and null, and the parties hereto shall have no further rights, burdens, duties, benefits, and/or obligations hereunder.

Paine was quite pleased with his work, after making numerous clarifications and changes, pointless though he believed them to be. He had covered all of the contingencies – if Ailsa's rink won, if they lost, if the bonspiel didn't take place, if it wasn't completed. When Ailsa and Lucas returned to the office on the ensuing Monday, Paine reviewed the contract with them clause-by-clause. Ailsa and Lucas were both satisfied that it accurately and comprehensively encompassed the entirety of their agreement and accounted for all contingencies. Solicitor Paine handed a pen to Lucas, who looked at Ailsa, smiled, and affixed his signature to three copies of the Agreement. He handed the pen to Ailsa. With her hand as steady as she could hold it, she affixed her signature to each of the three copies. Ailsa returned the pen to Solicitor Paine, who added his own signature in witness.

Paine handed one copy of the executed Agreement to Ailsa, and another to Lucas. "I shall keep one copy under seal here in my files." Paine placed his copy of the executed Agreement into a brown envelope. He retrieved his stick of wax, melted several drops onto the envelope, pressed his seal into the pool of wax, and sealed the envelope. "Each of you should take care that your copy is safeguarded," Solicitor Paine instructed before standing and escorting the pair to the door. "Good luck, Ailsa," he said. He did not wish the same to Lucas.

◆

Ailsa's mother and father knew that something was wrong. Ailsa had been so excited at the thought of Lucas's return, but now that he was back, she never mentioned him and he never came to see her. In fact, Ailsa didn't seem to want to talk about anything. It was Mrs. Maclaren who asked.

"Ailsa, dear, you haven't said a word about Lucas since you told us that he was back. Is there something wrong?" Ailsa's mother asked. She knew that there was.

Ailsa would have to make up something, although she had been working on a story in anticipation of the question. She didn't want to lie, but she certainly couldn't tell the truth. She settled on a middle ground of vagueness mixed with a touch of truth. "I don't think that I will be seeing him anymore," Ailsa said. Her mother was surprised to hear Ailsa say the words.

"Why is that? Did something bad happen?" Mrs. Maclaren asked.

"No, nothing bad happened, mother," Ailsa explained. "Lucas is just different now than before he left. He seems colder, more aloof. I can't really explain it except to just say he's different."

"What do you mean colder and aloof?" Ailsa's mother probed. "Is there someone else? Has he been untrue to you?"

The questions had to stop. Ailsa really did not want to talk about Lucas. There was a chance that she might say something that she shouldn't. "Mother, it's over. I won't be seeing Lucas anymore. Could we please not talk about him? Please?"

Chapter 14
The Scottish Curling Queen

The day that Ailsa had been anxiously awaiting, with both terror and excitement, finally arrived. Ailsa and her father, along with Sheenagh, Effie, Kirsty, as well as their fathers, boarded the Glasgow-Perth Railway Line train bound for Carsebreck Loch, the site of the first-ever Royal Caledonian Curling Club's Ladies' Championship. Ailsa seemed unusually nervous to her father.

To Ailsa, the train ride was endless. She wasn't sure whether she wanted it to end or just keep going forever. An eternity spent on a train would be far better than one spent in hell, even though the train car itself was hot and stifling. By sundown, her fate would be sealed, one way or the other. Perhaps all of Scotland's, too. It was impossible for her to think of anything other than her dangerous and reckless deal with Lucas.

The ice on Carsebreck Loch was in capital condition – hard, keen, and unbiased, and the weather was perfect for curling. There was no doubt that the championship would proceed. One of the contractual escape clauses which Pickering Paine had provided for Ailsa was out.

This would be the defining day of Ailsa's life, for reasons that she, and she alone, knew, even if she could not begin to fully understand. Once the train pulled to a stop at the Carsebreck railway station, Hugh Maclaren, the three other fathers, and the four young lasses retrieved their curling stones and exited the train, which had made a special stop for the curlers and spectators. There were far more women than men aboard the train, some of them participating in the bonspiel, but most there just to take in the most unusual spectacle of a ladies' bonspiel. It was an historic day for the women and girls of Scotland, and hundreds of people were coming to be a part of it. As far as Ailsa could tell – and she had been looking – Lucas Plotcok was not aboard the train. Solicitor Paine was aboard, though, out of an overwhelming curiosity at what might transpire. He had a vested interest in protecting his eternal soul from Old Clootie. The truth was, he had not led an entirely virtuous life. Ailsa spotted him, but made no effort at contact.

Ailsa's party, and all the others, made their way across the Allan Water and toward the ice. They all knew that they were to be a part of curling and Scottish history. Only Ailsa, and perhaps Solicitor Paine, knew what the true consequences of the outcome might be. She was excited and very scared. She also knew that she could not play out of fear. She tried, as best as she possibly could, to focus on curling.

There were sixty women entered into the championship, fifteen rinks of four women each. The smaller bonspiel the year before had aroused great interest and enthusiasm for ladies' curling, with more and more women and girls taking to the ice. Each of the other rinks had players who were older than the four young women comprising Ailsa's rink, but most had been playing for only a short time. Others, like the senior rink from Hercules, and the Lundin and Montrave rink skipped by Henrietta Gilmour, had actually been playing for a bit longer than Ailsa's rink. It was not going to be easy.

Ailsa, Sheenagh, Effie, and Kirsty had been thinking about this day and planning for this day seemingly forever, although it had been only a few months. They were ready. They had practiced on the Maclarens' pond at every opportunity, and it paid off. They roared through their opponents all morning. Once play began, Ailsa steadied her nerves, and by early in the afternoon, Ailsa Maclaren and the young lasses from Musselburgh were the talk of the bonspiel. Even some of the more skeptical men spectators grudgingly acknowledged how good they were – for ladies, that is.

By the time that mid-afternoon came, there were only two teams remaining in the championship – the senior rink from Hercules, skipped by Mrs. Scott Davidson, the wife of a noted curler, Major Scott Davidson, and Ailsa's. The Hercules rink was comprised of four women in their 30's, while Ailsa's had the four teenagers.

Most of the spectators expected the older women to exhibit more savvy and composure and win the day, but they would be proven wrong. Despite the eternal stakes for Ailsa, she summoned all of her will and courage, skipped a masterful game, and delivered her stones with a marksman's eye and steel. The crowd of nearly a thousand onlookers erupted when the game ended. The fathers ran forward and hugged their girls as tightly as they ever had. Both the fathers and daughters were crying. Ailsa was trembling. Pickering Paine was surveying the throng for any sign of Lucas Plotcok.

When the bonspiel ended at sunset, Ailsa's rink was formally declared the first-ever Scottish ladies' champions. They were presented with a modest trophy, nothing like the one awarded at the Grand Match or at other important men's bonspiels, but the young women could not have cared less about the size of their trophy. They only knew that they were the best – "the Queens o' a' the Core," as Robert Burns might have called them.

Ailsa scanned the crowd for any sign of Lucas Plotcok. Like Solicitor Paine, she saw none. Just as she had deep-down hoped, Lucas, or whoever he was, was long-gone, simply a prankster who spun an elaborate, ridiculous tale, never to be seen or heard from again. Why had she fallen for it? She guessed that it was simply her falling for a very handsome, very charming, very entertaining young man who seemed to genuinely care for her. Ah, well, it no longer mattered, anyway. If Lucas *were* actually the Devil, and if he could be trusted to keep his word, then Ailsa was the saviour of Scotland. At the very least, no matter who Lucas actually might be, Ailsa was no worse off than when the day had started. In fact, she was much *better* off. She had made history by winning. "Take that, Lucas," she whispered under her breath.

The four young women and their fathers made their way back toward the train which would return them to Musselburgh. As they were walking and talking excitedly, accepting congratulations, a young woman approached. "Excuse me, Ailsa," she said. "I'm Darcie. Darcie Gilday."

Ailsa shrieked. "Darcie. I can't believe it! Is it really you?"

"It is. I've been watching you and cheering for you all day. I've kept my distance so as not to intrude," Darcie said. The two young women hugged each other like old, dear friends, even though they knew each other only from their letters. And yet, they felt like kindred spirits.

When they let go, Ailsa turned to her father and said, "Father, this is Darcie Gilday. I've told you all about her. She's the one I've been writing to and getting letters from this past year." Looking back to Darcie, Ailsa said, "Darcie, this is my father, Hugh Maclaren. And this is Sheenagh, and Effie, and this is Kirsty." They all felt like they knew each other, since Ailsa had told Darcie all about her teammates and had told her teammates about Darcie. The five young women talked excitedly before Ailsa's father interrupted. "I'm afraid the train is leaving shortly, lassies. We must be going." Turning to Ailsa, he said, "Sweetheart, why don't you invite Darcie to come for a visit this summer?" Ailsa immediately embraced her father's suggestion.

Darcie said that she would love to visit with Ailsa and her friends, and the other young women all smiled and nodded their approval. "I will write to you in a day or two to make plans. I'm so glad that you came to see us! I can't wait to see you this summer! You can finally meet Magic!" Ailsa exclaimed. Ailsa and Darcie again hugged, tears forming in their eyes.

Throughout the entire journey home, Ailsa and her teammates were showered with congratulations and cheers from both their competitors and spectators. Pickering Paine even stopped to congratulate them, anonymously, of course. Ailsa caught his eye for a fleeting second. The newly-crowned Curling Queens revelled in their victory and in the praise being heaped upon them. They let people see their small trophy. They had little understanding yet of how important this day was for ladies' curling, although history would make note of it. The Canadians would learn of it soon, as well, and would be in touch with a grand proposal. There had still been no sign of Lucas Plotcok.

⸻ ◆ ⸻

Following their victory at the Scottish Ladies' Championship, Ailsa's rink was besieged not only with congratulations from all corners of Scotland, but with invitations and challenges. Even Queen Victoria took notice, and sent a telegram of congratulations to Ailsa's rink via the Royal Caledonian Curling Club. It seemed that every ladies' rink in the country wanted to play a match or have a re-match with the champions. There were even a few men's rinks, primarily rinks of bachelors, who wanted to test Ailsa's rink on the ice.

Hugh Maclaren and the other three fathers knew better than to accept any of the invitations or challenges. Their daughters needed a break from curling to let the magnitude of their accomplishment sink in and to have some time to enjoy what they had achieved. They had gone from the first ladies' bonspiel to the Royal Caledonian Curling Club's Ladies' Championship, with endless hours of preparation and practice. They needed some time to just be young ladies and do the things that young Scottish lasses should be doing. Hugh Maclaren responded to every invitation and challenge, politely, but unequivocally, turning them all down because Ailsa's rink was finished curling for the season. Perhaps next winter, he offered.

The weeks passed, and winter was morphing into spring. All around Scotland, everything was turning green. Curling season was over and life was gradually returning to normal for Ailsa and the other three. She resumed her Monday trips to the market. She continued going to church with her family on Sundays. Part of a sermon, delivered two weeks after the championship and entitled "A Grear Player in Life's Bonspiel," caught her attention. It must have been composed just for Ailsa:

> *Let strong assurance of future and heavenly rewards enter your mind and more and more control it. There is a visible line that girts us round and you know it. What lies beyond that line? What happens the moment after death? What enjoyments crowd upon the soul? What employments fill your hands? What station are you to occupy? These things need to be considered by us as being as real as the things we see about us in every day life.*

Ailsa spent more time lost in her books. She paid more attention to Magic. She thought less and less about Lucas Plotcok as time went by. She hadn't forgotten about him – she never would – but he now occupied a place in the background. She couldn't help but wonder, though, whether she had actually saved Old Scotia from the Devil's reach. On the slim, slim chance that he was who he claimed to be, she wondered whether Lucas was honoring their contract. There was no way to know, just as Lucas had explained, although he hadn't been seen or heard from since the championship.

Ailsa, Sheenagh, Effie, and Kirsty by now were close friends, and they did lots of things together. Common things. Fun things. Exactly the kinds of things that other young ladies did. Sometimes it was all four of them, sometimes three, or even just two. They went to the market together. They met for tea. Occasionally, they went to a play or a concert. They laughed and giggled. They looked at boys. They especially liked looking at boys. All of the things that they had largely missed out on while dedicating themselves to curling.

All along the way, Ailsa had told her friends about Lucas. The good things about Lucas. They knew that he was away and that he had been writing to her faithfully. Ailsa told them about Lucas's adventures on the continent. Whenever they saw each other, Ailsa's friends asked about Lucas and whether he had returned.

After the championship, Ailsa finally told her friends that Lucas had, in fact, returned, but that she wouldn't be seeing him anymore. The friends peppered Ailsa with questions, mostly the same ones that her mother had asked. Ailsa answered them the same way – that Lucas was different, colder, more aloof. There were lots of questions about whether Lucas was seeing someone else, or, perhaps, married even. Ailsa denied that there was someone else. Amongst themselves, Sheenagh, Effie, and Kirsty decided otherwise.

On a Saturday night in March, all four friends were at a ceilidh, a Scottish dance featuring fiddles, accordions, drums, and flutes. As Sheenagh, Effie, and Kirsty were dancing, Ailsa stood to the side, taking a break after the Highland Fling. A young man approached, unnoticed. "Hello, Ailsa," he began. "Are you having a good time?"

Ailsa immediately noticed that the young man had used her name. She froze in fear. It was exactly like her first encounter with Lucas Plotcok. Ailsa was terrified. It couldn't possibly be!

"How do you know my name?" Ailsa snapped. It was entirely out of character, for Ailsa was unfailingly well-mannered, but she immediately feared the worst.

"Everybody knows who you are, Ailsa. You're famous," the young man answered defensively, taken aback by Ailsa's sharp tone.

It was precisely the conversation that she had had with Lucas when they first met. Hesitantly, she asked, "Lucas . . . ?" She dreaded hearing the answer, although the young man looked nothing like Lucas Plotcok.

"Uh, no. My name is Colin. Colin Gibson," he answered. Ailsa wasn't completely convinced.

"We've never met before?" she asked.

"I don't think so," Colin answered. "I'd remember if we had."

Ailsa looked at Colin's eyes. They didn't seem familiar. "I'm so sorry, Colin. For a moment, I thought that you were someone else," Ailsa explained. "Someone that I'm not so keen on." Colin laughed. Ailsa relaxed.

Ailsa looked out at the dance floor and saw Sheenagh beckoning. Ailsa turned to Colin and said, "My friends are calling me. It was nice to meet you, Colin. I'm sorry that I snapped at you."

"It was nice to meet you, too," Colin answered. He thought that he might as well take his chance. "Perhaps you can make it up to me by sharing a dance later?"

"Perhaps," Ailsa coyly responded as she left to join her friends. Of course, the others had been watching and needed all of the details. Who was he? Was he nice? Did he ask her to dance? Giggling, they all agreed that he was very cute. Ailsa blushed. "It's true," she thought to herself. "He is rather cute."

As she had promised, Ailsa wrote to Darcie Gilday two days after the Ladies' Championship, thanking her for coming to watch and for introducing herself. She apologized for having to leave so abruptly. She told Darcie that she looked exactly as she had imagined. Ailsa went on to describe all of the excitement on the train ride home and the congratulations being received from all quarters. She told her about the telegram from Her Majesty Queen Victoria. As her father had suggested, Ailsa also invited Darcie to come and stay at her home during the spring and to visit with Sheenagh, Effie, and Kirsty, as well. There was so much mischief they could get into!

Ailsa and Darcie continued exchanging letters. Darcie was beginning to feel like the sister that Ailsa never had. Ailsa wrote about the aftermath of winning the Ladies' Championship; about all of the challenges being proposed by other curlers, mainly bachelors; about life on the farm; about riding Magic; and about all of the things she did with Sheenagh, Effie, and Kirsty. Darcie, in turn, wrote about life in Glasgow, cooking and gardening with her mother, and about life in a large family. She also wrote a lot about Murdock Ross, her beau and longtime friend from their early school days. Ailsa could tell that Darice was madly in love with him. They made their plans for Darcie's visit.

Darcie arrived at the Maclarens' farm in April of 1887. She would spend four days with the Maclarens. Ailsa, Sheenagh, Effie, and Kirsty planned things for the five young lasses to do. They all felt like they knew each other, since Sheenagh, Effie, and Kirsty had also begun writing letters back-and-forth with Darcie. The five young women walked the town and the markets in Musselburgh and Edinburgh, chatted endlessly about anything and everything, sat in the meadows on the Maclaren farm, and played parlor games together at night. With the days becoming noticeably longer and warmer, they spent as much time outside as they could. Darcie even helped Ailsa with some of her chores on the farm, particularly tending to the gardens. Darcie let Ailsa handle shoveling the manure in the barn. Scotland was becoming alive again and bursting in color – blue from the bluebells, yellow from the rapeseed and coconutty gorse, and green from the awakening grasses. Their time together flowed quickly and gracefully.

Most importantly, Darcie had an announcement to make, although she waited more than two days until she could no longer contain her excitement. In July – the 16th, exactly – she would be marrying Murdock Ross. The others shrieked when Darcie told them the news. For the rest of Darcie's visit, it was almost all that they talked about – the plans, Darcie's wedding dress, the reception, and the honeymoon. Darcie wanted all four of her new friends to come to her wedding in Glasgow in July.

On Saturday, the five young women put on their nicest dresses and went to a dance, another ceilidh. A young man approached Ailsa. He seemed somehow familiar, although Ailsa couldn't quite place him. "Hello, Ailsa," he said. "Do you remember me?" A reaction which Ailsa thought might never go away hit her. The fear that any person she met might be Lucas. Would she spend her entire life dreading someone approaching her and speaking to her? Ailsa just stared.

"Colin. Colin Gibson," the man said. "We met at a dance a few weeks ago. You promised me a dance, although I was never favoured with one."

Ailsa shook herself out of her stupor. "Oh, yes, I remember now. It was very rude of me. I'm very sorry."

"Would you like to make it up to me?" Colin asked. "I would be honoured." Other than on a very few occasions, Ailsa had never danced with a man, other than her father or an uncle or cousin. Not too long ago, she had dreamed of dancing with Lucas Plotcok.

"Certainly," Ailsa answered. They headed to the dance floor for the first of several times that night. After each time, Ailsa's friends wanted to know all of the details. Sheenagh, Effie, and Kirsty still agreed that Colin Gibson was very handsome. Darcie thought so, too. "If you don't want him, I'll take him," Sheenagh joked.

Darcie's visit was over all too soon. Ailsa, Sheenagh, Effie, and Kirsty immediately set about planning for Darcie's wedding, which was only two months away. The most important things were their dresses, they all agreed. The shoes were almost as important, although the dresses had to be chosen first. They spent hours and days shopping, first in Musselburgh, and then in Edinburgh. One-by-one, the choices were made. Each complimented the other three on their choice, although each secretly believed that their chosen dress was the prettiest. Each of the lassies looked beautiful. They arranged to stay at an inn near the wedding recommended by Darcie and they secured their train tickets.

On July 16th, Ailsa, Sheenagh, Effie, and Kirsty were at St. Andrew's Cathedral in Glasgow to celebrate Darcie's wedding with her. They were thrilled for their friend, a little jealous, maybe, and excited to meet Murdock, about whom they had heard so much. He did not disappoint. Murdock was tall and thin, with steely blue eyes. He was polite and charming, but not in a contrived way, and obviously loved Darcie. They watched as Darcie and Murdock were handfasted, literally having their hands tied together with tartan and the origin of the term "tying the knot;" exchanged their vows; kissed; and entered into their new life as husband and wife. They followed the piper to the reception, where they drank with Darcie from a quaich. Perhaps they partook a wee bit too much of the national drink, but who cared? They danced and laughed the entire evening. Everyone wanted to meet and congratulate the Curling Queens. Ailsa hoped to one day be celebrating her own marriage with her friends, and to be as lucky as Darcie Gilday, or Darcie Ross, as she would henceforth forever be known.

Chapter 15
Contract Revisions

Now that Ailsa and her rink were the Scottish ladies' champions, there was another challenge to be met, a challenge from afar. The Canadians – the women in particular – had heard about the Royal Caledonian Curling Club's Ladies' Championship in Scotland and were boasting that they had surpassed Scottish curlers in skill at Scotland's own game. The boasts were couched in the most respectful terms, but they were nonetheless serious. The Scots feared that it was probably true, for perfectly reasonable and understandable reasons. Canada's winters, much colder and longer than Scotland's, provided for a significantly longer curling season. Winters in much of Canada often afforded up to four, or even five, months of splendid ice, while Scotland's, even in a good year, might provide only a few weeks, or sometimes even none at all, when curling would even be possible. The lucky Canadians quickly became much more practiced and experienced curlers. The indignity of it all was that it was the Scots who had introduced curling to Canada when they emigrated there.

Nor did the Canadians often have to deal with wet, drug ice as frequently as the Scots. The ice in Canada was hard, thick, and fast. Much of Canada had taken to constructing sheltered sheets of curling ice, still outdoors, but protected from sun, wind, sleet, and snow. Wet, soft ice, like that encountered throughout Scotland, oftentimes ruined an otherwise perfectly good day for curling. Legend tells of a Scottish skip's diary which was found with this entry after enduring several consecutive days of wet ice:

Monday, cold and sloppy. Tuesday, cold and sloppy. Wednesday, cold and sloppy; shot grandma.

For more than twenty years, the Canadians had been attempting to convince the Royal Caledonian Curling Club in Scotland to send an envoy of curlers – men, of course – to Canada to take on the hosts in a series of bonspiels throughout the provinces. A grand welcome in Canada was guaranteed, given the very large number of Scots who now made Canada, particularly the Maritimes, their home. The invitations were always presented as a gesture of goodwill and tribute to the Scots, but the Canadians badly wanted to prove their curling superiority. The Canadians even sent a representative to the annual meeting of the mother club in Edinburgh on several occasions to personally present the invitation. The Scots always found reason to respectfully demur, whether due to distance, expense, or other purely logistical matters. The truth was that the Scots suspected that they would lose. Badly, perhaps.

On April 14, 1887, a communication to the Royal Caledonian Curling Club in Scotland, coming from the Canadian Branch of the Royal Club, arrived. It formally invited Scotland to send two of its best men's rinks, and now its best ladies' rink, as well, to Nova Scotia during the coming winter to determine who, in fact, could rightfully claim to have the keenest curlers in the world. The Canadians proposed that the event be called the Royal Caledonian Curling Club's World Championship. The expenses would be borne in their entirety by the Canadian hosts, who had received a most generous, unexpected, yet anonymous donation to sponsor the event. Passage across the Atlantic, food, hotel accommodations, incidentals – it would all be paid so that the Scots could come and curl in Canada. The Royal Club in Scotland was quite offended by the upstart Canadian Branch's brazenness, but found itself with no real choice but to finally accept the challenge. The Canadians had removed most of the impediments by assuming the cost and setting the venue at the nearest port to Scotland, in Nova Scotia. Nova Scotia, which translates to "New Scotland," boasted a population of which nearly fifty percent claimed Scottish origin. Rather reluctantly, the Scots accepted the invitation.

The Royal Caledonian Curling Club set about the task of selecting its three teams to send to Nova Scotia. Selecting the women's team was easy. Ailsa Maclaren's rink had just handily won the first Scottish ladies' championship. No one could really dispute their choice, although a few questioned the wisdom of sending such young lasses on so important a mission. The Royal Club asked Hugh Maclaren to communicate to his daughter their invitation for Ailsa's rink to represent Scottish women at the proposed World Championship.

Selecting the men's rinks would require a good deal more work and inspire some heated debate. The selection process had to result in assembling two formidable rinks to meet the Canadians. The Royal Club appointed a special committee, representing clubs from each district, to select the eight men who would represent Scotland in Canada. Above all, the committee wanted to fairly select who it considered to be the best curlers in Scotland, who would also behave and perform honourably in representing the flag. They also wanted rinks composed of curlers from different parts of the country. After long, occasionally contentious deliberations, the committee recommended eight men who agreed to meet the challenge. Eight very accomplished curlers were selected, each one being a skip from a different rink. None of the eight had ever played together, which would present a challenge. Those on the committee who favored sending the two best existing rinks were overruled. The Royal Club also selected the Reverend John Kerr as the team captain who would lead the delegation, although he would play only in the event of an illness or incapacity of one of the other men.

The Reverend John Kerr was an ordained minister and an avid sportsman, with a particular affinity for golf, skating, and curling. He was known as "the sporting Padre." The Reverend Kerr was also a distinguished man of letters, noted speaker, and unapologetic European imperialist. At the time when he was chosen to lead the Scottish curling delegation to Canada, he was the minister at Dirleton Kirk in East Lothian, as well as the Convener of the Literary Committee of the Royal Caledonian Curling Club. At the same time, he was just beginning to write his seminal book, *History of Curling – Scotland's Ain Game* to commemorate the Royal Club's fiftieth anniversary.

Hugh Maclaren presented the invitation to the four young women and their fathers, who unanimously, and without hesitation, agreed to accept the challenge. It was agreed that Hugh Maclaren would accompany the young women to Canada in January. Even though the young women were now nineteen or twenty years old, none of the men wanted their daughters traveling across the Atlantic unaccompanied. No matter what, they were still their fathers' little girls. The Royal Club booked passage for the entire Scottish delegation on the Allan Line's steamer *Parisian*, paid for in full courtesy of the anonymous Canadian benefactor, a cross-Atlantic journey from Liverpool to Halifax that would take nine days. It was doubtful that Ailsa's rink would get any practice time before traveling to Canada, owing to the vagaries of the Scottish weather. Ailsa's rink was confident nonetheless. The brash confidence of youth.

Sheenagh, amongst the four young women, was the most excited to be going to Nova Scotia. In addition to playing for the world championship, there would be relatives to see. Many in her extended family – uncles, aunts, cousins, nieces, and nephews – had emigrated to Canada in recent years, and many said that they would be coming to watch her curl. She knew that a few of her uncles and male cousins curled, but, as far as she could tell, none of the women or girls. Perhaps Sheenagh could convince them to give it a try. In the months leading up to her visit to Canada, Sheenagh exchanged letters with her overseas family and made plans to see many of them, time permitting.

The summer and fall dragged on endlessly for Ailsa, one day largely the same as the next, as she waited to head off to Canada to compete against the Canadians for the honour of being crowned the best lady curlers in the world. Her letters to and from Darcie Ross helped pass the time, as did the three days in September when the four lasses took the train to visit Darcie and Murdock in Glasgow. As feared, John Frost did not cooperate early that winter, exiling Ailsa's rink from the curling pond and providing scant practice time. At last, the day arrived. The party of Hugh Maclaren and the four women curlers travelled by train together to Liverpool, boarded the *Parisian*, settled in, and began the long, slow passage across the cold, dark North Atlantic to Canada,

The night before the delegation of curlers departed for Liverpool and their trans-Atlantic voyage, the Royal Club had arranged for a luxurious banquet at the Waterloo Hotel in Edinburgh, where the Royal Club had been born forty-nine years earlier. The banquet featured the traditional curling dinner of beef and greens; toasts to the Queen, country, and keen curlers everywhere; pipers, of course; speeches; and songs. The officers of the Royal Club were all there, as were officers from each club which was sending one of their men off to friendly battle. Ailsa's rink did not represent any club – ladies still being unwelcome as members. The Reverend Kerr gave an address, where he announced that two distinct groups of people awaited their arrival – those who were born in Scotland and those who regretted being born elsewhere. A special poem, composed by a Mrs. M'Nab, was read, sent by the Canadian Branch of the Royal Caledonian Curling Club:

A thousand welcomes, and a thousand more
To this new land – our wild Canadian shore:
Good brother Curlers all! – A welcome true
And hearty – we extend to you.

Our land is all before you, from the open door
At Halifax – a thousand welcomes more
Will greet you all along the snowy way;
New friends and hearty cheer, from day to day.

Some call our land "The Lady of the Snows" -
But, 'tis in truth The Kingdom of the Rose
Would you could see it in the early spring,
When ice breaks, flowers bloom, and the sweet birds sing.

Or in the rich, warm, glowing summertime,
When fragrant flowers and fruit are in their prime;
Or in the autumn, when the vast wheat fields,
The vines and orchards, each their harvest yields.

From ocean, far across the ocean grand,
It is a goodly, fair, and pleasant land;
To it we bid you welcome, Scotsmen true;
We'll do the very best we can for you -

For though we are not a' "John Tamson's bairns,"

Full well we love and reverence Scotland's cairns,
Her mountains, lochs, and glens – her purple heather,
The plaidie, bonnet blue, the kilt and feather.

"Noo play the game, wi' brooms and stanes and a'!"
"Play me and there, wi' juist a canny draw."
An' gin ye fin' ye're sometimes sorely pressed,
Play "elbow in" or "out," as ye think best!

O hey! for Scotland's dear and bonny name!
O hey! the pleasures o' the Roarin Game!
Shout, Curlers! make the very rafters ring!
"Scotland for ever!" and God save the Queen!

Each of the three rinks – Ailsa's and the two men's rinks – were showered with plaudits and hearty well-wishes in representing Scotland across the sea. In addition to the speeches, there were telegrams and letters from curling clubs, dignitaries, and royals from all parts of the country. The banquet went on for three hours. It was striking to see the men's rinks, with an average age of forty-six years, juxtaposed with Ailsa's, barely averaging twenty. The evening finally closed with a prayer for safe passage from the Reverend Kerr and a hearty singing of "Auld Lang Syne."

The next morning, upon leaving the Waterloo Hotel, the curlers were met with cheers and huzzas from the crowd gathered outside. Scottish flags flew everywhere. Ailsa, Sheenagh, Effie, and Kirsty were each presented with flowers, courtesy of the Hercules lady curlers, the rink which they had defeated to earn the Scottish Ladies' Championship a year earlier. It felt like a national holiday. There was a proud and patriotic fervor in the bracing morning air. An impromptu parade led the delegation to the station for the train ride to Liverpool.

Ailsa was assigned a tiny cabin aboard the *Parisian*, which she would share with Sheenagh, while Effie and Kirsty shared another, and Hugh Maclaren took a third, which he shared with the Reverend Kerr. Ailsa and Sheenagh had become best friends over their years of curling together, Sheenagh serving as Ailsa's vice, or second-in-command of their rink. Sheenagh was accomplished enough that she could have skipped and led her own rink, but she enjoyed playing with her three friends too much to even consider that. Besides, where would she find three other lady curlers in Musselburgh? Sheenagh also knew about Ailsa and Lucas. Not everything, but more than Effie and Kirsty knew. She knew that Ailsa used to be in love with him, but now wasn't.

There wasn't a lot to do aboard the *Parisian*. Ailsa had brought several books to read, but reading for too long at sea made her queasy. So mostly, the young women sat and talked – mainly about curling, but sometimes about more mundane things like boys and bits of gossip they had heard. Sheenagh talked a lot about the relatives she would soon be seeing. They asked Ailsa whether she had seen or heard from Colin Gibson. She had not.

Two-hundred and sixty other people were making the voyage, as well – children with their parents who were emigrating to Canada in search of a new life or to join with family, businessmen seeking riches in North America, vacationers, and the crew members. The voyage was unremarkable, for the most part. A later passage by the *Parisian*, in April of 1912, was not. The *Parisian* was just fifty miles southwest of the *Titanic* when the *Titantic* hit the iceberg, but the *Parisian* hadn't received the distress call and simply continued its westward passage, oblivious to the tragedy unfolding in the North Atlantic.

On the second night of the voyage, a Saturday, the Allan Line had prepared a special banquet in honour of the curlers. It was far from standard fare for an 1888 steamer trip between England and North America:

<u>Menu</u>

Norwegian Anchovies.
Pate de Foie Gras.
Jardiniere Soup.
Turtle Soup.
Boiled Salmon, Green Peas, Caper Sauce.
Jugged Hare.
Sweetbreads, Tomato Sauce.
Fowl and Tongue Patties.
Roast Sirloin of Beef, Horse-Radish.
Roast Saddle of Mutton, Red Currant Jelly.
Roast Turkey and Sausage, Cranberry Sauce.
Fillet of Veal, Lemon Sauce.
Roast Goose, Apple Sauce.
Cold Ham and Tongue.
Tomatoes.
Asparagus.
Mashed and Boiled Potatoes.
Pheasant, Bread Sauce.
Plum Pudding, Tapioca Pudding.
Gooseberry Tart.
Mince Pies.
Maraschion Jelly.
Queen's Cakes.

Ice Cream.

Grapes.

Pears.

Carlsbad Plums, Figs, Filberts.

Walnuts, Almonds.

Muscatelles.

Gorgonzola, Cheshire, and Stilton Cheese.

Tea, Coffee.

The twelve curlers, along with the Reverend Kerr, Hugh Maclaren, and the ship's captain, sat together at the captain's table for the feast. Ailsa and her friends had never seen so much food – nor had they ever eaten so much food. Once again, there were toasts, speeches, and songs honoring the curling ambassadors. The Reverend Kerr offered a few humorous remarks and thanked the passengers and crew for their warm wishes and hospitality. Making reference to the expansive menu, the Reverend Kerr reminded the passengers, lightheartedly, that gluttony was one of the seven deadly sins. He quoted from *Proverbs 23*, which admonishes, "Be not among winebibbers; among riotous eaters of flesh: For the drunkard and the glutton shall come to poverty . . ." Ailsa vowed to be more temperate for the rest of the trip.

Sunday morning church services aboard the *Parisian* were led by the Reverend Kerr, who never declined an opportunity to preach the Word. Normally, the Allan Line would have employed a clergyman to make the voyage and conduct services, but with the Reverend Kerr on board, and more than willing, there was no need. All of the curlers, still bloated from the prior evening's meal, attended.

The Reverend Kerr chose for his sermon to preach about the evils of being seduced by temptation. Perhaps he chose the topic as a reminder to the passengers to be circumspect in the choices they made in a foreign land. Perhaps it was a recycled sermon which could be directed to a new audience. Perhaps it was simply what he felt moved by the Spirit to speak about that day.

The scripture for the Reverend Kerr's sermon on temptation was a very familiar one, especially to Ailsa. She had asked Lucas about it. The minister read from *Matthew 4:1-11*:

[1] Then was Jesus led up of the Spirit into the wilderness to be tempted of the devil. [2] And when he had fasted forty days and forty nights, he was afterward an hungred. [3] And when the tempter came to him, he said, If thou be the Son of God, command that these stones be made bread. [4] But he answered and said, It is written, Man shall not live by bread alone, but by every word that proceedeth out of the mouth of God. [5] Then the devil taketh him up into the holy city, and setteth him on a pinnacle of the temple, [6] And saith unto him, If thou be the Son of God, cast thyself down: for it is written, He shall give his angels charge concerning thee: and in their hands they shall bear thee up, lest at any time thou dash thy foot against a stone. [7] Jesus said unto him, It is written again, Thou shalt not tempt the Lord thy God. [8] Again, the devil taketh him up into an exceeding high mountain, and sheweth him all the kingdoms of the world, and the glory of them; [9] And saith unto him, All these things will I give thee, if thou wilt fall down and worship me. [10] Then saith Jesus unto him, Get thee hence, Satan: for it is written, Thou shalt worship the Lord thy God, and him only shalt thou serve. [11] Then the devil leaveth him, and, behold, angels came and ministered unto him.

Ailsa snapped to attention upon hearing what the scripture passage would be. She had read it dozens of times since hearing Lucas explain that he never set temptations before people. Lucas even denied the account of tempting Jesus which the Reverend Kerr had just recited. She was no longer certain what to believe. She knew that she should believe the biblical account, but Lucas had been quite vehement in his denial. Ailsa tried hard to listen to the Reverend Kerr's admonishments about being tempted by the Devil, but her mind kept wandering back to Lucas's explanation of his involvement – or, rather, his lack of such – in presenting temptations. She would love to talk with the Reverend Kerr about her own experience, but knew that she never would.

During the long months leading up to the voyage, the Reverend Kerr had been in communication with curling clubs throughout Canada to learn as much as he could about the sport in that country. He would use the information to record the trip for posterity, but also to entertain the Scottish party during the long days at sea. One of the curious bits of information which he received concerned the Asylum Curling Club in Hamilton, Ontario, which was exactly what its name implied. The Asylum Curling Club was formed at the Hamilton Asylum for the Insane by Dr. James Russell, and was comprised of both patients and employees. Dr. Russell wrote the following to the Reverend Kerr, which he shared with the Scottish curlers:

> *The club was organized . . . as an experiment at an Asylum. We erected the curling shed by Asylum labour, and the Government was good enough to supply the stones for the patients. Officers and employers brought their own stones. The experiment proved an immense success. Our patients worked in the game with the greatest enthusiasm, and many of them developed into most skillful players. Of all*

the curative means employed for the restoration of mental health nothing has equalled the game on the ice. We played matches with all the surrounding clubs . . . In every rink there were at least two patients, and it was not easy to distinguish who was who on the ice. Our club won the Walker Trophy one year, which was open to all clubs in the Hamilton District. Another year our club came out ahead in the competition for the Ontario Tankard in our district.

Many amusing incidents have happened on the ice, which would take too much space to relate. The longest percentage of recoveries is from the curling club, and we have to deplore each year the loss of our best players who return home clothed and in their right mind.

It must have been difficult, the Reverend Kerr surmised, for Dr. Russell to discharge one of his best curlers from the asylum, especially as the curling season drew near and there were trophies to be competed for and won. Perhaps the patient would benefit from a few more months of care, just to be sure.

The Reverend Kerr had also collected a number of curling stories to share with curlers to help pass the time on the long voyage. He told a story of how disturbing the makeup of the rinks prior to the annual matches between married men and bachelors was not looked upon kindly, and how those who dared to do so were subject to penalties imposed by the clubs, all in good fun, perhaps. Curling clubs preferred that they be consulted before a bachelor went over to the other side. Kerr read a passage from a curling historian:

In nearly every annual minute book some luckless member is fined for having got married 'without having consulted the Committee of the Club.' In those days, when most of the matches were between Bachelors and Benedicts, it will be allowed that it showed a want of consideration for any one individual to disturb 'the balance of power.'

One particular story which the Reverend Kerr had found, he thought that Ailsa, Sheenagh, Effie, and Kirsty might particularly enjoy. He related that when women were brazen enough to venture onto the ice to play, they were often chastised, in no uncertain terms, for their temerity in participating in "the manly Scottish exercise." It reminded Ailsa of her own banishment from the Musselburgh Curling Club's ice. Kerr read from an 1826 account in the *Dumfries Weekly Journal*:

On Tuesday last, 28 blooming damsels met on Dalpeddar Loch in the parish of Sanquhar, to play a friendly bonspiel. They formed themselves into two rinks, and although wading up to the ankles in water, seemed to enter into the spirit of the game, and to contest it with as much intense anxiety as if the question that the losing party should all die old maids had depended upon the issue. At the conclusion of the game neither party became victors, the number of shots having been equal. Many individuals of the other sex were attracted to the scene of action; and as the ladies, like true curlers, had resolved to adjourn to the toll-house, where a het pint had been ordered, they kindly invited the gentlemen to accompany them. It soon became a matter of doubt if this was of sufficient potency to counteract the bad effects resulting from wet feet, and . . . our heroines resorted to whiskey toddy, and through its inspiration, a dance was proposed…and the ball was kept up with great vigour until far into the wee hours o' the morning. It may be true that there is no good reason why females should not have their hours of recreation as well as men, but it seems advisable that those recreations which they do engage in should be of a character befitting their sex. Ice playing is certainly not a game of this description – it has nothing feminine pertaining to it either in theory or practice. If, therefore, prudence and propriety are to be consulted, the fair maidens of the lower end of Sanquhar parish will not again resort to the same expedient for obtaining a day's relaxation and enjoyment.

On the sixth day of the trip, a Wednesday afternoon, despite the bitter cold and biting wind, Ailsa was spending a few minutes alone on the deck, taking in the salt air and staring out to the horizon. A woman approached. A woman whom Ailsa did not recognize as one of the other passengers. "Hello, Ailsa," the woman said. "It's been quite a long time. I've missed you. Have you missed me, as well?"

Ailsa was startled. It was the third time in a year that a stranger had approached her and used her name. Her body reflexively tensed. Ailsa was unnerved. She didn't want to believe it, but she immediately knew that it was true. The woman's eyes were the giveaway. The eyes never changed. "Lucas?" she asked. If she didn't know who Lucas really was before, she certainly did now, seeing him incarnate before her as a petite, middle-aged woman. She had hoped to never see Lucas again.

"Indeed. I'm so happy that you remember," the woman answered. The woman was a bit disheveled. She could have been mistaken for one of the many passengers hoping to begin a new, better life in a new country. But the eyes . . . It was the woman's eyes that confirmed for Ailsa that she was once again talking to Lucas Plotcok.

"I never had the chance to congratulate you on winning the ladies' championship last winter," the woman began. "I would have done it sooner, of course, but a deal is a deal. Our contract forbade me from remaining to Scotland, and, hence, from seeing you after the bonspiel. I departed as soon as your game ended. I must tell you that I've missed Scotland dearly this past year. It was one of my favorite stops. Solicitor Paine did a very thorough job on our contract. I tried to find a way out of it, regrettably with no success. But we're no longer in Scotland, are we Ailsa? You won the championship, for which your countrymen should be eternally grateful, if they only knew what you had done for them. I suppose that they never will, though." The woman stopped and waited for Ailsa's response.

Ailsa stood silently for a long time, lost in a tumble of thoughts, shivering – or was she trembling? – and not knowing what to say. Finally, she managed to speak. "You came here to see me and to congratulate me?"

"I did. I would have done it much sooner, for which I apologize, but I had no choice. You must think me terribly rude. I suppose that I could have at least sent a telegram." The woman smiled. "Oh, well, let's agree to let bygones be bygones, shall we?. But I can assure you that I have honoured every word of our contract. Yes, I've missed Scotland. Do you know what I've missed the most, Ailsa, aside from the obvious? The brogue. I've very much missed the brogue. It's quite nice to hear it again. I told you that you could trust me to live up to my bargain." The woman stopped talking and waited for Ailsa.

"Yes, you did," Ailsa said. "Yes, you did." And yet, she had no real way of knowing whether Lucas spoke the truth.

The woman reached into her coat pocket and produced a brown envelope. She handed it to Ailsa. "I want you to read this, Ailsa. After you do, I'll be back in touch. It was a pleasure to see you again. I'd almost forgotten how beautiful you are. Now, I must get out of this terrible cold. G'day." With that, the new incarnation of Lucas Plotcok turned and shuffled away. Before rounding a corner and disappearing, the woman turned and said, "And Ailsa, please tell the Reverend Kerr that his sermon on Sunday was dreadful. Absolutely dreadful."

Ailsa stared at the envelope that she really didn't want to be holding and that she knew she shouldn't even open. She had thought that she was done with Lucas Plotcok forever. She managed a weak grin at the thought of the handsome, dashing young man she thought that she was in love with now presenting himself as a beleaguered, dowdy woman.

⸻ ◆ ⸻

Ailsa sat alone, staring at the envelope, from the office of Solicitor Pickering Paine, terrified to open it, her hands numb and trembling. Finally, she opened it. Inside, she found four copies of a new contract, appearing very similar to the one she had signed a year earlier. She started reading, her hands still shaking:

> *The Party of the First Part, Lucas Plotcok [hereinafter "Lucas Plotcok"], being the Devil Himself, also known as, including, but not limited thereto, inter alia, Satan, Lucifer, the Deil, Beelzebub, Mephistopheles, Moloch, Shayton, Pluto, Loki, Old Clootie, Old Nick, the Prince of Darkness, Perdition, Baphomet, Iblis, el Diablo, and/or Lucas Plotcok, enters into this binding Agreement of his own free will and volition, and without reservation, intending to be forever bound by its terms, with no intent of evasion or deception, and covenants to be bound by its*

terms, conditions, duties, rights, and/or obligations for all time, from this day forward.

The Party of the Second Part, Ailsa Maclaren [hereinafter "Ailsa Maclaren"], an unmarried adult woman currently residing in Musselburgh, Scotland, enters into this binding Agreement of her own free will and volition, and without reservation, intending to be forever bound by its terms, with no intent of evasion of deception, and covenants to be bound by its terms, conditions, duties, rights, and/or obligations for all time, from this day forward.

As best as she could recall, so far it was precisely the same language as in the previous contract. That was about to change for the worse.

The Party of the Third Part, Sheenagh Gillie [hereinafter "Sheenagh Gillie"], an unmarried adult woman currently residing in Musselburgh, Scotland, enters into this binding Agreement of her own free will and volition, and without reservation, intending to be forever bound by its terms, with no intent of evasion or deception, and covenants to be bound by its terms, conditions, duties, rights, and/or obligations for all time, from this day forward.

Sheenagh?! What could Sheenagh possibly have to do with any of this? Why was she now involved? Had Lucas gotten to her? There was absolutely no way that Ailsa was going to allow Sheenagh to become entangled with Lucas. It was bad enough that Ailsa had allowed herself to be seduced into making a deal with the Devil. Terrified at what might be coming next, she continued reading.

First. Ailsa Maclaren and her rink, consisting of herself; the said Party of the Third Part, Sheenagh Gillie; Effie Lawrie; and Kirsty Barnett [hereinafter "Maclaren's Rink"], intend to compete in the Canadian Branch of the Royal Caledonian Curling Club's Ladies' World Championship in February, 1888, in Nova Scotia, Canada. Despite their names being set forth herein, for the sole purpose of identifying Maclaren's Rink, the said Effie Lawrie and Kirsty Barnett are not parties to this Agreement, and do not in any manner or form whatsoever assume any burdens, duties, benefits, rights, and/or obligations hereunder.

Second. In the event that Maclaren's Rink wins the said Canadian Branch of the Royal Caledonian Curling Club's Ladies' World Championship in February, 1888, in Nova Scotia, Canada, neither the said Party of the Second Part, Ailsa Maclaren, nor the said Party of the Third Part, Sheenagh Gillie, shall have any further burdens, duties, obligations, and/or debts of any kind or nature whatsoever, forever and always, to the said Party of the First Part, Lucas Plotcok, known by whatever name and/or in whatever form, as he may appear and/or be known.

Third. In the event that Maclaren's Rink wins the said Canadian Branch of the Royal Caledonian Curling Club's Ladies' World Championship in February, 1888, in Nova Scotia, Canada, the said Party of the First Part, Lucas Plotcok, known by whatever name and/or in whatever form as he may appear and/or be known, shall forever and always be barred from, and shall for all time, from that day forward, refrain from entering, manifesting, residing, and/or appearing anywhere and at any place and/or places, in the Dominion of Canada.

Fourth. In the event that Maclaren's Rink wins the said Canadian Branch of the Royal Caledonian Curling Club's Ladies' World Championship in February, 1888, in Nova Scotia, Canada, the said Party of the First Part, Lucas Plotcok, known by whatever name and/or in whatever form as he may appear and/or be known, shall forever and always be barred from, and shall for all time, refrain from taking, harvesting, collecting, claiming, securing, and/or in any other manner of any nature whatsoever, the soul, essence, spirit, and/or any other afterlife incarnation of any Canadian, whether man, woman, or child.

Fifth. The said Party of the First Part, Lucas Plotcok, known by whatever name and/or in whatever form as he may appear and/or be known, shall refrain from, and shall in no way, form, shape, or manner, interfere with, influence, effect, impact, alter, and/or manipulate the playing or outcome of the said Canadian Branch of the Royal Caledonian Curling Club's Ladies' World Championship in February, 1888, in Nova Scotia, Canada, nor shall the said Party of the First Part, Lucas Plotcok, cause, aid, and/or abet another party, in any way, form, shape, or manner whatsoever, to interfere with the playing, contesting, and/or outcome of the said Canadian Branch of the Royal Caledonian Curling Club's Ladies' World Championship.

Sixth. In the event that Maclaren's Rink fails to win the said Canadian Branch of the Royal Caledonian Curling Club's Ladies' World Championship in February, 1888, in Nova Scotia, Canada, the said Party of the Second Part, Ailsa Maclaren, and the said Party of the Third Part, Sheenagh Gillie, agree and covenant that at the conclusion of their natural lives and upon each of their deaths, which the said Party of the First Part, Lucas Plotcok agrees and covenants that he will in no way, form, shape, and/or manner whatsoever, either cause, hasten, accelerate, or precipitate, that the said Party of the First Part, Lucas Plotcok, shall take possession and control of each of their respective souls, essences, spirits, and/or any other afterlife incarnations, to possess and exercise full dominion over at his sole pleasure, to have and to hold from that day forward.

Seventh. In the event that the Canadian Branch of the Royal Caledonian Curling Club's Ladies' World

Championship fails to be contested in February, 1888, in Nova Scotia, Canada, fails to be completed, or fails to produce a winner as certified by the Royal Caledonian Curling Club, or in the event that Maclaren's Rink, as defined in Paragraph First herein, is unable or does not for any reason or cause whatsoever, enter and compete in the said Canadian Branch of the Royal Caledonian Curling Club's Ladies' World Championship, this Agreement shall be void and null, and the parties hereto shall have no further rights, burdens, duties, benefits, and/or obligations hereunder.

Ailsa didn't move, couldn't move. Her heart raced furiously. She just stared at the papers in her hand, reminding herself to breathe. Did Lucas really expect her to get her best friend involved in this now? There was no way that Ailsa would ever do that. Her biggest fear was that Sheenagh was already involved somehow. And yet, she didn't tear the contract apart and throw it into the ocean, as she knew she should. Rather, she slid the papers back into their envelope and stuffed them into her coat. She needed time to think. Lots of time.

After a fitful night, and looking for any sign that something was different or unusual about Sheenagh, Ailsa went to the same spot on the deck at the same time as the day before. She waited. There was no sign of Lucas, in either of his guises. She waited a little longer. Nothing. She wanted to see Lucas to tell him to go to hell. He just might appreciate the irony of such a thing. He had once told her that even though he did not possess a great sense of humor, his sense of irony was highly-developed. Ailsa went back inside, disappointed and surprised that Lucas had not appeared. Had she imagined all of this? She slipped her hand into her coat pocket and felt the envelope.

Sheenagh's growing excitement about arriving in Canada was beginning to wear off on Ailsa, Effie, and Kirsty, and even on Hugh Maclaren and the Reverend Kerr. It was getting a little bit tiring, although contagious. She talked constantly of hearing from her relatives about how beautiful the country was and how wonderful the people were. The air in Canada was crisp and clear, the water clean and blue, the ice hard and sparkling. It was nearly as beautiful, they told her, as Auld Scotia herself. Sheenagh couldn't wait to see Canada and to see her relatives again.

That night, alone in their cabin, Ailsa once again listened as Sheenagh went on and on about Canada and her relatives, Ailsa trying her best to follow who was who, where in Canada all of them lived, and where in Scotland they were from. It was obvious how much Sheenagh seemed to love Canada, even though she had never been there and even though it was still hundreds of miles away. Nothing was different about Sheenagh, at least that Ailsa could perceive. As Sheenagh talked, Ailsa kept glancing at her closet with her coat hanging inside, Lucas's new contract tucked away in a pocket.

Ailsa didn't want to say anything to Sheenagh. Sheenagh hadn't confided anything unusual. It didn't appear that Lucas had gotten to her yet. Ailsa could simply tell Lucas that she wouldn't agree to any deal, and that would be the end of it, because Lucas's new contract required the agreement of both she and Sheenagh. Lucas, mercifully, might then be gone forever. And Sheenagh would never know and would never be in any jeopardy. Ailsa calculated that it was highly unlikely that Lucas would deal with Sheenagh directly, since he clearly wanted both of the young ladies, and Ailsa in particular, not just Sheenagh.

Slowly, against her will, Ailsa's thinking began to change. Partly, she felt like Sheenagh deserved to know, but mostly, Ailsa simply had to tell someone about Lucas. Who better to tell than her most trusted friend? Ailsa had made her own decision about dealing with Lucas. She wouldn't have wanted someone else making her decision for her. Didn't Sheenagh deserve the same? After all, Sheenagh was every bit as smart and deliberate and mature as Ailsa was. Sheenagh would make a good decision. The right decision. She wouldn't be as reckless as Ailsa had been. Besides, after more than a year of keeping her secret inside of her, Ailsa desperately wanted to tell her story to someone. She *needed* to tell it to someone.

Ailsa finally decided to do it. She would tell Sheenagh everything. Sheenagh was the one person who might possibly believe her. She would tell Sheenagh everything about Lucas Plotcok, her deal with the Devil, and the new deal that he was proposing. Ailsa summoned her nerve and resolve, but also her faith and trust in her friend to do the right thing. She hoped that Sheenagh believed her, but also thought that she might think that Ailsa had gone mad. Who wouldn't? It was not a story to be readily believed.

Ailsa sat down across from Sheenagh and took both of Sheenagh's hands in hers. Sheenagh sensed Ailsa's fear and apprehension. Ailsa's hands were cold and clammy. They were trembling and her pulse was pounding. "Sheenagh, I need to talk to you," Ailsa began, her voice unsteady. "And I need for you to please, please listen to me and to believe me, even though what I will tell you will seem unbelievable. But every single word is true, I swear to you. Everything I tell you is true."

Sheenagh had no idea what Ailsa might be about to tell her. "What is it, Ailsa? Are you ill?" Sheenagh asked. All kinds of terrible thoughts raced through Sheenagh's head. She had never seen Ailsa so shaken.

"I'm fine, Sheenagh, believe me, but you might not think so after I tell you what I need to tell you." Ailsa managed a faint smile. "Please, just listen and try to believe me. You know that you can trust me, don't you?" Ailsa asked. "You know that I would never lie to you. You know that, right?"

"Of course I trust you. You're my best friend. I'd trust you with my life," Sheenagh answered. If she only knew.

"Then let me tell you. Just listen and try to believe me. Please just listen," Ailsa begged. Ailsa began recounting her story of meeting Lucas Plotcok, of beginning their courtship, of Lucas's revealing his true identity to her, of the boy who fell through the ice, of their meeting with Pickering Paine, of their contract, and of what the Scottish Ladies' Championship *really* meant for all of Scotland. She fought through her tears as she told the story, her voice quivering, her breaths infrequent and shallow. Sheenagh didn't say a word. Nor did she believe what Ailsa was telling her.

Ailsa finished that part of the story and looked up. Finally, Sheenagh spoke. "I want to believe you, Ailsa, I really do, but it's just not possible. Whoever he is, he's not the Devil. He played a trick on you. He's just a liar or a charlatan. He's had his fun and he's lost interest. He's probably in Aberdeen or Glasgow playing a joke on someone else."

"I thought so, too, at first," Ailsa responded. "But he's not. He's on this ship, Sheenagh. At least he was. I saw him yesterday, although he was different. He was a woman this time. But it was him. I know it was him. I saw him in the woman's eyes. She knew everything, Sheenagh. Everything." Sheenagh did, in fact, wonder whether her friend was ill. Try as she wanted, Sheenagh simply couldn't believe it. Ailsa's story was becoming more and more preposterous. She knew that Ailsa wouldn't lie to her, but the whole story just wasn't possible. She considered telling Mr. Maclaren that Ailsa might be sick.

"What does he want? Why would he be traveling with us on a boat to Canada?" Sheenagh asked. She asked not because she believed any of it, but because Ailsa obviously had more to tell.

"He wants to make another deal. But not just with me. He wants to make a deal with both of us this time. Here, read this." Ailsa retrieved the envelope she had been hiding and offered it to Sheenagh. Sheenagh removed the contents and began reading, trying to make sense of the legal jargon. When she finished, she was trembling.

"Why, Ailsa? Why does he want us? What did we do wrong?" Sheenagh asked, her voice unsteady. It was the same question Ailsa had asked of Lucas a year earlier. It was also a question that suggested Sheenagh was starting to maybe believe.

"That's the really odd part. It doesn't mean that we've done anything wrong. It just means that he sees in you what he claims to see in me. A leader. Someone strong and sure enough to manage some of his flock. An asset in his work." Ailsa went on and explained everything that Lucas had told her about his Counterpart and the afterlife and their agreement about collecting souls.

"My God, Ailsa, you really believe all of this, don't you?" Sheenagh finally asked. "You actually believe it."

"I do," Ailsa answered. "I actually do."

"Who else knows about this, Ailsa? Who else have you told?" Sheenagh asked.

"No one. You and I are the only ones. Oh, and Solicitor Paine, I suppose."

<hr>

Neither Ailsa nor Sheenagh slept much that night. Sheenagh peppered Ailsa with questions about Lucas and his Counterpart, what the contract meant, Lucas's explanation about the afterlife, what she thought hell might be like, why she thought Lucas to be trustworthy. On and on, question after question, much like Ailsa herself had asked of Lucas. Ailsa answered them all, in painstaking detail, sometimes repeating verbatim what Lucas had told her.

Sheenagh finally insisted upon meeting and judging Lucas herself, or so she said. What she really wanted to do was to show Ailsa that Lucas wasn't really on the ship, or, at the very least, that he wasn't the Devil. She needed to prove to Ailsa that she had imagined it, or that someone was playing an elaborate joke on her. Sheenagh intended to get to the bottom of it. Ailsa didn't want Sheenagh meeting Lucas – the risk was far too great – but Sheenagh was relentless. Ailsa gave in.

That afternoon, Ailsa and Sheenagh made their way to the deck, at the same time and in the same place as Ailsa claimed to have encountered Lucas as a middle-aged woman. There was no one there when they arrived. They stood and they waited. After more than half an hour, Sheenagh had had enough. She had made her point. "I told you, Ailsa. Whoever it was that you think you met here, you didn't. You imagined it. You simply imagined it. You were probably just anxious or seasick. Now let's go back inside, get some rest, and forget about all of this." They had been staring straight out to the horizon. Maybe Sheenagh was right, Ailsa tried to convince herself, but she knew otherwise.

Sheenagh turned and bumped into a woman, almost knocking the woman off of her feet. "Oh, my God! I'm so sorry!" Sheenagh blurted out. "I didn't see you. Are you alright?"

"Now, now, Sheenagh, it's quite alright, dear. I'm fine. It was an accident. Don't worry yourself," the woman said. Sheenagh froze. The woman was exactly as Ailsa had described her.

"Wait. How did you know my . . . " Sheenagh stopped and looked at Ailsa. Ailsa nodded.

"I hope I haven't kept you two waiting for too long. Please accept my sincerest apology. Unfortunately, I had some unexpected business that required my immediate attention," the woman said. She paused before asking, "Am I to surmise that this meeting is not simply by chance? Is there some business that we need to discuss?"

Ailsa answered. "I've told Sheenagh all about us, Lucas."

"Splendid! I hope that you told her nothing but good things," Lucas said with a grin. "First impressions are so important."

"I told her everything," Ailsa snapped. "And I told her that she should have nothing to do with you. But she insisted upon meeting you, anyway. Sheenagh can be quite adamant sometimes."

"You two seem to have many things in common," Lucas said. "It's one of the reasons I wanted to meet you, Sheenagh. You appear to have many of the same admirable traits as Ailsa. Until now, I've only been able to observe them from afar, I'm afraid, but I have been very impressed. It's why I've made my offer to you. I trust that Ailsa explained it to you and that you are now familiar with it? It turned out very nicely for Ailsa and for your homeland. Now, you have a similar opportunity. An even grander opportunity. I understand that you have a great many relatives awaiting your arrival." Sheenagh had already decided what she was going to do, although she hadn't told Ailsa.

"I'll do it!" Sheenagh blurted out. "I'll do for Canada precisely what Ailsa did for Scotland."

"Marvelous!" Lucas said. "But unfortunately, the Agreement requires consent from both of you, not just from you alone." Lucas turned and looked to Ailsa. "Ailsa? What do you have to say?"

Ailsa was blindsided. She had no idea that Sheenagh was actually going to agree to the deal. She needed time. Time to think and time to talk Sheenagh out of making a pact with the Devil. She had to get Sheenagh away from Lucas. Quickly. "We'll meet you here tomorrow at the same appointed time. Don't be a minute late, Lucas, because we're not going to wait around again. Let's go, Sheenagh." Ailsa grabbed Sheenagh's arm and hustled her away.

***

Safely ensconced back in their cabin, Ailsa tried and tried to convince Sheenagh not to do it. "Don't sign the contract." She pleaded with Sheenagh not to get involved with anything having to do with Lucas

Plotcok. It was too dangerous, too eternal, too final. "Please, please, Sheenagh, I'm begging you not to do this. I can't let you do this, I won't do this," Ailsa pleaded.

"You did it once, Ailsa. And you won! If Lucas is really who he says he is, think of what you've done for all of Scotland for all time! I want to do the same thing for Canada, for my family. Do this with me, Ailsa. We can do this together. Please," Sheenagh begged. They spent the entire day and night talking about nothing else – Sheenagh pleading and Ailsa refusing.

Ailsa knew that she shouldn't do it. She knew that she couldn't allow Sheenagh to do it. How could she live with herself if they lost in Canada and her best friend was condemned to an eternity in hell? "I can't. I can't," Ailsa finally said. "I just can't let you do this. Please don't ask me to do it. I would do anything for you Sheenagh, you know that, but not this. I love you too much."

Sheenagh was persistent and relentless. She wanted to do it. She wasn't afraid. She could save her entire family, and millions of others, from the Devil's clutches for all time. How could she be so selfish as to not try? Ailsa was weakening. "I have to think, Sheenagh. Give me some time to think about this," Ailsa replied. Ailsa got up and left the cabin to be alone and to figure out what she would do.

— ◇ —

The next afternoon, Ailsa and Sheenagh went to the appointed spot at the appointed time. Lucas – the woman – was waiting. Right on time. Early, in fact. "G'day, Ailsa. G'day, Sheenagh. Let's get right down to business, shall we? Tell me, have you come to any decision?" she asked.

"We have," Sheenagh answered. "We've both signed your papers. Let's see if you dare to do the same." Sheenagh handed the signed Agreements to Lucas, who seemed quite pleased, and also quite impressed by

Sheenagh's brashness. She would make an excellent addition to his collection. Sheenagh produced a fountain pen from her coat pocket. A fountain pen she had borrowed from the Reverend Kerr. For some reason, Sheenagh thought that it might bring some good fortune. She handed the pen to the woman, who removed her mittens and affixed the signature of Lucas Plotcok to all four copies. The woman handed one to Ailsa and one to Sheenagh. "I shall send his copy to Solicitor Paine for safekeeping," the woman announced. "I would prefer to deliver it in person, but I'm afraid I'm not permitted." Lucas smiled at Ailsa.

"If you don't mind, Lucas, we'll send it," Ailsa said. Lucas handed Pickering Paine's copy to Ailsa.

"As you wish," Lucas said. "You really need to be more trusting, Ailsa. Perhaps we'll be able to work on that at a later time." Before turning to leave, the woman said, "I would wish you luck against the Canadians, but I'm afraid our interests in the outcome are quite opposite." The woman turned away, then looked back at the two young women. "Enjoy the rest of your journey," she said.

"Excuse me, Lucas," Sheenagh said.

"Yes?" the woman asked.

"Could I have my pen back?"

"I'm so sorry, Sheenagh," the woman apologized. "It's a terrible habit, taking things that don't belong to me." She handed Sheenagh the pen. Lucas was extremely impressed by Sheenagh. He had made a wise choice. She seemed absolutely fearless.

Chapter 16
Canada

Finally, after nine days at sea, the *Parisian* slowly made its way to the deep water terminus in Halifax. Sheenagh raced up to the deck as soon as Canada appeared on the horizon. The bagpipers, faint at first, grew louder as the steamer approached. Ailsa, Effie, and Kirsty soon joined Sheenagh on the deck. Most of the other passengers were there, too, with one notable exception. They had made it, and the thought of playing the Canadians for the world championship suddenly became more immediate. Sheenagh's anticipation was even greater, for she would soon be seeing her relatives and sealing her, and their, eternal fates. The thought of her contract with Lucas had now become strikingly real.

A large delegation greeted the Scottish curlers when they disembarked from the *Parisian*, led by a special deputation from the Halifax Curling Club, which formally welcomed them to Canada, Nova Scotia, Halifax, and the World Curling Championships. The Canadians had been waiting more than twenty years for this day, when they would finally be able to prove to the Scots that they had surpassed them at their own game. They would not do so with ill-will or animous, for many were sons and daughters of Scotland, but with pride at how they had attained near-perfection at the game. The Canadians would treat the Scots with the utmost honour and respect. Then they would best them.

It hadn't always been easy for the Canadians when it came to curling. While ice was generally plentiful and strong, settling on curling stones was a challenge. In some places, eager curlers who had no access to good curling stone granite fashioned their "stones" from blocks of wood. Curlers in western Canada preferred oak. In others, stones were made out of iron, primarily from melted-down cannon balls. The first two Canadian curling clubs – in Montreal and Quebec City – exclusively used irons. In yet other places, curlers continued with the old Scottish practice of finding suitable rocks in nature and affixing handles. In the Maritimes, though, curling was played almost exclusively with imported curling stones made of Ailsa Craig granite. It was one of the reasons the championships would be played there. In fact, the *Parisian's* cargo included six dozen new Ailsa Craig stones for use throughout the Maritimes.

The Scottish party of fourteen – two men's rinks, Ailsa's rink, Hugh Maclaren, and the Reverend Kerr – loaded onto horse-drawn sleighs and were driven through the streets of Halifax to the Queen Hotel on Hollis Street, where they would spend their stay. The entire hotel, inside and out, was adorned in a Scottish theme. Along the route, hundreds of people lined the street and cheered. Pipers played and toasts were shouted. Scottish flags, a white saltire over an azure field, flew everywhere. Although the party had been told to expect a warm and hearty welcome, they were nonetheless overwhelmed by the showing. Intent on winning, the Canadians were also intent on being perfect hosts. Along the route, Ailsa and Sheenagh both scanned the crowd for Lucas.

Sheenagh was greeted in the lobby of the Queen Hotel by a large group of relatives, more than a dozen, most of whom lived in New Brunswick, around Moncton. Sheenagh hugged each of them tightly, excited to finally see them again. Some had left Scotland many years ago, others, only recently. They sat and exchanged news about family and friends back in Scotland and family now living in Canada, and about Sheenagh's curling exploits. The older uncles and male cousins talked about curling at the Moncton Curling Club, although they admitted to not being nearly as accomplished as Sheenagh.

Sheenagh talked with her cousins, mostly. She couldn't believe how much different they looked – so much taller and more mature. They offered the same assessments about her. With all of the attention, she felt like a celebrity. She realized how much she missed them. She also hoped to give them the most incredible gift.

Sheenagh talked mostly with her cousin Fiona, the cousin she had been closest to before Fiona's family left for Canada two years earlier. "Guess what, Sheenagh," Fiona whispered when no one else was listening.

"What?" Sheenagh asked.

"I have a boyfriend! No one knows about him, though, so . . . " Fiona put her index finger in front of her lips, signaling Sheenagh not to say anything.

"Really?!" Sheenagh replied in a hushed tone. "What's his name? Is it serious?"

"His name's Scott. He's really nice. And his family's pretty rich, too," Fiona answered mischievously. "Plus, he's awfully good-looking. It's getting serious, too. I'm going to have to tell my parents soon."

"Does he have any brothers?" Sheenagh asked jokingly. Fiona's younger sister approached before Fiona could answer.

After nearly two hours, Sheenagh's extended family announced that they would have to be heading home before darkness fell. They promised to be at the world championship bonspiel to cheer her and her friends to victory. After another round of hugs and kisses, they exited the magnificent hotel lobby and headed home. Sheenagh finally went up to the room that she would share with Ailsa, opened the door, and found her friend fast asleep, still wearing the same clothes that she had been wearing when she disembarked from the *Parisian*. The two hours with her family had flown by – two hours in which Sheenagh hardly thought about Lucas.

Strewn about Ailsa's bed were several telegrams addressed to her which the Reverend Kerr had collected upon the party's arrival at the hotel. The Royal Caledonian Curling Club wished her, "Good Curling!" William Beveridge conveyed the best wishes of the Musselburgh Curling Club. Henrietta Gilmour implored Ailsa to "Do Us A' Proud!" A telegram from Colin Gibson was in Ailsa's right hand. It read, "Best of luck, Ailsa. You can do it."

Yet another banquet had been prepared for the evening of their arrival to honour the Scots and the Canadians who would be playing for the men's and ladies' world championships. It was even more extravagant than the one at the Waterloo Hotel in Edinburgh and the one aboard the *Parisian*, if that were possible. Curling dignitaries from all parts of the Dominion were there, offering greetings, messages of goodwill, speeches, songs, and yet another poem:

> *Nae game can mak' your blood run quick*
> *As when ye draw a port or wick,*
> *Or run the winner out, and stick*
> *Upon the tee, that's Curlin'.*
> *Oh, hapless Wretch who ne'er has known*
> *The music o' the curlin' stone;*
> *To heavenly songs ye'll no be prone,*
> *That's what ye'll lose, no Curlin'.*

The menu for the feast seemed fit to feed the entire Province. It most certainly was not simply a traditional "beef and greens" affair, although beef and greens were on the menu. Remembering the Reverend Kerr's admonition about gluttony after the feast aboard the *Parisian*, and recalling the bloated feeling for the two ensuing days, Ailsa was more judicious about how much she ate. The lobster salad was the best thing that she had ever tasted. The strawberry ice cream was almost as good.

<u>Menu</u>

Oysters on the Shell.
Sliced Lemon.
Queen Olives.
Scotch Broth.
Salted Almonds.
Chicken Halibut aux Carottes.
Creamed Potatoes.
Macaroni au Gratin.
Pineapple Fritters, Port Wine Sauce.
Boiled Sugar-Cured Ham, Sauce a la Essence.
Boiled Leg of Mutton, Caper Sauce.
Roast Turkey, Cranberry Jelly.
Roast Loin of Beef au Jus.
Lobster Salad.
Roast Grouse, Dressed and Larded.
Roast Red Deer, Black Currant Jelly.
Mashed Potatoes.
French Green Peas.
Celery and Cheese.
Plum Pudding, Brandy Sauce.
Snow Pudding, Soft Custard.
Apple Pie, Lemon Pie.
Madeira Jelly.
Maraschino Cream.

Strawberry Ice Cream.
Apples, Oranges, Malaga Grapes, Nuts, Raisins.
Confectionery.
Coffee, Sauterne, Port, Claret, Sherry.

During the banquet, Ailsa's rink was introduced to the attendees with a quote from Robert Burns:

Her 'prentice han' she tried on man.
And then she made the lassies, O.

There was thunderous applause. Although many had heard about Ailsa's rink, most were shocked at how very young they were. Most observers doubted that they would be able to stand up against the older, sturdier Canadian women.

Ailsa's rink was then introduced to their opponents, a rather stern-looking group of women who had been rigorously vetted and selected as the four best women curlers in Canada. They appeared to be in their mid-to-late thirties. Finally, after more than two hours, the banquet ended. The four Scottish lassies, sated and exhausted, headed quickly for their rooms. The men stayed in the banquet hall to enjoy one more round of Canadian whisky and curling stories, a few of which may have actually been true. The Reverend Kerr had a story at the ready, as always. A sad story:

John Menzies had for years been recognized as the most reliable skip of the Burnfoot Curling Club; he was also an elder in the kirk, and a very worthy man, held in great respect in the community. One time, the occasion being the annual match between the Burnfoot Club and their old rivals of the Braehead, he was very unwilling to take his place in the rink, as one of his children was dangerously sick; but being hard pressed by his curling friends, and urged to go by his wife, who told him 'it would do him guid, and she could manage fine hersel,' he reluctantly took his place at the Tee-head, to contend with his old opponents of the Braehead Club. The game opened well, the two rinks were finely matched, and every man seemed to be in his best playing form, and it was a neck to neck struggle . . . when, just as John was about to play his stone in the last end but one, Jeanie, his wife, came on the ice, looking half distracted, and said to him, 'Come away hame, John, oor wee Jamie's died.' John paused in swinging his stone, he rested it on the ice at his foot, and without relaxing his grip of the handle, looked up to his wife, saying calmly, 'Hoots, woman, dinna mak sic an ado; yae bairn mair or less in a faimily is neither here nor there; gang yeer wa's hame, I'll no be lang.' She quietly withdrew, and he, taking another searching glance at the ice and at the directing broom, shot his stone with perfect aim, and proper force. It grazed the outlying stone, swung round inwards at the point of contact as on a pivot, and counted one more shot in that end. The Channel-Stane: Or Sweepings from the Rinks [John MacNair 1883].

Fortunately, the men did not convene a Curling Court after the banquet.

The newspaper the next morning announced the arrival of the Scottish delegation on its front page. It described them as "splendid specimens of Scottish architecture, somewhat angular, and in spots a little bulgy . . ." Hopefully, the description was of the Scottish men, not Ailsa's rink.

—◆—

The rules for the World Championship were clear and straightforward. Royal Caledonian Curling Club rules would apply. The games would be played only with Ailsa Craig granite stones. The men's and ladies' rinks would play five games each over the course of three days. The men's games would consist of ten ends each, the ladies' would be eight ends. The rink winning the majority of games would be declared the victor and proclaimed to be the best and keenest curlers in the world. One game for each of the four men's and two ladies' rinks would be played on Friday, two on Saturday, and either one or two on Sunday, if necessary. The president of the Halifax Curling Club, a Scotsman by birth, would serve as umpire. The Scots would be afforded one day's practice time before the tournament began.

The matches would all be played on Dartmouth Lake. The Halifax Curling Club deemed Dartmouth Lake to have the best ice and to be the most suitable for safely bearing the rinks and the anticipated large crowds. The ice was in splendid condition. Chocolate Lake was examined and determined to be satisfactory, but less so than Dartmouth Lake. The first games would be played on Friday, February 17th, commencing at noon.

There was one very significant difference between Scottish curling and Canadian curling as played in the Maritime Provinces. Because the outdoor ice in Canada was generally much, much thicker than the ice in Scotland, the Canadians had abandoned the use of the crampits which were widely used in Scotland for curlers to stand on when delivering the stones. The Canadians utilized hacks carved two or three inches into the ice surface to serve as footholds. Rather than playing with two feet on the crampit, one foot was positioned in the hack and the other was on the ice. Ailsa's rink had never played from hacks. It had a much different feel. Her rink had just one day on which to practice and make the adjustment. Fortunately, both Hugh Maclaren and the Reverend Kerr had played from hacks, and were able to provide instruction.

Late Friday morning, the Scottish curlers once again climbed onto horse-drawn sleighs, which would deliver them to Dartmouth Lake, where a crowd was already gathering. Again, as it was all along their odyssey from Edinburgh to Liverpool to Halifax, the curlers' procession was led by pipers. It turned out to be the best part of an absolutely horrible day for Ailsa's rink.

Ailsa's rink lost their first game to the Canadian women in spectacular fashion in front of a large assemblage of Canadians, including many of Sheenagh's relatives. Ailsa's rink was *soutered*, failing to score even a single point, and losing 11-0. At least the two rinks of Scottish men managed to score in their first games, losing 9-3 and 10-3. To the Canadians, it was affirmation of their vast superiority at the game. To Ailsa and Sheenagh in particular, but to Effie and Kirsty as well, it was unthinkable. They had come all of this way only to discover that they were simply no match for the Canadians. It could have completely broken their spirits. It was Hugh Maclaren who got the dispirited young women into a better frame of mind in time for the next day.

"The most important thing," he said, "is to believe in yourselves and in each other. Allow no negative thoughts or doubts to creep in. The reason you are here is because you are the best. All that remains to be done is to play like it."

"But we couldn't even score a single point against them," Effie said.

"It's not that you couldn't," Hugh replied. "It's that you didn't. Next game, you will."

He encouraged them, he consoled them, he let them get their disappointment out, he reminded them of how good they were, and he told them that one game is one game, and that the next one could be theirs if they were brave enough to take it. The Reverend Kerr chimed in by reciting *1 Corinthians 9:34*: "Know ye not that they which run in a race run all, but one receiveth the prize? So run that ye may obtain."

Ailsa's father's counsel almost succeeded. The lasses battled and summoned all of their skill and intensity, but fell short again in the second game on Saturday morning in front of an even larger crowd than the day before. Early on, they actually led the match, capitalizing on the Canadians' overconfidence, before the Canadians came back and earned an 8-6 victory. What might have been Ailsa's best chance to win even a single game had slipped away. She feared for herself, but just as much for Sheenagh, because now everything was all too real and impending. The thought of winning even one game seemed impossible, much less winning three.

Ailsa didn't really think too much about how the game itself had played out. That wasn't important now. Instead, she thought about her friend. Why had she allowed Sheenagh to get involved? Lucas had preyed on her, used her confidence and hubris against her, and she had been weak. Now, she and Sheenagh were facing the consequences.

Before the third, and possibly final, game on Saturday afternoon, Hugh Maclaren and the four young women again sat and talked. Ailsa and Sheenagh were terrified, much more so than Effie and Kirsty, and Ailsa's father could see it. He assumed that it was simply their fear and disappointment at the thought of not winning the championship. That was the least of it, though. He again worked on building back their confidence and resolve.

"Now," he began, "it is simply a question of which rink wants to win more badly. I believe that that is you. What do you think?" Hugh looked at each of the four lasses. No one said anything.

Finally, Sheenagh spoke. "It's us, Mr. Maclaren. It's us."

Hugh Maclaren smiled warmly at the young women. They could win, he told them, if they stuck together and trusted and believed in each other. They could face the moment and prevail. Ailsa tried to believe it and desperately needed to believe it. Sheenagh actually did believe.

Alone on a bench after lunch, Ailsa and Sheenagh sat silently, each thinking of nothing but what the next game meant for their earthly, and eternal, lives. "Sheenagh," Ailsa finally said. "I'm so, so sorry for what I've done to you. I didn't want any of this to happen. I shouldn't have ever told you about Lucas. I could have stopped this." Ailsa was sobbing. Effie and Kirsty saw them, but kept their distance.

"You have done nothing to me, Ailsa. Nothing. I decided to do this, not you. And I would do it again," Sheenagh said. Ailsa lifted her head at those words. It was Sheenagh's turn to be strong and to be the leader. She had learned so much about leadership and togetherness and strength from Ailsa over the years, and it was time to summon those things for her friend. "We're going to win, Ailsa. I know it and you know it. We're going to go out onto that ice and win. Those hens have no idea what's coming. Now clear your head and get ready. We're all counting on you to guide us through."

Hugh Maclaren's and Sheenagh's words worked. Down 2-0 after the first end, and facing both elimination and damnation, at least for Ailsa and Sheenagh, Ailsa's rink focused, fought, and climbed out of their hole with an intensity that their more experienced opponents had never before encountered. After seven ends, trailing 9-3, the Canadian women conceded the third match. There were stunned looks on the faces of the defeated women and their supporters who already had their celebration planned. Ailsa never so much as hinted at a smile. Somewhere in the crowd, disguised in some hideous way or another, Ailsa assumed, an unhappy Lucas Plotcok had been watching.

The fourth game, on Sunday morning, was the most fiercely contested yet. The Canadian women now knew that it was not, in fact, going to be as easy as they had come to believe, and that the Scottish women could match them shot-for-shot. The Canadians arrived at the ice with a renewed focus after their drubbing the day before. The championship was going to be decided by will as much as by skill. The game went back-and-forth, but Ailsa's rink, behind the most masterful game Sheenagh had ever played, won 8-7, evening the championship series at two games apiece. The final, deciding game would be played that afternoon.

Ailsa and Sheenagh knew that something momentous was going to happen that afternoon. They just didn't know what it might be. It would be something unbelievably wonderful or unspeakably tragic. Whatever it was going to be, at least they would be facing it together. They once again sat on their bench, each lost in an ever-changing cascade of emotions, bouncing from absolute terror to glorious hope. The championship match was imminent.

"What are you thinking about, Ailsa?" Sheenagh asked her friend.

"I'm thinking that we're going to do this. I'm thinking that it's going to be the best day ever for Canada, although they don't know it," Ailsa answered confidently, flashing a huge smile. "And for us, too." She paused for a second before adding, "We're going to walk out onto that ice and play the best game we've ever played. We're going to win. I know it and you know it." They were the same words that Sheenagh had used the day before. Both of them laughed, wanting and needing to believe.

The championship game came down to the final stone from Ailsa's rink. As word of the women's epic series had spread, the afternoon brought a crowd of more than 2,000 spectators, including Sheenagh's relatives. They were all watching the ladies' match, both rinks of Scottish men having lost their series three games to none. It had been a tense and taught battle, the ladies' rinks exchanging shots and points, the Canadians up, then Ailsa up, then the Canadians up again. The crowd, largely favoring the home team, cheered heartily and enthusiastically.

Wagers, still considered taboo, were in place. If the crowd only knew what was truly at stake, they would have been rooting for Ailsa, both for their own sakes and for their entire country.

Ailsa prepared to play her final stone, Sheenagh standing at the mark and shouting instruction and encouragement down the ice to Ailsa and the sweepers. Ailsa and Sheenagh made eye contact, and Sheenagh nodded. The crowd fell silent as Ailsa prepared to throw the stone which would determine the outcome. She positioned herself in the hack, oblivious to the crowd, drew her final stone back and then forward, and released it, her hand steady and her eyes fixed only on the target. It was a shot which Ailsa had practiced many times. She thought of nothing but the shot and the mark.

Ailsa's stone went roaring down the ice. The crowd was still hushed, four thousand eyes tracking Ailsa's stone. Lucas, in yet a new guise, was in the crowd, watching with them. He had a lot riding on this shot. Ailsa's stone held its line and speed, headed with precision for exactly where it was intended to go. The sooping by Effie and Kirsty was flawless. Ailsa's rink was going to gain the day! In just seconds, they were going to be world champions, and Lucas Plotcok would have to find somewhere else to ply his trade.

Just like that, it was over. As the stone slowed and began curling toward its winning spot, Lucas closed his eyes and concentrated. As he did, Ailsa's stone, even while clear of all of the other stones, suddenly shattered, fragments scattered everywhere, none of them anywhere near the mark. Ailsa, Sheenagh, Effie, and Kirsty gasped, stopping in place, staring at the pieces of granite strewn across the ice. The crowd, too, was dead silent, confused. Suddenly, it erupted. Canada had won! Hugh Maclaren and the Reverend Kerr began to push forward to protest; Lucas quickly disappeared from the crowd. Ailsa stood on the ice, staring at the pieces of her stone. Her legs wobbled. She could barely stand. She managed to catch Sheenagh's eye. What in the hell had just happened?

The officers of the Royal Caledonian Curling Club and the umpire huddled with Hugh Maclaren and the Reverend Kerr, whose protests would be to no avail. Rule 9 of the Royal Caledonian Curling Club's "Rules of the Game" was very clear and directly applicable to exactly the current situation:

> *All Curling Stones shall be of a circular shape. No stone must be changed throughout the game, unless, it happens to be broken, and then the largest fragment to count.*

Clearly, the largest fragment of Ailsa's final stone was far from the mark. The points in the eighth end were won by the Canadians, who were officially declared the victors in the deciding fifth game. Ailsa's rink had lost. Maclaren broke the news of the Royal Club's decision invoking Rule 9 to Ailsa, Sheenagh, Effie, and Kirsty. No one, it seemed, had a rational explanation for what had just happened.

Chapter 17

Renunciation

It only took an instant, though, for Ailsa to understand what had happened. Sheenagh knew, too. 'Twas the Devil that had smashed Ailsa's stone. There was no other possible explanation. Fine Ailsa Craig curling stones didn't just shatter on their own.

At the beef and greens banquet and the gathering of the curlers that night following the Ladies' Championship, every single person who spoke with Ailsa asked her what she thought had happened and offered their condolences over how the final match had ended. It was a pity, everyone agreed, even those who favored the Canadians. Ailsa knew exactly what had happened, of course, and why, but didn't say. She simply thanked everyone for their kind words. Ailsa, Sheenagh, Effie, and Kirsty could only stand and watch helplessly as the Canadian women formally accepted their trophy. The Scottish lasses knew that the trophy was rightfully theirs. It was only because of her love and respect for the game, and her father's and the Reverend Kerr's insistence, that Ailsa even managed to attend the banquet. She had no appetite for the beef and greens. She had no appetite for anything.

Ailsa and Sheenagh were particularly despondent over the outcome. They had made a terrible mistake. An irrevocable mistake. Lucas had lied to them, tricked them, and now they faced the prospect of eternal damnation, with no possible recourse. What were they going to do, try to haul Lucas into court for breaking the contract? Solicitor Paine had warned Ailsa that that would be folly.

Well into the evening, when Ailsa wanted nothing but to run to her room and cry, an elderly gentleman, stooped, frail-looking, disheveled, and walking with the aid of a cane, approached her. "I'm very sorry for your loss," he offered. Just like everyone else. "You are an extraordinary curler. As good as 'most any man I've seen. And I've been around for a long while." Ailsa took him for a veteran "knight of the broom" whose infirmities had finally vanquished him from the ice.

"Thank you, sir," Ailsa responded rotely. "You're very kind." She was so tired of hearing words of supposed comfort. They provided none at all. They simply made things worse. She just wanted to leave the banquet and lock herself in her room. She was ready to leave Canada, too.

The old man chuckled. "'Kind' is not a word often said of me." His eyes sparked to life.

Ailsa immediately recognized the eyes. She had looked into them many times before. "Lucas . . . " she finally said.

"It's so good to see you again, Ailsa. Especially on *terra firma*. I'm not really keen on riding the high seas," he smiled. "You must be exhausted. And very disappointed, I'm sure. You and Sheenagh both played magnificently. It certainly appeared that you were going to win until things went catawampus."

Ailsa looked around to see if anyone was listening. "We had a deal!" Ailsa admonished. The old man just smiled.

"Indeed, we did," the old man replied. "Indeed, we did. And a most unusual one at that. Unfortunately for you, though, you lost the championship and our little wager. Which means that I won. You are quite the worthy adversary, though, I must say. Sheenagh, as well. She played an extraordinary game, given the circumstances. But I just wanted to let you know how much I have enjoyed my time with you and that I very much look forward to working with both of you. In due time, of course, as per our contract. There is no hurry. No hurry at all. You have a long and fruitful life to look forward to."

"You broke the contract. You interfered with the outcome. Article Fifth of our contract – you were to 'in no way, form, shape, or manner interfere with, influence, effect, impact, alter, or manipulate the outcome,'" Ailsa protested. She had studied the contact so often that she had memorized its terms. "That's why my stone went a-flinders. You did it."

"Perhaps," the old man offered. "But you certainly can't tell anyone that now, can you, Ailsa? Who do you suppose would believe such a ridiculous thing? Why, they'd think you had gone stark mad. And it would display very poor sportsmanship to blame Old Clootie for your loss and deny your gracious hosts the full enjoyment of their victory. I'm afraid that it must forever remain our secret."

Ailsa knew that the old man was right. What was she going to do, run to the Royal Caledonian Curling Club and protest that the Devil Himself had smashed her stone in mid-journey because he didn't want her to win? It was a preposterous notion, and one which would not speak well of either Ailsa or of ladies' curling. The old man knew that Ailsa had nowhere to turn, no recourse, and that he would receive his bounty when the time finally came. The full, final ramifications of her loss were setting in deeper and deeper with Ailsa. The old man looked at her. His eyes seemed to glow. "It was nice talking with you," he said. "I'm afraid that I'll not see you again until your time comes. But be certain that I very much look forward to it. And, if it is any consolation, my dear, our time together might not be as bad as you imagine. There are some perquisites to being among my specially chosen ones. And remember, Sheenagh will be right there with you, if that is of any consolation." It was the cruelest thing he could have said, invoking Sheenagh. It was intentionally so. With that, the old man turned away.

And then something dawned on Ailsa. Something Lucas had told her shortly after they first met. "Lucas," Ailsa said to the old man as he began shuffling away. "May I ask you something?" Lucas was certain that Ailsa would propose yet a third wager, which he had no interest in considering. Firmly in possession of the rights to Ailsa's and Sheenagh's souls, he was not about to bargain them away. He had secured what he wanted – why would he put his spoils at risk? Lucas couldn't blame her for trying, though. He had long admired Ailsa's tenacity.

"What is it, Ailsa?" he asked impatiently. "Quickly, please. Our business is concluded. For now, at least."

"Well," Ailsa began, "you once told me that your Counterpart honours the contracts that you enter into with people like me, didn't you?"

"Yes," the old man answered. "It's an arrangement that we settled into long ago. It works out very satisfactorily for both of us."

"And you also told me that you had never breached one of your contracts, which was plainly a lie, wasn't it? I just watched you break one," Ailsa said. "Frankly, I very much doubt that it was the first time."

Being called a liar never sat well with Lucas. It was a sore spot, for he took great pride in being an honest businessman. "I beg your pardon, but I did not lie to you, Ailsa. Until this very day, I had never violated a single term of any contract with any person, including you. Not a single one. Then again, I had never entered into a contract in which the stakes were quite this high. I mean, another country that I would be barred from? Losing Scotland was bad enough. I could have lost a lot of lucrative business had you won and exiled me from Canada, too. You might say that I gave in to temptation, which is quite ironic when you stop to think about it. Now, is that all? I really must be going."

"Just one more thing, Lucas, if I may," Ailsa answered.

"Quickly, please," snapped the old man. "I have other pressing business to attend to."

"Certainly," Ailsa said, the beginnings of a smile forming. "I'm just wondering what your Counterpart is going to think about your little arrangement now that He's seen that you do not honour all of your contracts, only the ones that work to your advantage. Do you think that

He might wonder whether you are taking advantage of Him? Might He not think that you're actually stealing from Him? What if He was planning on taking Sheenagh and I for Himself?" Ailsa looked at the old man for any sign of concern. She thought that she might have detected one. "Do you think that He's still going to abide by your little understanding, or do you suppose that He might reconsider now that He knows how you are conducting your business? I mean, you claim that you've never been in this situation before. If that is true, then neither has your Counterpart."

Lucas hadn't considered the possibility. He had been working his contract business for so long, unimpeded even by his Counterpart, that he simply assumed that he would always be at liberty to continue it, free of all worries. The thought of being put out of business, at being forever consigned to taking only the leftovers after his Counterpart collected all of the prime souls, infuriated him. It wouldn't be fair. The mere notion was unnerving. He surely deserved some of the choice ones that he worked so hard to identify and bargain with. Lucas's face turned red. An eerie red. A shade of red which Ailsa had never seen before.

Ailsa saw Lucas's angst, she felt it, she loved it. She had never seen Lucas's confidence waver. She pressed on. "Is that a risk you really want to take, Lucas? I know that I wouldn't. But maybe He will overlook it, this time, anyway, and you'll be just fine. Who knows? It's just one breach, after all. Just two silly Scottish lasses. Everyone makes a mistake sometimes. Perhaps you could ask Him for forgiveness."

Lucas thought and thought. He still said nothing. Ailsa didn't relent. "Let's consider all of your options, Lucas, calmly and rationally. When my time comes, hopefully a long time from now, your Counterpart will have two options. First, He'll see that you made a contract with me, and He'll decide to honour it, just like always. That's certainly one possibility, I suppose. *Or*, He'll see that you've broken it, take me for Himself – and Sheenagh, too, of course – and put an end to your dishonest wheeling and dealing. I know that He would not appreciate being played the fool. No more contracts, no more haggling, no more having to prove yourself to get people to believe, no more trying to convince people to trust you, no more trips to a solicitor's office. Your life would actually be much simpler, if you stop and think about it. All you would have to do is wait for your Counterpart to make His selections and pick through the leftovers. Then, you'll have lost me, Sheenagh, all of Scotland, and who knows what He'll do about Canada. I must be quite a catch for you to risk all of that, Lucas. I'm very humbled. But I wonder if that's what you really want – a lifetime of leftovers."

Lucas was unsteady, his confidence and bravado gone. No matter how much he prized Ailsa and Sheenagh, it might simply be too big of a risk. What if his Counterpart *did* decide to put an end to their arrangement? Ailsa was right. He certainly wouldn't countenance being made the fool. What would He do after watching Lucas break one of his deals? There would certainly be consequences. No more bargaining, no more collecting some of the prime dearly-departeds. Why, the only thing left for Lucas to do would be to choose from the scraps left unclaimed by his Counterpart. What a horrible thought it was. His only real bit of say over who joined his ranks would be gone. He would spend eternity feeding off leftovers. He deserved better. It would be humiliating and it simply wouldn't do. Not even Ailsa Maclaren and Sheenagh Gillie were worth the risk. Lucas came to a conclusion that he detested.

"Alright, Ailsa. Enough. You win," Lucas said with disdain. "I renounce our contract and my claim to you or Sheenagh for all time." Lucas was agitated, fuming, even. Ailsa thought that she caught a whiff of sulphur as Lucas turned away.

"Lucas," Ailsa said. By now, she was far more composed than he. "All of Canada, too, right?" Sheenagh would be thrilled. It was an abasement the Devil had not known before. "Yes! That, too," he barked.

"B'gone now, Lucas," Ailsa commanded for the third and final time. "And get rid of that cane. You look ridiculous." And with that, the old man threw down his cane and was gone. Ailsa looked up at the ceiling. "You heard all of that, right?" she whispered.

Ailsa was bursting to tell Sheenagh the news. Sheenagh had been inconsolable ever since losing to the Canadians. She was upset about losing, of course, but that was the least of it. She had somehow consigned herself to an unimaginable eternity in hell. Sheenagh couldn't begin to comprehend what that might actually mean. Ailsa raced to find Sheenagh, who was sitting with Effie and Kirsty, who in turn were trying their best to comfort her, without any success. "May I speak with Sheenagh alone for a moment?" Ailsa asked the other two. It was more of a command than it was a question. After Effie and Kirsty left, Ailsa looked at Sheenagh, her eyes twinkling at being able to share her news. She took hold of Sheenagh's hands.

"Sheenagh, look at me. I just spoke with Lucas," Ailsa began. Sheenagh looked up. "We're free from him, Sheenagh! He's agreed to free us from the deal, even though we didn't win. It's over. We're done with him. He's gone. We never have to worry about him again."

Sheenagh didn't know what to think. "Why? How?" she finally managed to ask.

"I can be very persuasive, Sheenagh. You know that." Ailsa was beaming. "And guess what else? He agreed to leave Canada alone, to boot. We did it, Sheenagh! We actually did it." Ailsa threw her arms around Sheenagh and squeezed as hard as she could. It was as if they had actually won the championship.

After Ailsa's news sank in, Sheenagh finally asked, "What happened? What did you do?"

"I'll tell you the whole story someday, Sheenagh. I promise I will. Right now, though, can we not talk about Lucas anymore? I'm so sick of him."

<hr>

Back home in his realm, the Devil sat cogitating on his throne, his forked tail tucked between his legs, his horns regrown, and his hooves resting on the molten floor. Lucas's clothes hung in the corner. He let loose a howl. He was humiliated, disgraced – embarrassed, even. He had been outwitted by a mere mortal. *And by a woman, no less.*

The Devil occupied his time thinking about what had gone wrong. He had revealed too much. In his zeal to convince Ailsa who he was, he had said things he didn't need to say. Things that Ailsa didn't have to know. He vowed to be more judicious in the future. Other than to gloat, there was no reason why he had even gone to see Ailsa after her loss in Canada. He had allowed his ego to get the best of him. He had to torment her instead of simply enjoying his victory. The Devil took a small measure of consolation in the knowledge that people would continue to present a multitude of opportunities to avail themselves of his services.

Chapter 18
Two Deaths

It was March by the time that the curling ambassadors finally arrived back home in Scotland. Mercifully, no banquet awaited them. The voyage home was far less eventful for Ailsa than the one to Canada had been. There were no surprise introductions by strangers and only a few passing questions about the shattered curling stone. Spring was arriving, curling season was over, and the four lassies were eager to resume their normal lives, none more so than Ailsa and Sheenagh. Ailsa received a lot of letters from curlers throughout Scotland, women mostly, congratulating her for performing so well and bringing honour to the mother country. What they all really wanted to know was what Ailsa thought had happened in the final game, of course. Some proposed their own novel theories.

Ailsa eventually answered all of the letters, but not before writing a long one to Darcie Ross. She described for Darcie the Atlantic crossing, the banquets, the world championship, and her adventures in Canada. She wrote of all of those things without ever mentioning Lucas Plotcok. Ailsa asked about Darcie's married life with Murdock and about her work in the mills. She apologized for not writing more often, and promised to be more faithful in the future. Darcie responded with a long letter of her own in which she described her new life with Murdock. It was more wonderful than she had imagined. They were even beginning to talk of a larger family. Darcie wrote of visiting with each other again.

In June, at the dinner table, Hugh Maclaren mentioned the tragic collision of two steamships in the Firth of Clyde. The disaster had sunk the *Princess of Wales*, built by Barclay, Curle & Company, taking down with it three workers, who had not been found and were presumed dead. Ailsa ran to retrieve the newspaper. She found the story. It identified one of the three men as Murdock Ross, Darcie's husband of eleven months. It couldn't possibly be, Ailsa thought. How could it be?

Ailsa tried to imagine what Darcie must be going through, but knew that she couldn't possibly comprehend. She had no experience in dealing with death and this kind of grief and loss. She tried to write a letter to Darcie, but found it impossible to find the words. Each time that she started a letter, she read her words and tore up the paper. Finally, she understood that all she could say was how terribly, terribly sorry she was. And so she did. She also invited Darcie to get away and come visit her on the farm. It was a visit that would never come to pass.

As horrible as the news of Murdock's death at sea had been, even more unthinkable news would reach Ailsa barely a year later. It was August 9, 1889, and it was the worst day of Ailsa's young life. It was the day that she learned that Darcie was dead. The newspapers reported that the body of a young woman named Darcie Ross had been found atop the island of Ailsa Craig. She had been murdered, apparently. The authorities were investigating. Ailsa was devastated and in shock. There had to be a mistake. Just two years earlier, Ailsa had celebrated Darcie's wedding at St. Andrew's Cathedral in Glasgow. Less than a year later, Darcie was widowed when the *Princess of Wales* went down. They had been faithful friends ever since Darcie first wrote to Ailsa three years earlier.

Ailsa and Darcie had continued to write to each other after Murdock's death. Just six months after the accident, Darcie had left Glasgow to make a new life in Girvan, on the west coast of the Scottish mainland. Darcie explained that she simply needed to escape Glasgow and the looks of pity which seemed to always be directed her way. She didn't want pity and didn't want to be "Poor Widow Ross." She wanted to find peace and understanding. She enjoyed Girvan, and had made a new friend in Father O'Shaughnessy, who seemed to understand.

The last letter Ailsa received before learning of Darcie's death told of Darcie's excitement about going to live on the island of Ailsa Craig for the summer to cook for the quarrymen who worked there for Kay's Curling. Father O'Shaughnessy had arranged the job for Darcie. It was another means of escape from the unwanted attention she sensed from strangers for being widowed at such a young age and in such a tragic way, for her story had followed her to Girvan. Ailsa was so happy for her. Darcie even invited Ailsa to come and visit her on the island.

Now, at just twenty-one years old, Ailsa was again sitting in St. Andrew's Cathedral, this time attending her friend's funeral. Ailsa's mother went with her. So did Sheenagh, Effie, and Kirsty. How was any of this fair? Just a month ago, Ailsa had received the letter from Darcie about starting her work on Ailsa Craig, about how much she enjoyed working for the quarrymen, about tending to her garden on the island, and about how good it felt not to be stared at and pitied.

When Ailsa returned home from Darcie's funeral, there was another letter waiting for her. It was from Darcie, and had been written on August 5th, just two days before she was murdered. Darcie sounded so hopeful, so happy, so excited. Darcie wrote about how she would go to the ruins of an old chapel atop Ailsa Craig and read her Bible and pray for Murdock's soul, as well as for her own. She was keeping Ailsa in her prayers, too, she wrote. She sought peace and healing when she went there, and felt as though she were finally beginning to find some. She was looking forward to returning to the mainland when the summer was over and starting to build a new life. It was the most hopeful and at peace that Darcie had sounded since Murdock's death. Ailsa couldn't stop her tears as she read and re-read the letter. She kept looking at the date. Her mother sat with her, her arm around Ailsa's shoulder, and wept along with her until there were no tears left.

Chapter 19
The After-Years

The games in Canada in February of 1888 were the last ones that Ailsa, Sheenagh, Effie, and Kirsty ever played together. They were adults now, and their circumstances changed quickly. Shortly after returning home to Scotland, Effie fell in love and became engaged to Gavin Stirling. A short while later, they were married. Ailsa and Sheenagh were bridesmaids, while Kirsty served as Effie's maid of honor. Gavin Stirling had made clear to Effie that he expected her to spend her days tending to household responsibilities and to raising their children, of which he expected many. There would no longer be any time for curling, he assured her. Effie, very much in love, agreed that foregoing curling would be necessary as they started to raise their family. Effie never again threw another curling stone.

Kirsty's family left Musselburgh for Glasgow a year after the curlers returned from Canada. Her father's work took him to Glasgow, and the entire family went with him, including Kirsty. Kirsty continued to curl for many years, although not with Ailsa and Sheenagh. She simply lived too far away. She joined a ladies' curling club near Glasgow and became skip of her own rink, calling on the skills and leadership which she had learned so well from Ailsa.

Ailsa and Sheenagh, though, continued to curl together. Given their accomplishments and stature, the Musselburgh Curling Club, over the loud and vitriolic objections of John Carswell, admitted them into auxiliary membership. They were the first two women to be admitted to the club. One time, five years later, at another Scottish Ladies' Championship, Ailsa and Sheenagh's rink, now including Maesie Duncan and Aileen Muir, actually met Kirsty's rink in the championship game. It was the most fun that any of the young women ever had on the ice. Even given the stakes and their competitive spirits, Ailsa, Sheenagh, and Kirsty smiled and laughed and hugged each other throughout the entire match. After all, the three women – pioneers – forever shared a place in history as well as a bond which would never be broken.

For her twenty-first birthday, Hugh Maclaren presented Ailsa with a copy of James Taylor's recently-completed book about curling and its history, *Curling – The Ancient Scottish Game*. Little did Ailsa know that later writers on the subject would speak of her role in the sport's history. In reading the book, Ailsa came across this story about an unusual event in Kilmarnock:

> *The landlord of the Sun Inn, John Bryan by name, was a keen, keen curler, and missed no opportunity of enjoying the sport. On one occasion when the frost set in somewhat late, and there was only one bit of ice where a game could be had, Boniface went out at a very early hour in the morning to take a spell at the curling along with a blacksmith, a wee, black, towsy, ill-washed body, whom he had persuaded to accompany him. Bryan was a tall portly person of dignified appearance, and always wore ruffled shirts, and powdered hair with a pigtail. The contrast between him and his curling companion must have been somewhat striking. A collier who, on his way to the pit, was passing the pond where the pair were absorbed in their game, was so alarmed at the spectacle that he at once returned home with all speed, and informed his wife that 'he had seen a sicht that would keep*

> *him from going farther that day; he had seen Bryan o'*
> *the Sun Inn and the devil [curling] on the Auld Water.'*

Ailsa laughed at reading the account, for she knew that the Devil wasn't really a curler. She conjured up an image of Lucas as a blacksmith – dirty, wee, towsy, and ill-washed. She liked the image. Not as much as recalling him as a dowdy, middle-aged woman aboard the *Parisian*, but she liked it nonetheless.

⸻ ◆ ⸻

Not long after returning home from Canada, Ailsa was at the market doing her weekly shopping for her mother. Life was resuming a sense of normalcy. A vaguely familiar voice greeted her. "G'morning, Ailsa," the man said. "It's good to see you again." The familiar fear immediately gripped her. She had thought that she was finished with Lucas forever. She turned and saw Colin Gibson, the man she had danced with when Darcie had come to visit her in Musselburgh. Relief washed over her. The tension which had shot into her neck and shoulders dissolved.

Barely two years later, Ailsa and Colin were married. Colin worked in construction and had earned a reputation for being an extraordinarily hard worker and for the fine quality of his work. He was very supportive of Ailsa and her curling, and always went to watch her compete. He also became an expert in constructing artificial curling ponds, much more sophisticated than the primitive one built by Ailsa and her father. Colin learned how to build artificial ponds with concrete or tar and macadam bases. He also constructed coverings for his curling rinks to protect them from the elements. As curling in Scotland proliferated, Colin was hired by clubs around the country which wanted access to more frequent and reliable ice. Indoor curling rinks were still some time away, but artificial outdoor ponds were the rage, and Colin Gibson built the best.

Ailsa and Colin, shortly after their marriage, decided that there was no better place to start and raise a family than right on her parents' farm. They presented their idea to her parents, who needed no time at all to embrace it. What grandparents wouldn't want their future grandchildren living so close by? Colin set about his two building projects almost immediately. The first was selecting a spot and preparing the site for a house. Colin, along with Ailsa's father, settled on a location about 300 yards to the north of the existing house. Over the course of a year, Colin, Hugh, Ailsa, and Mrs. Maclaren, with the occasional help of some neighbors, meticulously erected and finished the new house. Colin even included a special shelf for Ailsa's curling trophies and medals. Magic, now entering middle age, seemed glad to have Ailsa home.

The other project for Colin was building an improved curling pond on the site of the existing one. While the existing pond was more than adequate, it wasn't built to last. After a few years, worms and weeds began to ruin the clay and earth base. Colin reworked the base of the pond with concrete, which would hold up for much longer. If Colin and Ailsa were going to raise a family of curlers, they would need a better pond to play on.

Colin also had something very special that he would place at the new curling pond. He commissioned a mason to create a marble marker:

On this site in 1880, at the age of 12, Ailsa Maclaren,
4-time Scottish Ladies' Curling Champion, constructed a
curling pond with her own hands.

Before their marriage, and during its early years, Ailsa continued to curl on a rink with Sheenagh and the two new teammates who had replaced Effie and Kirsty. Even after the birth of her first two sons, they competed. By the time that Ailsa retired from competitive curling at the age of twenty-nine, she had three young boys at home, along with four Scottish Ladies' Championship trophies. Sheenagh retired then, too. They both knew that it was time.

There was another matter that Ailsa wanted to attend to. There was a trip that she needed to take. She called on her father to fulfill a promise that he had made to her when she was a young girl. Ailsa asked him to take her to the island of Ailsa Craig, the island from which Ailsa had derived her name, the island that is home to the blue hone and common green granite used to make curling stones, and the island atop which her dear friend Darcie Ross had been murdered. Hugh Maclaren knew that Ailsa wanted to visit the island for all of those reasons, but especially the last. He called on his contacts and made the arrangements for them to visit Ailsa Craig.

On August 7, 1892, Hugh and Ailsa embarked on the long train ride from Edinburgh to Girvan. They left before the sun rose. Already, it was hot and humid. It was three years to the day since Darcie's murder. Through his many curling connections, and being the father of Scotland's most decorated lady curler, Ailsa's father was able to arrange for a boat ride from Girvan to Ailsa Craig, ten miles at sea to the west, on one of Kay Curling Company's vessels. A team of twenty quarrymen who lived on the island during the summer was engaged in harvesting curling stone granite. Ailsa and Hugh Maclaren were welcomed to Ailsa Craig by the foreman, John Greenlaw. John Greenlaw knew to a near-certainty who had killed Darcie Ross. Ailsa and Hugh were completely unaware of that fact, and of the fact that Greenlaw had been instrumental in making sure that the killer evaded punishment.

Greenlaw gave the visitors a quick history of the island, pointing out the quarries, lighthouse, castle ruins, living quarters, and foghorns. He pointed out the cave where his men had discovered two guano-covered human skeletons. He let them watch some of the mining operations from a distance. Finally, Ailsa asked, "Can you show us how to get to the summit? To the old chapel?" Greenlaw had not been there for three years. Intentionally. He had no desire to ever go up there again. Nevertheless, he knew the path well and pointed it out. "Keep an eye out for the rats. Nasty little *bassas*. There are quite a few of them," Greenlaw advised.

Ailsa and her father began the slow, winding walk to the top of the island. The air was thick and still. They came to what clearly at one time had been the chapel, although not much of it remained. Ailsa was lost in the horrifying thought of what had happened to Darcie on the very place where she stood. She almost wished that she had never come. She knelt down with her father and said a silent prayer for her friend. When she stood, she reached into her pocket and withdrew a rose petal. She had taken it from one of the flowers at Darcie's wedding to keep as a momento. Ailsa placed the petal on the ground. "We can go now, father," she said, taking his hand.

They made their way down from the chapel together and to the dock, where the boat was waiting to return them to the mainland. Ailsa and her father boarded the boat without speaking. Hugh Maclaren knew that Ailsa needed to be alone with her thoughts, and he went to speak with some of the other men. As the boat made its way across the firth, Ailsa stood at the railing, gazing back to the top of Ailsa Craig. She reached into her pocket and withdrew the gold necklace with the curling stone pendant. She looked at the inscription on the back. She had brought it with her so that she could throw it into the sea and be done with it forever. She remembered how she had felt when Lucas had given it to her, how in love she had been. It really was beautiful. She could never again wear it, she knew. She wasn't quite ready to throw it away, either. She slipped the necklace back into her pocket.

Ailsa, Sheenagh, Effie, and Kirsty's true and lasting legacy was that the first women's bonspiel, the Royal Caledonian Curling Club's Scottish Ladies' Championship, and the World Championship in Canada had combined to create an explosion of interest and participation in women's curling in Scotland. Their exploits were noted, usually with approval, by newspapers around the country. No longer content with only ice skating for winter recreation, hundreds of women took to playing the "manly Scottish game." It would take a few years before the Royal Caledonian Curling Club and its member clubs fully embraced their participation. Ailsa's rink's contribution was of great significance, but they were by no means alone.

It was, ironically, a Canadian woman, Henrietta Gilmour, who helped to lead the way in Scotland. Henrietta Gilmour didn't need to change her name when she married John Gilmour, a wealthy Scot engaged in the Canadian timber trade, since John Gilmour was her first cousin. Henrietta Gilmour left Canada with her new husband, and the couple settled in Montrave House on an estate in Fife owned by John Gilmour's father. John Gilmour was an avid curler and had a curling pond constructed on the estate several years after Ailsa and Hugh Maclaren had built theirs. The Gilmours' curling pond was much larger, suitable for use by an entire curling club, not just four girls.

As persons of wealth and influence, and now proprietors of their own curling pond, the Gilmours formed the Lundin and Montrave Curling Club in 1885. It was the first curling club in Scotland which admitted both men and women as full members, and was the first club with women members to be accepted into the Royal Caledonian Curling Club. Henrietta Gilmour was one of those members. It was not, however, the first curling club *exclusively* for women to join the

Royal Club. That honour belongs to the Hercules Ladies Curling Club, formed as an adjunct to the exclusively-male Hercules Curling Club. The Hercules Ladies Curling Club was granted membership into the Royal Club in 1895. The Boghead Ladies Curling Club followed in 1897, followed by the Balyarrow Ladies Curling Club in 1898 and the Cambo Ladies Curling Club in 1899.

It was Henrietta Gilmour, however, who had the greatest influence on the growth of women's curling. She had both the time and resources to travel throughout Scotland, having formally become Lady Henrietta Gilmour in 1897, playing matches against other women wherever she could arrange them. Almost invariably, her rink won. For her influence and accomplishments, Lady Henrietta Gilmour was one of only two women, out of sixty-one persons, included in the painting *Curling at Carsebreck*, commissioned by the Royal Caledonian Curling Club in celebration of its diamond jubilee in 1898. The other woman was Mrs. Maxwell Durham, the first president of the Boghead Ladies Curling Club. Ailsa Maclaren was not included in the painting.

Henrietta Gilmour and Ailsa Maclaren were fierce rivals on the ice. Together, they dominated ladies' curling in Scotland for more than a decade. They also grew to be good friends off of it, despite the fifteen-year difference in their ages and their different social classes. Between the first Scottish Ladies' Championship in 1887 and the last one that Ailsa and Sheenagh competed in in 1896, the two rinks met each other for the title seven times, Ailsa's rink winning four times and Gilmour's winning three. On two occasions, Henrietta Gilmour invited Ailsa and Colin to stay at her estate and to curl on her pond. She also granted Ailsa an honorary membership in the Lundin and Montrave Curling Club. One of the earliest known photographs of women curling depicts Henrietta Gilmour and Ailsa standing side-by-side at the tee, besoms in hand.

Chapter 20
A Very Secret Secret

Sheenagh would be the first of the four members of Ailsa's rink to pass away. She and Ailsa shared a lifelong friendship, a unique place in curling history, and one incredible secret. Long, long ago, the ruthlessness of age had forced Sheenagh to give up curling. Through it all, she and Ailsa remained dear and trusted friends, sharing all of life's grandest and worst moments – weddings, children, illness, loss of parents – and the death of Sheenagh's oldest son, Stewart.

Stewart, at the age of twenty-three, volunteered to join the Scottish army shortly after Great Britain declared war on Germany at the onset of World War I. He was assigned to a unit which, with little training and even less experience, would be sent to fight the Germans in France. On July 1, 1916, the Battle of the Somme began, a battle that would last for five bloody, horrific months and leave more than 300,000 people dead. Stewart was one of the "Ladies from Hell," a nickname bestowed by Germans on the kilted Scottish soldiers. He was also one of the 19,240 British soldiers who died that day in France.

As the assault began on the morning of July 1st, British soldiers were sent on foot toward the heavily fortified German defenses. The Allied commanders had grossly underestimated the German fortification, subjecting their soldiers to overwhelming artillery and machine gun fire from the trenches. It was a turkey shoot for the Germans, and Stewart was one of the very first casualties.

Sheenagh didn't receive the news until several weeks later. News that no parent should ever hear. She never fully recovered from the loss of Stewart. Her belief that she could do anything she set her mind to was gone, because for the one thing that she wanted to do – the only thing she desperately wanted to do – bring Stewart back, she was powerless. Her grief was partly because Stewart was never returned to Scotland, but was buried in a military cemetery on the Somme. Stewart didn't belong in France, he belonged in Scotland, where Sheenagh could visit his grave and be with him and talk to him. He should be at home with his family, not buried far, far away amongst a legion of fallen strangers.

Knowing that the end would soon come for Sheenagh, her family, at Sheenagh's request, invited Ailsa to come and see her for one final time. It was difficult for Ailsa, who was now forced to use a cane to walk, which she detested. Her body, which had spent months digging and moving rocks to build her curling pond, which had delivered curling stones as well as any man, and which had borne three children, now mocked her with its frailty. Nevertheless, Ailsa was there the very next day. Sheenagh's family gave them some time alone.

As best they could, with Sheenagh lying in bed and speaking in a whisper, the lifelong friends reminisced one last time about their lives together. They talked very little about curling, but about all of the other wonderful times that they had shared. Random things, silly things, long-forgotten things, the kinds of things that make for a well-lived life. Of course, they talked about Stewart, too. Ailsa couldn't recall a conversation in which they had not talked about Stewart. They spoke not a word about Lucas or any of that, until Ailsa finally said, "Do you see this cane, Sheenagh? Guess where I got it." Sheenagh offered only a shrug and a soft grunt. "I got it from Lucas in Canada. He left it behind after I told him that he looked ridiculous with it. I took it and brought it home with me. It turns out that it's come in quite handy. I guess he didn't know that he was doing me a favour." Both women chuckled, Ailsa more heartily than Sheenagh.

After a short silence, Sheenagh finally said, "Well, Ailsa, I guess I'm going to find out first."

Ailsa didn't know what her friend meant. "Find out what?" she asked.

"You know, Ailsa, whether Lucas has kept his word." Sheenagh smiled ever-so-slightly and weakly before offering, "Goodbye, Ailsa." Sheenagh closed her eyes. Ailsa slowly rose from her chair beside Sheenagh. She bent over and kissed her on the forehead.

"Goodbye, Sheenagh. I love you." Ailsa picked up her cane, steadied herself, and left Sheenagh for the final time.

⬥

Ailsa and Colin's oldest son, Graeme, had graduated from Edinburgh Law School with distinction and embarked on his legal career. Ailsa and Colin were so proud. Soon after beginning his career, Graeme entered into a partnership with the aging Pickering Paine, with an understanding that Graeme would take over the practice upon Paine's retirement. That day finally arrived. Ailsa was not happy about the arrangement, but had no real say in Graeme's professional life.

Shortly after Pick's retirement, Graeme undertook the task of sorting through all of Pick's files and deciding which needed to be kept and which could finally be disposed of. Most were decades old and of no further use. There were thousands of files, as Pick kept almost everything from his forty years of practice. Each day, Graeme tried to devote an hour or so to the chore. Pick had meticulously labeled and alphabetized his files. Some were quite large, others only a page or two. They all still reeked of decades-old pipe tobacco smoke, which had permanently infused the paper.

More than halfway through the undertaking, Graeme reached the "P" files, and then came to one labeled, "Plotcok, Lucas." The file was in a brown envelope, closed with a wax seal. Very few of the files which Graeme had reviewed were sealed, Last Wills and Testaments mostly, to be opened upon the testator's demise. Graeme broke the wax seal and removed the contents. There were several pages of notes, in Pick's unmistakable handwriting, along with a signed contract. Graeme began reading. "The Party of the First Part, Lucas Plotcok [hereinafter "Lucas Plotcok"], being the Devil Himself, also know as, including, but not limited thereto, inter alia, Satan, Lucifer, the Deil, Beelzebub . . ." Graeme was puzzled, yet fascinated. It didn't make any sense. What could it possibly mean, writing a contract for the Devil? He continued reading. "The Party of the Second Part, Ailsa Maclaren [hereinafter "Ailsa Maclaren"], an unmarried adult woman currently residing in Musselburgh, Scotland . . ." His mother? Graeme had no idea that his mother had ever had any dealings with Pick. He had even less of an idea why she might be party to what professed to be a contract with the Devil.

He continued reading, now even more confused as to what it could possibly mean. He wasn't confused by the legal terminology or jargon, but rather by the notion of his mother thinking that she was actually making a contract with the Devil. What had she been thinking all those decades ago? Had she been ill? Tricked, perhaps? And what was Pick thinking? Was it an elaborate ruse planted by Pick as a joke, knowing that Graeme would find it? Graeme returned to the cabinet and found a second "Plotcok, Lucas" file, similarly sealed. Again, he broke the seal and began reading. The terms were nearly identical, except that they also implicated his mother's friend, Sheenagh Gillie.

Graeme, of course, knew all about his mother's curling exploits, the Scottish Ladies' Champtionship, and the World Championship in Canada, but not about *this*. Who else knew about the contracts? Who, exactly, was this Lucas Plotcok? He had never heard the name. Graeme had to find out. He would talk to Pick first. For the rest of the afternoon, Graeme did nothing but sit in his office – Pick's old office – read and re-read the contracts, and think.

The next day, Graeme paid an unannounced visit to Pick at Pick's home. The retired solicitor greeted him at the door. "Hello, Graeme. It's good to see you, my friend. I've been wondering when you would finally be coming to see me," Pick said. "I've been expecting you for some time. Frankly, I thought that you would have come months ago."

"What do you mean?" Graeme asked.

"You've come to ask about your mother, haven't you?" Pick asked. There was no need to make small talk or reminisce. They both knew why Graeme was there.

"Yes. I need for you to tell me what it means," Graeme answered. He stepped into Pick's home, which smelled of decades of pipe tobacco smoke, both fresh and ancient, like his office always had.

"Have a seat, please, Graeme. Would you care for a drink before we start?" Pick offered.

"No, thank you," Graeme answered. Pick poured one for himself anyway. The two men sat. "Why don't I just tell you the whole story, beginning to end, as best as I can recollect," Pick offered. "Save your questions for the end." Pick began by relating the story of the visit decades ago when Ailsa and Lucas Plotcok first arrived at his office. Pick narrated the story in vivid detail, as if it had happened very recently. He remembered what each one looked like and wore. Some parts of the conversation he recited verbatim. Graeme simply let him tell the story, as Pick had suggested. Pick concluded by saying, "I have neither seen nor heard from either party for over thirty years."

When Pick was finished, Graeme asked, "And you believed them? You can't possibly have believed them. You actually believed that Lucas Plotcok was the Devil Himself?" Pick removed his spectacles and cleaned the lenses, a ritual which Graeme was intimately familiar with. Pick was thinking about his answer.

"What I believed was of no consequence. My only concern was in providing the service that they requested. And that was paid for up front, I should add. I made certain of that," Pick answered.

"I'm asking you, as we sit here now, whether you believe that Lucas Plotcok was who he claimed to be," Graeme pressed.

"I simply don't know the answer to that, Graeme. I simply don't. From all appearances, he was simply a well-dressed, well-mannered, normal-looking young man. But what I do know is that your mother certainly believed that it was true. And I can also assure you that she was well and very cogent. I had no doubts about her mental state. None whatsoever. I don't know why she believed that Lucas was the Devil, but I have no doubt that she did. No doubt whatsoever. She was deadly serious throughout the entire matter," Pick explained. Taking a sip, he added, "But I hope for her sake that she was wrong. As you know, she did not win the World Championship in Canada."

"Yes, I know," Graeme said. The two men stood. "Does anyone else know about this, Pick?"

"Not from me, Graeme. I would have to be mad to have told the story to anyone. I had a respectable practice to run. And I always took confidentiality very seriously, as you well know," Pick answered. "Tell me Graeme, was the seal on the envelope intact?"

"It was," Graeme answered. "I broke it."

"Good," said Pick. "Then we can be fairly sure that no one else knows. Unless your mother said something, which would surprise me. I can't vouch for Sheenagh Gillie. I never met her."

"Thank you, Pick. It was good to see you again."

"It was good to see you, too, Graeme," Pick replied. "Please give my best to your mother. I liked her very much."

Graeme visited his parents at least once a week, and on his next visit, only his mother was at home. Graeme needed to ask the question and to hear his mother's answer, although it would be very uncomfortable for both of them. Ailsa sensed that something particular was on her son's mind. Finally, as they were talking and enjoying their tea, Graeme asked, "Mother, I have to ask you something." For some reason, Ailsa knew what the question was going to be. "Who is Lucas Plotcok?" Even though she was expecting it, hearing Graeme ask made her body stiffen. She didn't like hearing the name, especially from her son. "How do you know?" she asked in resignation. "Did Paine tell you?"

Her son related the story of sorting through Solicitor Paine's files and finding the two contracts. Ailsa silently cursed Paine for keeping them. She had assumed, or at least hoped, that they were destroyed years ago. "Tell me everything, mother," Graeme said calmly. Reluctantly, but in minute detail, Ailsa began. She remembered every detail and every conversation she had ever had with Lucas. "I first met Lucas at one of your father's bonspiels, in February of 1886." For twenty straight minutes, Ailsa related everything from that moment through the last time that she had seen him, as an old man, following the World Championship in Canada. She even told Graeme about the cane.

Graeme took everything in. The story was nearly identical to the one Pick had related, although Pick only knew a small fraction of it. His mother actually looked relieved after telling the story. She had never told it to anyone other than Sheenagh. "Do you believe it, mother? Do you actually still believe that Lucas Plotcok was the Devil Himself?" Graeme asked.

"I do, Graeme. I believe that it is all true." As much as he tried, Graeme couldn't believe it. But he could tell that his mother surely did.

"Why?" Graeme asked. "Why do you believe it? It's not possible."

"It's more than possible, Graeme. It's all true." Ailsa could tell that her son didn't believe her, and she didn't like it. Ailsa went on to remind Graeme about how his father had rescued the boy who fell through the ice, about Lucas's appearance as a woman on the *Parisian*, and about the old man with the cane in Canada. "But honestly, Graeme, it was the eyes. The eyes were the same every time."

"Who else knows about this?" Graeme asked.

"No one. Absolutely no one other than Sheenagh, Paine, and now you, unfortunately," Ailsa answered. "And it has to stay that way, Graeme. No one can ever know. No one. Ever."

"What about father?" Graeme asked. "Shouldn't he know?"

"No! Absolutely no one else. I need you to promise it to me, Graeme. Promise me that you will never tell anything at all to anyone." Ailsa stared directly at Graeme. "Promise me, now." Graeme looked at his mother. Even though she was begging him, she was also commanding him.

"I promise, mother. On our family's honour, I will never tell anyone."

<hr>

Nine years passed. Sheenagh was gone. Pick, as well. Hugh Maclaren and Mrs. Maclaren, too, had passed. Ailsa was spending her final days with Colin in their home on the Maclaren farm. Graeme was visiting, sitting next to his mother's bed. As her time grew closer, at the gloaming, Ailsa asked her son, "Have you kept your promise, Graeme?"

He looked into his mother's now clouded eyes. "I have, mother. And I always will."

Afterword

Reading historical fiction presents some unique challenges, the most significant of which is trying to discern, amongst all of the people and events, which parts of the story are "historical" and which parts are "fiction." For the author, who already knows the answers to those questions, the task is easier – find some historical places, events, and people and weave them into a story, or weave a story around them. Not that writing a novel is easy – I can assure you that it isn't – but at least the author knows what is real and what is simply a product of imagination.

As to the characters in this story, almost all are entirely fictional. Ailsa Maclaren, Hugh Maclaren, Mrs. Maclaren, Sheenagh Gillie, Effie Lawrie, Kirsty Barnett, John Carswell, William Beveridge, Darcie Ross, Murdock Ross, Pickering Paine, Colin Gibson, John Greenlaw, Sheenagh's son Stewart, and Graeme Gibson are all fictional. Three of those characters – Darcie Ross, Murdock Ross, and John Greenlaw appear in much larger roles in my prior curling-centric novel, *The Stones of Ailsa Craig*. The exceptions, in order of their appearance, are Her Majesty Queen Victoria, the Reverend John Kerr, Sir John Gilmour and Lady Henrietta Gilmour, and Mrs. Maxwell Durham.

Her Majesty Queen Victoria was the Queen of the United Kingdom of Great Britain and Ireland for more than 63 years, from 1837 to 1901. Her reign roughly defines the contours of the Victorian Era. It was Queen Victoria who bestowed the title "Royal" on the Grand

Caledonian Curling Club in 1843 after viewing a demonstration of the sport on the wooden floor at Scone Palace and actually giving it a try herself. Her "delicate arm" was reported to make that attempt at throwing a curling stone unsuccessful.

The Reverend John Kerr was one of the most notable Scottish curling figures of the late-nineteenth and early-twentieth centuries. He played the game, promoted the game, compiled an extensive history of the game, and chronicled the game. During the Scottish mens' goodwill tour of Canada and the United States in 1903, the first official curling delegation sent by the Royal Caledonian Curling Club, the *St. Paul Dispatch* described the Reverend Kerr as follows:

> *The most striking figure among them is the Captain of the team. He is the Rev. John Kerr, minister of Dirleton Parish, East Lothian. He is a man of splendid physique, fifty years of age, six feet tall, with the shoulders of a Hercules, and weighs 224 pounds. He said in his broad Scotch accent, when asked how many pounds he weighed, 'I am sixteen stones; I don't know how much that is in pounds.'*

Like all of us, Kerr was both a product and a victim of his times. He was a highly educated man with a master's degree in divinity from Glasgow University, a protestant minister, sportsman, and author of three seminal books about curling – *History of Curling: Scotland's Ain Game; Curling in Canada and the United States: A Record of the Tour of the Scottish Team 1902-03;* and *Ailsa Craig: Its History and Natural History.* He was also an unabashed European imperialist. His recounting of the Scottish curlers' tour of the United States contains this unfortunate passage:

At this hotel [in Chicago] we found that all the waiters were 'darkies,' and it must be confessed that the feeling was rather 'eerie' in having one's food served all round from Ethiopian hands. The 'black men,' however, are very efficient at their work, and if any one among them makes a blunder at any time, his neighbours seem most unmerciful in their condemnation of him as a 'stupid old nigger.'

The Reverend Kerr, more than perhaps anyone else of his generation, promoted and elevated the sport of curling in Scotland. His historical accounts and writings are still referenced today, as is his meticulous mapping of the island of Ailsa Craig.

Henrietta Gilmour was the most famous woman curler of the late 1800s and early 1900s. Her influence on the rise in popularity and acceptance of curling by women is almost impossible to overstate. She was truly one of the pioneering curling ladies. Henrietta Gilmour is pictured in what is believed to be the oldest photograph of women curling. As an example of the blending of history and fiction, Henrietta Gilmour really is in the picture. Ailsa Maclaren, who is entirely fictional, is not, despite being portrayed as such in the story. Henriettal Gilmour was able to exert her enormous influence largely because of her wealth and social status.

Henrietta Gilmour was a Canadian by birth. She married her first cousin, John Gilmour, a wealthy Scot working in the Canadian timber trade, and returned to Scotland with him. They took up residence in Montrave House, on John Gilmour's father's estate.

Henrietta Gilmour, together with her husband, founded the Lundin and Montrave Curling Club in 1885 and built a large curling pond on their estate in Montrave, which served as the club's pond. The Lundin and Montrave Curling Club is the first club known to have admitted both men and women into membership. When John Gilmour received a baronetcy from Queen Victoria in 1897, Henrietta Gilmour became *Lady* Henrietta Gilmour, with yet further stature and influence.

Sir John Gilmour eventually became president of the Royal Caledonian Curling Club in 1912. Upon the expiration of his term in 1913, the Gilmours presented two trophies to the Royal Club. The Sir John Gilmour Cup, as it would come to be called, was presented as follows:

> *Sir John Gilmour, as President, should present to the Royal Club a Trophy, value £25, open only to the Lady Members in Scotland and England. The match to be played either in the open or in an Ice Rink. The Trophy if won three times by the same Club, not necessarily in succession, becomes the property of the Club.*

The Lady Gilmour Cup was announced at the same time:

> *Lady Gilmour, wife of the current President, who is a Canadian lady and has always taken the greatest interest in the game of Curling, and especially in Canada, desires also to present a Trophy to the value of £25, to be played for by the lady Members of the Royal Club in Canada . . . In presenting these Prizes both Sir John and Lady Gilmour have in view the hope that as a result, greater interest may be taken in the game by ladies.*

The first Sir John Gilmour Cup was won by the Balerno Ladies Curling Club in 1914. The trophy, naturally, was presented by the Reverend Kerr. The competition for the first Sir John Gilmour

Cup, played at the Haymarket Ice Rink in Edinburgh, was the first competition exclusively for women that was conducted under the auspices of the Royal Caledonian Curling Club. It took place twenty-seven years after the fictional bonspiel won by Ailsa Maclaren in 1887. That is another example of the license granted to the writer of historical fiction. Due largely to the outbreak of World War I, the Sir John Gilmour Cup was not contested for again until 1925. When the Edinburgh Ladies won the cup for the third time in 1928, it became their property under the terms of Sir John Gilmour's gift, and was given to their skip, Mrs. J. E. Crabbie. In Canada, the first Lady Gilmour Cup was won by the Heather Curling Club in 1914. The cup is still awarded today to the winner of the Canadian Branch of the Royal Caledonian Curling Club's Mixed Championship.

Lady Henrietta Gilmour is one of only two women, out of sixty-one people, included in the Royal Caledonian Curling Club's 1898 painting, *Curling at Carsebreck,* commissioned for its Diamond Jubilee. The Reverend Kerr, of course, is also depicted. As mentioned, the Reverend Kerr was ubiquitous in Scottish curling.

The last of the real people appearing in the story is Janetta Durham, or Mrs. Maxwell Durham, who was the first president of the Boghead Ladies Curling Club. The Boghead Ladies Curling Club was the second ladies' club to be granted membership in the Royal Caledonian Curling Club, in 1897. She is the second woman, along with Henrietta Gilmour, depicted in *Curling at Carsebreck.*

Readers are left to decide for themselves whether they believe that Lucas Plotcok, the incarnate *Devil Himself*, is real or fictional. His recitation to Ailsa of what happens in the afterlife, and of his arrangement with his Counterpart, however, should be viewed with a healthy dose of skepticism.

All of the books mentioned and cited, as well as all of the newspaper accounts of events, are real. Events such as the sinking of the steamer the *Princess of Wales* really happened, although there was no one named Murdock Ross on board. The *Parisian* was a real ship and really did miss the distress call from the *Titanic* after it struck the iceberg on the night of April 15, 1912. The sermon quoted in Chapter 13 was actually delivered before the Grand National Curling Club in New York City by the Reverend S. B. Possiter, D.D. on January 9, 1896. And, yes, there really was an Asylum Curling Club in Canada.

The actual history of women's curling is far more complicated than portrayed in the story, and has played out on a significantly different timeline. What is no doubt true is that women were not generally encouraged or oftentimes even permitted to play in the 1700s and 1800s, although there are the occasional accounts of times when women in Scotland did play. There was the 1740 match in Nithsdale between the married and unmarried women; the 1826 bonspiel between the "blooming damsels" in Sanquhar; and the 1841 match in Buittle between the married and unmarried, all cited in Chapter 3. While there are hundreds, if not thousands, of accounts of men's games during that time period, the fact that there are only a handful about women speaks to the rarity of women playing.

David B. Smith, in his book, *Curling: An Illustrated History* (1981), claims that the first all-women curling match was held around 1823:

> *The earliest recorded all-female match is to be found in the pages of The Dumfries Weekly Standard of 7 January 1823, where a match at Sanquhar 'within these very few years' is noted in which 'the sides were pretty numerous, and comprised exclusively of women – the wives against the lasses.' After the match the curleresses retired to a tavern. 'How the husbands relished this unusual display of masculine prowess, and convivial dispositions, on the part*

of the wives, need not be enquired into. A similar occurrence has not happened since.'

A more detailed and accurate description of the history of women's curling, particularly in Scotland, would begin around the middle of the nineteenth century and would roughly be as follows. That history is difficult to reconstruct, though, because comprehensive information on the subject is not easy to come by. The history of women's curling is found mostly in snippets, gathered from a few scattered sources, and is almost always buried within a different story.

What seems fair to deduce is that women's curling began to gain acceptance and increased popularity toward the latter part of the 1800s. The Scottish Curling Trust is in possession of watercolor paintings of Scottish women curling in Eglinton from 1859 and 1860. One of those paintings is shown on the cover of this book. It is one of the earliest, if not *the* earliest, depictions of women playing the game. Perhaps the oldest photograph of women curling, from 1895, shows Henrietta Gilmour herself, along with three other women, standing around the tee with curling stones and besoms.

When women first began to play in any significant numbers, they did so as a social or recreational activity, not a competitive one. Women were not expected to excel at the game, and they were still considered too weak and fragile to play the game as well as men, despite the fact that they "could dig potatoes, scrub floors, chop wood, feed chickens, and milk cows" according to *The Stone Age: A Social History of Curling on the Prairies* (Vera Pezer 2003). Their more common roles remained as food preparers at men's bonspiels or as spectators. Some curling clubs even constructed separate viewing areas away from the men for women. Separate, but equal, if you will.

It was not until 1895 when the first all-women's curling club in Scotland, the Hercules Ladies Curling Club, with eighteen members, was admitted into membership by the Royal Caledonian Curling Club. The logical conclusion is that by that date, it was no longer considered unusual or taboo for ladies to be playing the game. Hercules was followed into membership by the Boghead Ladies Curling Club, with sixteen members, in 1897; the Balyarrow Ladies Curling Club, with eleven members, in 1898; and the Cambo Ladies Curling Club, with fourteen members, in 1899. At the time, the ladies' clubs were not permitted to compete against men's clubs, only against other ladies' clubs. The Montreal Curling Club claims that the first women's curling club anywhere in the world, the Ladies Montreal Curling Club, was formed in 1894, making *it* the oldest women's curling club in the world.

The *Dundee Courier* of February 12, 1895, mentions a ladies' match in which both Henrietta Gilmour from Montrave and the ladies from Hercules played against each other. The report read as follows:

> *MONTRAVE v. HERCULES – A friendly match was played on Montrave Pond yesterday, when the ice was in capital condition and a splendid game was heartily enjoyed. The players of Montrave rink were Mrs. Gilmour (skip), Miss Gentle, Mrs. Carew Yorston, and Miss Martin, who ran up a total score of 21. The Hercules players were Mrs. Scott Davidson (skip), Mrs. Borrowman, Miss Campbell, and Mrs. Peterson, who ran up a total score of 9. Thus Montrave rink won by a majority of 12.*

The inference that it was becoming more common for women to be curling in the 1890s is confirmed by an article in the London Magazine *Hearth and Home*. The article relates that Henrietta Gilmour's rink played ten matches against other women's rinks over the winter of 1894-95, winning seven. At the time, Gilmour was in her early 40's. There only appear to be records describing two of the matches, both against the Hercules Ladies Curling Club. Henrietta Gilmour's rink won those matches by scores of 23-7 and 42-5. Apparently, she and her rink were quite good.

Henrietta Gilmour continued curling for a number of years, although records of her accomplishments are scarce. A 1901 account in the *Dundee Courier* reports that her rink defeated a ladies' rink from Balyarrow by a score of 21-14. Gilmour was also one of the first women to compete with and against men. In February, 1902, three women, including Gilmour, took part in a friendly match between four rinks from Cupar Curling Club and the Lundin and Montrave Curling Club. Lady Gilmour played lead on her husband's rink.

By 1900, the records of the Royal Caledonia Curling Club indicate that a few women had been accepted as members of non-ladies' curling clubs. Perhaps two dozen or so, categorized as "Regular," "Occasional," or "Extraordinary" members. Not everyone was pleased with this development. At the Annual General Meeting of the Royal Caledonian Curling Club in July, 1901, the Glasgow Lilybank Curling Club introduced the following motion: "That ladies not be eligible to compete in any matches held under the auspices of the Royal Club, unless by arrangement, and against rinks composed entirely of their own sex." Representatives of the Bathgate Curling Club, Airthey Castle Curling Club, Bonhill Curling Club, and West Lothian Curling Club argued against the motion, which was defeated. In theory, women were now free to compete alongside and against men in Royal Caledonian Curling Club matches.

The novel's account of the Scottish curling delegation's journey to Canada in 1888, where Ailsa and Sheenagh made their deal with Lucas Plotcok, to play for the fictional "World Championship" never happened. It was not until the winter of 1902-03 that the Scots, after years of rejecting invitations from the Canadians, actually sent a delegation of curlers to Canada. The Canadian Branch of the Royal Caledonian Curling Club had first sent an invitation forty-five years earlier, in 1858. The entire 1902-03 delegation, comprised of 24 curlers, consisted of men. Of course, it was the Reverend Kerr who was selected to lead the delegation and to record it for posterity. He did so, in a tome of more than 800 pages, *Curling in Canada and the United States – A Record of the Tour of the Scottish Team 1902-03 and of the Game in the Dominion and the Republic*. It is from Kerr's book that the menus for the various banquets in this story were taken.

It is also in Kerr's account of the Scottish curlers' tour of Canada that one of the very first references to a men's rink playing against an all-women's rink is found. On January 8, 1903, an impromptu match was arranged. It was decided that two rinks of Scottish bachelors would play against two rinks from the Quebec Ladies Curling Club. And the Quebec Ladies won. The Reverend Kerr reported on the match as follows:

> *When it became known that there were many keen curlers among the Quebec ladies who were anxious to have a game with the Scottish curlers, it was arranged that two rinks of the bachelors should be told to play the ladies, the married contingent being strongly desirous that the ladies should score a victory. In this they were not disappointed, for while the bachelors had a tie in one rink . . . they lost by 9 shots in the other . . .*

Kerr went on to describe one of the reasons he perceived for the bachelors being defeated:

Apart from the point of gallantry, the result was not to be wondered at, for here and elsewhere in Canada, the ladies play the game with small iron stones about half the size and weight of the irons used by the gentlemen, in the use of which, by long practice, they are past masters, while the Scotsmen were considerably at sea at what might be regarded as a pingpong form of curling.

One of the men who played against the Quebec ladies was Provost D. R. Gordon from the Bathgate Curling Club. After returning from the tour of Canada, Gordon published a small booklet – *With the Curlers in Canada*. In it, he described playing against the ladies:

Here we were invited to engage in a match with the ladies – two rinks a side. There were heard the usual voices who counselled that no match should be played for fear that the colours of the team would be lowered . . . The rinks were surrounded by all the youth and beauty of Quebec, who enjoyed the novel spectacle of big brawny Scots in knickerbockers and tam o' shanters contesting for all they were worth for supremacy. As you know, victory rested with the ladies, who well deserved it . . . Like a vanquished general who hands over his sword to the conqueror, I handed over my curling besom or cowe to the skip of the ladies' rink to be hung in her boudoir with a Gordon tartan ribbon tied round it, in token of surrender and as a remembrance of the historic meeting between the sons of the Thistle and the daughters of the glorious Maple leaf.

Why, exactly, he expected his besom to be hung in the boudoir, Provost Gordon does not venture to say. News of the men's defeat at the hands of the Quebec women was not well-received back home in Scotland. The *Dundee Courier* called the result a "crowning humiliation" for the Scottish men. The Alloa Curling Club proposed that the team be recalled from Canada immediately and that the balance of the tour be cancelled.

A few days later, the Scottish men again took to the ice against the ladies. Three rinks of Scottish men played three rinks from the Ladies Montreal Curling Club. The men won one match, the women the other two. Kerr reported:

> *Over 1200 spectators were said to have witnessed the match. The play of the ladies was excellent, and was much applauded by their opponents, who all agreed they could curl as well as the gentlemen.*

The *Edinburgh Evening News* headlined its story, "Beaten Again by the Ladies." A Canadian newspaper ran the headline, "Noo They'll No Craw Sae Crouse. The Scottish Carles likkit by the Montreal Leddies yesterday." You can no doubt divine the meaning. Provost Gordon, whose team again lost, wrote that, "Those who have felt the influence of the ladies most will readily believe that their charm, aided by their great skill, accounted for the defeat of the Scotsmen." Along with the respect for how well the women played, there were not-so-subtle excuses buried within each of the accounts – the men's gallantry, the women playing with small iron stones, the women curlers' "charm."

One final occurrence during the tour of Canada is noteworthy, historically speaking. On January 15, 1903, matches were played in Montreal between rinks composed of two Scottish men and two

Canadian women each. It may well be the first recorded mention of a mixed curling match.

Although more women were taking up the game, their role was still primarily to support the men who curled. Witness this account of a match on Strathpepper Pond from the *Highland News* on February 10, 1912:

> *The pond was beautifully illuminated, and the scene was an animated one, skaters and curlers having a delightful time. A rink skipped by Mr. Wotherspoon had motored from Kildary, and after a keen game finished two up. Refreshments were served by a willing band of ladies...*

Even though more and more women were taking to the ice, and even forming their own curling clubs, they were by no means treated as equals. In fact, some of the treatment was downright condescending and insulting. For example, at a charity bonspiel at the Victorian Curling Club in Canada in 1911, women were allowed to participate with the men. However, one of the rules required that if a man was playing opposite a woman, the man was required to deliver his stone left-handed. In 1914, in Moose Jaw, Saskatchewan, a charity bonspiel attracted seventy women curlers who competed on eighty-one teams. Each skip received two extra points for each woman on the team. At another Canadian bonspiel in 1915, women were again allowed to play. In this particular bonspiel, each experienced male skip was assigned three inexperienced curlers. If one of the inexperienced curlers happened to be a woman, the team received a one point bonus.

Vera Pezer, in *The Stone Age: A Social History of Curling on the Prairies*, recounts this event:

Jim Gorrie entered the 1933 Calgary Curling Club Men's Open Bonspiel with three women. The team was considered a joke and allowed to play. After its fifth consecutive win, 'panic set in' and a hastily convened executive voted the team ineligible for further competition.

Although clergy, particularly in Scotland, were extremely influential in curling's growth, they were not universally helpful. In Birtle, Manitoba, women had been curling alongside men for several years in the early twentieth century. An Anglican minister did not approve, and went on record that the women should not be permitted to continue because curling alongside the men put them at great risk of hearing the men swear. God forbid! Some of the men, on the recommendation of the church, seized upon the opportunity to deny the women any further access to their curling ice.

It is also noteworthy that most men's curling clubs in the 1700s and 1800s had chaplains. Women's curling clubs, when they finally came into being, did not. First, there were no women clergy to serve as chaplains. Second, the women reasoned that they simply did not need chaplains like the men did.

Interestingly, World War I provided a boost to women's curling. Many clubs, particularly smaller ones, found their membership depleted because of all the men who were enlisted and sent to fight. To make up for the decreased membership, some clubs elected to allow women inro membership to help make up for the shortfall in membership fees.

Curling was first contested at the Winter Olympics in Chamonix, France in 1924. Only men curled at the 1924 Winter Olympics. Just three teams competed – Great Britain, France, and Sweden. The Great Britain team, comprised of four Scots, won the gold medal by defeating Sweden 38-7 and France 46-4. For eighty-two years, it was believed that curling was only a demonstration sport at the 1924 Winter Olympics. However, in 2006, the International Olympic Committee determined that curling had been an official event, and posthumously awarded full gold medals to the Scottish men.

Curling was again played at the 1932 Winter Olympics in Lake Placid, New York. This time, curling was officially demoted to demonstration sport status, and it was once again exclusively for men. Curling did not return to the Winter Olympics until 1988, again only as a demonstration sport, this time for both women and men. When curling became a medal sport in 1998, the Canadian women, skipped by Sandra Schmirler, took the first women's gold.

During the twentieth century, the game itself gradually changed. Stones were no longer being delivered from a standing position on either a crampit or from a hack, but were being delivered with the modern-day slide. A Canadian, Ken Watson, is credited for popularizing, if not inventing, the slide on the leather sole of his shoe.

In Canada, it was not until 1960 that the first official Canadian National Women's Curling Championship was played. The first official men's championship, the Brier, was first played thirty-three years earlier, in 1927. In 1982, the women's championship was re-branded as the Scott Tournament of Hearts (sponsored by Scott Paper) and in 2007 it became the Scotties Tournament of Hearts.

Although the television ratings in Canada for the Brier and the Scotties were similar, it was not until 2019 that the men and women played for equal prize money. The year before, the purse for the Brier was 77% more than the purse for the Scotties.

It took until 1977 for the Royal Caledonian Curling Club to officially recognize a Scottish women's champion. An official men's champion, naturally, had first been crowned many years prior. In the United States, it was the same. The first men's championship was held in 1957, the first women's in 1977.

It was not until 1979 that the first official world curling championship for women would be held. The men's world championship, as one would suspect, had been held twenty years earlier. At the time, the women's championship was known as the Royal Bank Ladies World Curling Championship. The inaugural event was held in Perth, Scotland, and was won not by Scotland or Canada, but by Switzerland. Eleven countries took part.

The history of women's curling reflects society at large. Women began participating in the sport later than men, were admitted into curling clubs later than men, were playing in sanctioned events later than men, and assumed governing roles in the sport later than men. All along the way, they faced resistance and reprobation for their efforts at full inclusion. Today, various studies indicate that in Scotland, Canada, and the United States, at least, around 36-40% of all curlers are women. There remains progress to be made.

⬥

Lastly, a word about the self-publishing journey. Self-publishing holds a lot of advantages for the author who simply wants to tell a story, not try to somehow eke out a living by writing. The sad fact is that the odds of making any significant amount of money as an author are long, although there is a non-zero chance of that happening. A few self-published works have found great commercial success. *The Martian*, *Fifty Shades of Grey*, and *Still Alice* all began their literary lives as self-published works, so it is possible. With more than two million titles self-published each year, though, be forewarned.

The disadvantages of self-publishing are many, but not insurmountable. The main drawback is that the author is responsible for each and every single detail involved in bringing a book to market, not just the writing. In fact, many find the writing to be the easiest part. There is editing to be done, multiple rounds of proofreading and proofreading some more, formatting to be chosen, decisions about fonts and line spacing and book dimensions, ISBN numbers to buy, Library of Congress Control Numbers to secure, a cover to create, advance reviews and blurbs to gather, press releases to write and send, book signings and author events to schedule, a launch party to plan, credit card readers to install, book award contests to enter, an email list to grow, and an author website to be created and constantly updated. You should probably write some guest blog posts, too, and see if you can cajole and convince a few bookstores and libraries to carry your book. That's the short list of things to do. And be prepared to spend some money on printing and shipping your book.

On the other hand, self-publishing provides an exhilarating amount of freedom to the author. The author can tell her or his story exactly as they like, without an agent, editor, and publisher all meddling in what the author wants to say and exactly how they want to say it. That is a two-edged sword, though, since it is precisely those said agents, editors, and publishers who know what a professionally-produced book should look and read like. Plus, the self-published author can release the book whenever they feel like it, not on a publisher's timeline. It is perhaps the single biggest advantage to self-publishing – getting the book to market at the author's pace. So, if you don't care about making money and are persnickety enough to want absolute control over everything about your book, self-publishing just might be for you.

Appendix

For readers who aren't intimately familiar with the sport of curling, a brief introduction to its origins and history, how it is played, the surface that it is played on, and the equipment that it is played with, should prove helpful. Its spirit, too, is an essential part of the game. Curling's nickname – *The Roarin' Game* – comes from the sound of the forty-pound granite stones rumbling down a sheet of pebbled ice.

The very first thing that you are likely to notice in watching curling is that almost everyone looks happy. Whether they are learning to curl for the first time or are experienced curlers playing in a league or a bonspiel, people are generally smiling and laughing. Curling, above all else, is fun. How could it not be – playing on a team, sliding stones down a 150-foot-long sheet of ice to a target that looks like a bullseye, and watching and hearing the stones as they crash and carom into each other?

Curling is probably most familiar to people from being prominently featured on television every four years during the Winter Olympics. It has become one of the most-watched events during the Olympics. To many, it is simply a curiosity. To many others, though, it is mesmerizing. Although the overwhelming consensus is that the game originated in Scotland more than five centuries ago, there are still occasional heated and emotional arguments favoring the Netherlands as its true home. Regardless of which is correct, it was in Scotland where the game took root and flourished. A quick primer on the history of the game is in order.

The earliest *physical* evidence of curling being played comes from a curling stone inscribed with the date "1511," which was discovered when a pond in Dunblane, Scotland, was drained hundreds of years later. It is the oldest known curling stone still in existence, although it bears little resemblance to the stones that are used today. The "1511" curling stone now resides at the Sterling Smith Art Gallery and Museum in Stirling, Scotland.

The earliest known *written* reference to curling also comes from Scotland and dates back nearly 500 years. In 1541, a notary named John McQuhin recorded a challenge made by John Sclater, a monk at Paisley Abbey outside of Glasgow, to Gavin Hamilton, the lay governor of Paisley Abbey. It seems that Gavin Hamilton was thoroughly and rather intensely disliked by nearly everyone, but because a monk could not possibly challenge a governor to a duel, the monk decided to challenge him to a curling match instead. History does not record whether the challenge was accepted, or who may have won the match, if indeed it was contested, but the monk had nonetheless made his point.

The first *artistic* depiction of curling comes from 1565, when Flemish artist Pieter Bruegel the Elder completed two paintings, *Winter Landscape with Ice Skaters and Bird Trap* and *The Hunters in the Snow*. Each of the paintings depict outdoor curling scenes and they represent the oldest known visual representations of curling.

The first reference to curling in *literature* is found in a 1639 poem by Henry Adamson. Adamson wrote in *The Muses Threnodie*, that James Gall "was much given to pastime, as golf, archerie, curling; and Joviall companie." Scottish poet David Gray wrote of whisky-drinking curlers at the Luggie Water, a stream in Kirkintilloch. Of course, they were drinking whisky. They were curling and they were in Scotland.

The first formal curling society, or club, was apparently established in Kilsyth, Scotland in 1716. Only apparently, because, as with most things related to curling, that honor is disputed by others claiming to have been the first, including curling societies in Kinross and Muthill. The Kilsyth Curling Club, at more than 300 years old, is still in existence today.

The earliest known written description of the game itself is found in Thomas Pennant's 1772 book, *A Tour in Scotland and Voyage to the Hebrides*. Two-and-a-half centuries later, the description ably and succinctly depicts the modern game:

> *Of the sports of these parts that of Curling is a favorite;*
> *and one unknown in England. It is an amusement of the*
> *winter, and played on the ice, by sliding from one mark*
> *to another great stones of forty to seventy pounds weight, of*
> *hemispherical form, with an iron or wooden handle at top.*
> *The object of the player is to lay his stone as near to the mark*
> *as possible, to guard that of his partner, which has been well*
> *laid before, or to strike off that of his antagonist.*

Poets have long celebrated the sport of curling, including Robert Burns, the 18th century Scottish poet, in 1786's *Tam Samson's Elegy*:

> *When winter muffles up his cloak,*
> *And binds the mire like a rock;*
> *When to the loughs the Curlers flock,*
> *Wi' gleesome speed,*
> *Wha will they station at the cock?*
> *Tam Samson's dead!*
>
> *He was the king o' a' the Core,*

To guard, or draw, or wick a bore,
Or up the rink like Jehu roar,
In time o' need;
But now he lags on Death's hog-score
Tam Samson's dead!

Curling, by the early 1800s, was also claimed to have definite medical benefits. Dr. Alexander Pennecuik wrote:

To Curle on the ice does greatly please;
Being a Manly Scottish Exercise,
It clears the Brains, stirs up the Native Heat,
And gives a gallant Appetite for Meat.

On July 25, 1838, the Grand Caledonian Curling Club, which would become the national governing body for the sport in Scotland, was founded at the Waterloo Hotel in Edinburgh. The Grand Caledonian Curling Club was formed to bring some sense of order to the chaos of each individual club playing by its own particular set of rules and with its own particular kinds of stones. It was granted a royal charter in 1843 by Queen Victoria, who became fascinated by the game after viewing a curling exhibition on the wooden floor of Scone Palace in Perth. The Queen even tried to throw a stone, but it "proved too heavy for her delicate arm." After the exhibition, Prince Albert was presented with "a splendid pair of Curling Stones, made of finest Ailsa Craig granite." Renamed the Royal Caledonian Curling Club after receiving a royal charter, the first formalized set of curling rules was adopted.

Around the time of the Royal Club's formation, stones made of Ailsa Craig granite were becoming increasingly popular, both in Scotland and

Canada. Ailsa Craig is a small island ten miles to the west of the Scottish mainland, the remnant of a volcano which erupted sixty million years ago as Europe and North America separated from each other and Pangea was completing its disassemblage. When the volcano cooled, it left two kinds of granite. Varieties of granite which have never, to this day, been found anywhere else in the world.

Blue hone granite is the rarer of the two, and holds the main key to making curling stones. Blue hone granite, because of its molecular structure and mineral composition, is completely impervious to water penetration. Water infiltrating the stone would repeatedly freeze and thaw during the stone's lifetime, causing it to weaken, crack, and ultimately fail. Blue hone granite, used for that part of the curling stone contacting the ice, eliminates that issue.

The bulk of the curling stone is made from the slightly more abundant common green granite, also found exclusively on Ailsa Craig. Common green granite is very similar to blue hone granite, although slightly better suited to absorbing the non-stop collisions with other curling stones during the course of a game and a stone's useful lifetime. Because of these unique characteristics, Ailsa Craig curling stones may last upwards of forty or fifty years. Today, the only stones used in Olympic and other high-level competitions are Ailsa Craig stones, and they are manufactured exclusively by Andrew Kay & Co. Ltd.

Just as they have done with curling, poets have long celebrated Ailsa Craig, including John Keats in his poem, "To Ailsa Rock":

> *Hearken, thou craggy ocean pyramid!*
> *Give answer from thy voice – the sea-fowl's screams!*
> *When were thy shoulders mantled in huge streams?*
> *When from the sun was thy broad forehead hid?*
> *How long is't since the mighty Power bid*
> *Thee heave to airy sleep from fathom dreams –*

Sleep in the lap of thunder or sunbeams –
Or when gray clouds are thy cold coverlid?
Thou answerest not, for thou art dead asleep.
Thy life is but two dead eternities –
The last in air, the former in the deep!
First with the whales, last with the eagle skies!
Drown'd wast thou till an earthquake made thee steep,
Another cannot wake thy giant size!

Prior to 1838, there had been few serious attempts to unify or codify the rules of curling, although the Duddingston Curling Society had drawn up a set of regulations several years prior. Each club played by their own particular rules, and matches between different clubs required extensive negotiations over how the games would be played. With the formation of the Royal Caledonian Curling Club as a governing body, a uniform set of rules was finally adopted. With a uniform set of rules now the standard, the modern sport of curling rapidly evolved and grew in popularity in Scotland and beyond.

One of the initial rules had an enormous effect on the game. Rule 9 required that "All Curling Stones shall be of a circular shape." Before the adoption of the rules, curlers played with any stones they pleased. One such stone was named "Whirlie," a large, triangular stone. A man who played with Whirlie wrote this sad tale of playing with the stone. It reads like a love letter:

It was the first stone which the writer of this ever played with.
It being our first attempt at curling, we were appointed
to lead, which we happened to do in such a manner that
Whirlie was uniformly laid on or near the Tee; to remove
it from the position on which it had taken rest was no

easy matter; because, if the stone which was destined to remove it strike any one of the angled corners, round went Whirlie, round and round, without ever shifting from its position. Stimulated with the success of our first attempt at curling, we went early next day on the field of action with Whirlie in our hand. But to our utter disappointment, dear fellows, a Curling Court was held upon him, and he was unanimously condemned to perpetual banishment. This, however, we could not stand. We got him mounted in a more modern and fashionable uniform, by rounding his more acute angles, and in this capacity we introduced him as a stranger on his ancient domain. A bad character and bad habits, however, have a mark put upon them, and are not easily surmounted. The rogue, in spite of our endeavours, was still seen in his new shape and in his habits likewise, for his roundabout way of going to work never forsook him, and again and again has he been banished from, and restored to the society of his fellows; until at last we had the galling mortification to hear his final doom decreed by the present Baronet that this favourite stone should be played with no more. Since then, the Ice, and all the curlers, except ourselves, who well knew him once, know him no more. and perhaps forever. But many are the lingering emotions and fond affection with which we have sought after him; nor will we desist from the search until we in our turn shall be consigned to oblivion.

Curling was introduced to North America, primarily to eastern Canada, by Scottish emigrants, in the eighteenth and nineteenth centuries. The first Canadian curling club was established in Montreal in 1807. During the 1800s, curling expanded across the entire breadth of Canada, where curlers played with "stones" made of iron, granite, or even wood.

In order to understand modern curling, it is necessary to understand both the surface on which it is played and the specialized equipment which it requires. Curling is played on a much different kind of ice surface than hockey or figure skating, which require smooth ice. Curling ice is different. Curling is played on "pebbled" ice, which is created and maintained through a meticulous combination of art and science. While hockey and figure skating ice is smooth and renewed using a Zamboni, curling ice is a different animal altogether. First and foremost, curling ice must be completely level. A variation of one-eighth or one-quarter of an inch would make a curling sheet virtually unplayable in competition. Slanted, unlevel ice is sometimes called "biased" ice. The second notable feature is that a Zamboni is *never never ever* used on true curling ice. Curling ice also requires a very specific temperature, controlled by thousands of feet of piping or tubing a few inches below the surface of the ice, through which a very cold brine or glycol is pumped. Most curling ice is only around two inches thick.

Once a level sheet of ice at the proper temperature is laid down, the real, tedious process of making curling ice begins. "Pebbling" is what makes a curling stone travel as far as it does and enables it to curl, or turn, by reducing the area of the stone actually touching the ice and thus reducing friction. Ice technicians use warm, purified, deionized water with as few dissolved solids as possible to pebble the curling ice. Pebblers walk backwards down each sheet, with a tank of warm water on their backs, heated to around 120 degrees Fahrenheit, while waving an attached wand, similar to the aspergillum used by priests to sprinkle holy water, dispersing tiny droplets of warm water onto the ice. The droplets adhere to the ice and freeze almost immediately, creating tiny bumps on the ice. It may take several passes to apply sufficient pebble to the ice. The result is a sheet of ice which resembles the skin of an orange.

When the pebbling is done, a scraper is pushed up and down the ice. The scraper is a large, expensive piece of machinery with what amounts to a four or five-foot wide razor blade attached to the bottom. As the scraper is pushed down the ice surface, it shaves off the top of the pebble so that the remaining pebble is of a completely uniform height, creating consistency in how a stone behaves as it travels down the ice. Uneven pebble would cause the curling stone to wobble and misbehave as it slides down the sheet. After the ice has been shaved, a soft, wide, dry mop is pushed across the length of the sheets to remove the bits of ice which were shaved off of the top of the pebble by the scraper. At last, the ice is ready for play. The stones will glide across the top of the pebble.

Curlers use two kinds of specialized equipment unique to the game – curling shoes and brooms, which really aren't very similar to what are commonly thought of as brooms, although they once were. Curling shoes have a different sole on each shoe. When curlers push out of the hack to deliver a stone, which is essentially like a starting block in track, but embedded into the ice, they push off with their dominant leg. The shoe that is used to push out from the hack has a gripper on the sole, enabling the player to walk on the ice without slipping and to maintain the traction needed for sweeping. The grippers are made of a high-traction rubber, which provides the curler with stability when walking on the ice. On the sole of the other shoe, which remains flat on the ice, is a slider, usually made out of Teflon. Teflon has an extremely low coefficient of friction, so that it can slide down the ice without slowing down the curler. Teflon on ice is an extremely slippery combination. Balancing on the slider foot, the player slides down the ice with the stone in hand to deliver it.

The broom, or "besom" in old Scotland, is a bit like a sponge mop. Attached to a handle made of lightweight fiberglass or carbon fiber is a brush often made of cordura nylon over foam, which is the part of the broom which actually touches the ice. By applying downward pressure on the broom and quickly sweeping (or "sooping" in old Scots vernacular) it back and forth in front of the sliding stone, the sweeper warms the ice, which reduces friction and allows the stone to travel farther and straighter. Through the use of sweeping, players can guide the sliding stone to its desired location. Sweeping is the aerobic exercise part of the game, requiring more energy than delivering the stone. You might occasionally still hear some old-time skips yelling, "Soop, soop!" to the sweepers. Sweeping can add as much as eight or ten feet of distance to a shot if done properly. What a sweeper may never do is touch the stone with the broom.

Yet another bit of curling equipment, not often seen on the ice in modern play, is noted by the Reverend John Kerr in his 1890 *History of Curling*:

> *An indispensable equipment, according to a majority of curlers, is a flask . . . A flask is useful, but not indispensable. It is certainly dangerous to the feet if it affects the head . . . [E]very skip must take special care to keep this equipment in its proper place.*

With the ice prepared, curling shoes on, broom in hand, and stones in place, the game can finally begin. Curling rules are fairly simple, although execution is quite complex, much like chess. In fact, curling is often referred to as "chess on ice." The ability to envision two or three shots ahead is critical to success at higher levels of competition and helpful at lower levels.

A curling match is generally scheduled for eight or ten ends, similar to innings in baseball. In a normal match, each team consists of four players, who alternate taking shots, although there is also mixed doubles curling, with two-person teams consisting of one man and one woman. Each player on a four-person team – lead, second, vice, and skip – takes two shots per end, meaning that a total of sixteen stones, eight per team, will be thrown by the two teams in each end. The skip stands in the house, which consists of a twelve-foot wide circle, within which are smaller four-foot and eight-foot circles, as well as the button, or bulls-eye, which together comprise the scoring area. The skip directs the shooter and the sweepers as to what kind of shot to attempt and exactly where the skip wants the stone to come to rest.

The skip may want a shot to land in the house, but might also want the shooter to place a guard in front of a stone that is already there or to place a guard in anticipation of protecting a future stone placed in the house. A guard protects the stone which is in the house from being "taken out" by an opponent's stone. The end continues with teams alternating shots, setting guards, knocking opponents' stones out of the house, and tapping their own stones closer to the button, trying ultimately to get the highest number of stones closest to the center of the house (the "tee"). Players control how their stones behave by gently turning the stone's handle either clockwise or counterclockwise upon release. A clockwise spin will make a stone curl from left to right, while a counterclockwise spin will make it curl from right to left. Whether or not that is the origin of the game's name is another matter of some dispute. The sound of the forty-pound stones rumbling down the ice, and they are noisy, gave curling its nickname of *The Roarin' Game.*

There are at least two competing theories as to how curling got its name. The one which is most often told is that the name derives from the way that shooters can make the stones turn, or curl, by turning the handle upon release. Another theory is that it derives from the Scottish word "curr," which describes a low, rumbling sound. The first theory makes for a better story, but the second may very well be more accurate.

Once all sixteen stones have been played, the score for that end is tallied. Scoring begins with the stone that is closest to the button, or the center of the house. The stone need not be on the button, just closest to it. If a red-handled stone is closest to the button and a yellow-handled stone is the second closest, the red team gets one point. If a red stone is both the closest *and* second closest, red gets two points, and so on. In theory, therefore, one team could garner as many as eight points in an end, although that very, very rarely happens. A three or four point end is a significant score. With the score tallied, the process repeats itself for the next end.

Obviously, it is a big advantage to be taking the final shot in an end, which is known as having "the hammer." The hammer goes to the team which lost the previous end. Teams with the hammer would like to score two or three points in an end, while the team without the hammer would prefer to limit their opponent to one point, or even to "steal" a point for themselves when playing without the hammer.

That, in very abbreviated form, is the history of the game, along with a description of the modern game. Now, you can begin the story.

Glossary

The following terms, commonly found in Scottish writing and in writing about curling, are used in this book:

Ain: *Own*

Bassa: *Slang for bastard*

Besom: *Broom*

Biased Ice: *Ice which is slanted rather than flat*

Blae: *Blue*

Bonspiel: *A curling tournament, usually involving multiple clubs*

Cannoning: *Striking a guard so that it takes out the opponent's stone which is sitting as the winner*

Cauld: *Cold*

Chafts: *Jaws, cheeks*

Channel-stane: *Old Scottish term for a curling stone*

Chipping a winner: *Avoiding a guard and taking out a winner*

Crampit: *A flat board upon which a curler used to stand when delivering a stone; largely replaced by hacks*

Craw sae crouse: *Crow so loudly; boast*

Dull ice: *Wet, slow ice*

Drug ice: *Wet, soft, slow ice*

Flinders: *Small fragments, splinters*

Guard: *A curling stone placed in a position to protect other stones from being struck*

Hack: *The foot-hold from which a curling stone is delivered*

Hammer: *The final stone thrown in an end of curling*

Hog: *A stone which stops short of the hog-score, or hog-line, and which is therefore removed from play*

Hog-score: *The line which a stone must completely cross in order to remain in play; sometimes called "hog-line"*

I'm fair puckled: *I'm out of breath*

In-wick: *To strike a stone lying near the tee on its inside edge and carom toward the tee*

Keen ice: *Fast ice*

Lead: *The person on a rink, or curling team, who delivers the first stones*

Out-wick: *To strike a stone lying near the tee on its outside edge and carom toward the tee*

Rink: *A curling team, or the surface that curling is played on*

Running a port: *Shooting a stone through the space between two other stones*

Second: *The person on a rink, or curling team, who delivers stones after the lead*

Shut yer geggie: *Shut your mouth*

Skip: *The person on a rink who calls the shots and traditionally delivers the finals stones; sometimes called the "director"*

Soop: *Sweep*

Soutered: *Failed to score a single point in a curling match*

Stane: *Stone*

Tapping: *Gently striking another stone to move it to a different location, generally closer to the tee, or button*

Tawse: *A small leather strap used in Scottish schools for corporal punishment*

Ticking: *Moving a guard without removing it from play*

Vice: *The person on a rink who delivers stones after the second*

Wicking: *Touching another stone enough to change the played stone's direction*

Acknowledgements

A very special thanks go to my advance readers, Scotte and Paul Mason, whose insights and thoughtful comments were of immense value. Thank you so much for taking the time to help me craft a better story.

To Cheryl Bernard, the first curler I recall ever seeing, who graciously and enthusiastically volunteered to write the Foreword for a complete stranger.

To reigning United States champion, Tara Peterson, and three-time United States champion, Jamie Sinclair, for their kind advance praise and their contributions to women's curling.

To the amazing Scottish Curling's Historical Curling Places database (*https://sites.google.com/view/historicalcurlingplaces/home*), which contains thousands of historic newspaper accounts, photos, and maps, dating back into the 1700s, which provided a wealth of information about the historical record for curling in Scotland.

A very special thanks go to the Scottish Curling Trust for granting their kind permission to use the cover painting, "Eglinton Ladies 1859."

To Bob Cowan and the late David B. Smith's The Curling History Blogspot (*curlinghistory.blogspot.com*), which offers fascinating insights into the history of the sport, including several entries exclusively devoted to women's curling. It is from this blogspot that I learned so much about the early women curling pioneers.

With gratitude for their heartfelt generosity toward the people of Lewiston, Maine, I want to thank the dozens of Maine authors and illustrators who joined *Maine Authors for Lewiston* following the horrific events of October, 2023. I owe them thanks for their service, and also for encouraging me along my writing journey.

The following books have been drawn on for information about the history of curling and about the history of women's curling in particular:

Brown, Richard. *Memorabilia Curliana Mabenensia*. Dumfries 1830.

Cairnie, John. *Essay on Curling and Artificial Pond Making*. Glasgow 1833.

Grant, John G. *The Complete Curler*. Adam and Charles Black 1914.

Hill, Allen M. *Sweeping Frae the Yarmouth Curling Rink*. Herald Press 1910.

Kerr, John. *Curling in Canada and the United States: A Record of the Tour of the Scottish Team 1902-03*. George A. Morton 1904.

Kerr, John. *History of Curling – Scotland's Ain Game*. Edinburgh 1890.

MacNair, John. *The Channel-Stane or Sweepings from the Rink*. Edinburgh 1883.

Morris, Matt and Alladdyce, John. *Curling Capital*. University of Manitoba Press 1989.

Pezer, Vera. *The Stone Age: A Social History of Curling on the Prairies*. Fifth House Publishers 2003.

Ramsay, John. *An Account of the Game of Curling*. Edinburgh 1882.

Smith, David B. *Curling: An Illustrated History*. John Donald Publishers 1981.

Taylor, James. *Curling. The Ancient Scottish Game*. Second Edition, Edinburgh 1887.

The Kilmarnock Treatise on Curling. Edinburgh 1828.

Of course, there is W. O. Mitchell's classic, *The Black Bonspiel of Willie MacCrimmon*, a 1951 radio play later made into a novel, which provided some of the inspiration for the story.

Lastly, to everyone who was kind enough to purchase and read *The Stones of Ailsa Craig* and to offer their kind and supportive words. Without them, I never would have tried it again. Thank you.

About the Author

DAVID S. FLORIG lives in Ocean Park, Maine. He is a member of the Maine Writers and Publishers Alliance. Florig is also a member and past-president of the Pine Tree Curling Club in Portland, as well as a member of the Belfast Curling Club in Belfast, Maine. *The Stones of Ailsa Craig* was his debut novel and paid homage to Belfast, Maine; the glorious Maine coast; and the ancient Scottish sport of curling. Set in present-day Belfast, Maine and 1880s Scotland, the novel took a sometimes dark look into one man's loss, loneliness, obsession, and quest for vengeance. Rich in curling and Maine history, *The Stones of Ailsa Craig* is a work of historical fiction.

The Stones of Ailsa Craig was named Best Historical Fiction of 2023 by *Indies Today*; was a 2023 Finalist for the *American Writing Awards*; and was nominated for a *Maine Literary Award* and the *Eric Hoffer Award*.

The Stones of Ailsa Craig has been featured on Newscenter Maine's *207* and Maine Public Radio's *Maine Calling*.

More recently, Florig organized and led a group of ninety Maine authors as *Maine Authors for Lewiston*. Between November 25th and December 16th of 2023, the group held ten book sales/signings in public libraries around the state to raise money to support victims and families of the tragic events in Lewiston on October 25th. Each author donated all, or a portion, of their proceeds to charities in Lewiston.

David grew up and lived in South Jersey before retiring to Maine, where he lives with his wife, Nancy, and their sometimes ill-mannered rescue dog, Molly Malone. No, he has never been to Scotland. Adopted as an infant by Charles and Marjorie Florig for $130, he has seen just a single, black-and white picture of his birth mother.

For years, David practiced law in Pennsylvania and New Jersey. Following his legal career, he served as the Executive Director of two nonprofits - *Court Appointed Special Advocates of Burlington County* (New Jersey) and the *West Philadelphia Alliance for Children*. *WePAC* utilized volunteers to open shuttered elementary school libraries in Philadelphia, and for his work on behalf of Philadelphia's children, he was honored as one of the inaugural *GameChangers* by KYW Newsradio in celebration of Black History Month.

David Florig can be reached at david@davidflorig.com.